Photographer: Brandon Bishop

Claudia was born in London and is of St Lucian parentage. She has enjoyed a career on stage as an actress and singer for over thirty years, performing in prolific West End productions such as *Cat on a Hot Tin Roof* at the Novello Theatre; *The Big Life* at Apollo Theatre and Theatre Royal Stratford East; *RENT* at Shaftesbury Theatre; the original cast of *Miss Saigon* at Theatre Royal Drury Lane; and *The Phlebotomist* at Hampstead Theatre (2019). Claudia has also performed in notable productions at the National Theatre, London. Claudia's television guest appearances include ITV's *Coronation Street* and *Emmerdale*, and

BBC's *Doctors* and *Holby City*. Claudia graduated with a *BA (hons) Degree in Social, Cultural & Creative Processes* from Goldsmiths, University of London in 2006. She then qualified as a Primary Teacher in 2007 and she has taught in many primary schools in both London and Kent. Claudia graduated with a *MSc in Psychology* from Canterbury Christ Church University in January 2020.

Spectrum of Colours

Claudia Cadette

Spectrum of Colours

Vanguard Press

VANGUARD PAPERBACK

© Copyright 2023
Claudia Cadette

The right of Claudia Cadette to be identified as author of this work has been asserted by her in accordance with the Copyright, Designs and Patents Act 1988.

All Rights Reserved

No reproduction, copy or transmission of this publication may be made without written permission.
No paragraph of this publication may be reproduced, copied or transmitted save with the written permission of the publisher, or in accordance with the provisions of the Copyright Act 1956 (as amended).

Any person who commits any unauthorised act in relation to this publication may be liable to criminal prosecution and civil claims for damages.

A CIP catalogue record for this title is available from the British Library.

ISBN 978-1-83794-002-8

Vanguard Press is an imprint of
Pegasus Elliot Mackenzie Publishers Ltd.
www.pegasuspublishers.com

This is a work of fiction. Names, characters, businesses, places, events and incidents are either the product of the author's imagination or used in a fictitious manner. Any resemblance to actual persons, living or dead, or actual events is purely coincidental.

First Published in 2023

Vanguard Press
Sheraton House Castle Park
Cambridge England

Printed & Bound in Great Britain

To those who dream to dare and others who dare to dream

Acknowledgements

Thanks Pegasus Publishers and all the team for putting these words out there, and for your support, sometimes shown in the subtlest of ways, yet having the hugest impact. This book is dedicated to my late Daddy: Wenceslaus Cadette. *I owe everything to my Daddy.* You have always been and always will be my true guide and inspiration. Our Celebration Day of your Life was filled with love and was as beautiful as you are: we will cherish the loving memory forever. Thanks, Daddy, for your support and encouragement towards me completing *Spectrum of Colours.* And here it is. Thanks Mummy, for spurring me on with the book and teaching me how to possess a soul filled with unwavering empathy and compassion for others, and for shining the light in the darkest of times. Thanks to my friends (you know who you are), siblings and my sister-in-law Carole for providing me with the catalyst for this creation — your support has been tremendous and greatly appreciated since Spectrum of Colours' evolution over eight years ago! And finally, thanks to my love, Si, for your continual support. I am humbled by your wealth of talent and your passionate, tireless input to my works which has greatly contributed to shaping my creations. Thanks also my love for all what you have selflessly provided for my nearest and dearest since the moment we met…

Prologue

Four dark brick walls. A large brown desk occupies most of the space. The long strip of fluorescent light creates stilted shadows against the walls. A panel of officials sit stiffly in their chairs exuding as much personality as the décor of the boardroom.

'Sorry, can I just add something?'

The speaker stands. Heads turn to face the speaker who has taken it upon herself to interrupt the usual proceedings. She continues with an air of optimism and addresses the panel without their consent.

'Now that we've gathered all the information and the panel have reviewed Miss Healey's case, I'd like to say on her behalf that she is very keen to get back to her accommodation and be in the comfort of her home surroundings. I must also stress that Miss Healey has agreed to continue with her medication and understands the importance of this in light of what has happened.'

The speaker scans the room and quickly continues, deterring anyone from interrupting her flow. Her delivery is both deliberate and measured.

'I'm confident that, with the support of the health care officials here at Maudsley and her family, together with the support of her key worker (and of course myself as social worker), Miss Healey will overcome her… setback, and is on the road to living a fruitful life.'

There is a brief pause, and everyone can hear the sound of a clock ticking.

'Miss Healey has also asked me to inform you that she has already made enquiries about starting a course in Textiles in September at Morley College, which I'm sure you'll agree will keep her focused on something positive.'

The speaker senses that she has over-run her time and speedily rounds of her 'speech'.

'I'm sure you'll agree that Miss Healey's keenness to occupy her time productively is to be commended, and this will undoubtedly have a positive impact on her recovery.' The speaker smiles weakly as if to apologise for taking up so much time and sits back down.

'Thank you.'

A lady holding a clip board opens a window, allowing stifled air in the boardroom to escape. Everyone in the room exhales in unison, including the speaker. The room is released of its stuffy officiousness if only momentarily. One of the three grey-haired officials on the panel intervenes.

'Is there anything you'd like to add, Miss Healey?' he proposes with steeped authority. A fragile woman, dressed in a dark-blue trouser suit with a starched white shirt, coughs into her delicate brown hand. Her eyes barely lift off the boardroom table. Her monotone voice is determined and well-rehearsed but sounds more like she's struggling to be heard over loud music in a packed nightclub.

Sophia Healey speaks. 'Erm, yes, I'm feeling much better now, and the nurses have been fantastic!' She glances sideways to her social worker to see how well she is doing and then concludes, 'I feel so much better now.'

Sophia sits next to the window in her bedroom overlooking the garden below. A young family occupies the ground floor of the two-storey apartment. Sophia admiringly watches the children as they play and blow bubbles into the fresh spring air. A bubble travels past her window and she is transfixed by the spectrum of colours of the wobbly liquid ball. It lingers for a while, and she follows the bubble as it's carried higher into the sky until it disappears from view. She smiles, then gazes at her reflection in the mirror.

Today's a good day.
The mist is clearing.

Although life has tried hard to destroy my being,
memories are clear.
I still have those...
I haven't been rid of everything...

Chapter 1

Hop Farm: Lister Ward

The nurse placed the two miniature-circular white pots on the side table. I reached out and knocked back the white liquid, followed by the pills washed down with lukewarm water.

My eyes grew heavier and heavier as I hazily watched the nurse disappear around the corner…

'Lauren!'

I turned around, shaken by the presence of someone emerging from the darkness.

'It's me. Sophia,' I tremored.

'Oh gosh, *Soph*. You all right?' Devon asked, adjusting his eyes to find mine.

'Look what I found…'

I thrusted the boater barely visible in the dark into his hand. Devon froze for a moment, then took the hat, and hastily searched for my other hand, urgently pulling me along the pathway.

'Maybe she's gone the other way — round the driver's route.'

We scurried in the darkness through the alleyway to the front of the estate. The palm of my hand was bruised further as Devon squeezed it tightly, making sure he didn't let go — calling out Lauren's name as we went. Our voices evaporated into the night air. We stopped and stood in the middle of the racing track, panting in unison, doing a last scan of the area.

'She must have gone back inside. Let's go back to the house, Soph,' Devon relented.

'Ok, but don't tell Mum Lauren ran off with my hat — I don't want her to get into trouble,' I pleaded.

'Course, Soph, I won't say anything,' Devon comforted. I gripped my boater tightly between my thumb and forefinger, searching the corners as we went.

As we bolstered through the open front door, I noticed the same couple huddled together near the entrance. Devon nearly knocked over the loved-up duo as he urgently headed to the party room. I hid my boater down by my left side as I hastily ran up the stairs scanning the kitchen as I went — eager to reach my bedroom — our sanctuary. Before long Devon crept up behind me shaking his head uncontrollably. We stood side by side in the bedroom doorway.

The only sign of life was the gentle movement of the curtains flapping in the prevailing wind…

It was now 12:35 a.m. Devon and I scoured the house from top to bottom. Party revellers were in full swing and didn't take much notice of us — they must have thought we were just playing around again. I paced into Mum and Dad's bedroom overlooking the playground and drew back the curtains searching into the distance for a sign of Lauren; Devon checked our bedrooms again at the front of the house. Rapidly losing hope, I ran back into my bedroom wiping my tears as I went. Devon appeared at my bedroom doorway.

'We gotta tell Mum, Soph,' he urged. 'We gotta search the estate.'

We found Mum in the middle of the dance floor — her outstretched arms dancing in the air, hypnotically *Rocking* to Janet Kaye's *Rhythm* — magnetised by her beautiful vocals — contented in her own world. Even though time was of the essence, I stood paralysed, unable to move or utter a word and just stared at her. Mum grabbed my hands and joyously motioned me to dance with her, but my feet were immobilised. My arms limply swung from side to side as if detached from my body when Mum's palms met mine.

In an instant, Devon fiercely pulled on Mum's arm and pushed his mouth against her ear. I could see his lips moving ten-to-the-dozen. His face animated. Expressionless, I stood looking at them both as the music swelled around me. Mum cocked her head to the side and stood face-to-face with Devon. She paused for a second; her eyebrows lowered and gathered in the middle. Devon leant into Mum again, his lips frenetically opening and shutting in quicker succession and in closer proximity to her ear than before. As Mum released me from her grip, my arms collapsed by my side. Mum quickly weaved her way through the crowd from the dance floor towards the passageway near the front door.

'What do you mean she's not here?' Mum asked in confusion.

'Lauren ran off out of the house. We were just playing a game in Soph's bedroom, and she just ran off — out the front door.'

'Why would she just run off?' Mum perplexed.

Devon looked at me then continued, 'I don't know... we were just playing a game. Soph and I ran straight after her... We've looked around the estate playground, but can't find her anywhere, Mum,' Devon emoted.

'Have you checked upstairs?' Mum questioned. 'She might be in the bathroom or something...'

'We've checked, Mum, she's not there. We've checked over and over,' Devon persisted.

Mum turned to me and noticed my reddened eyes.

'Over and over? What do you mean? How long has she been missing?'

'I don't know... erm... about fifteen/twenty minutes,' Devon guessed.

In haste, Mum paced up the stairs, leaving us standing in the passageway. Moments later, she raced back down and told us to stay inside whilst she checked around the estate. Mum sped out the front door, taking the two chain-smokers, who were standing on the outdoor communal balcony in tow.

Devon and I glanced towards the living room and then decided to run back upstairs. We figured as Mum didn't say anything we wouldn't mention anything to Dad yet either — hoping Lauren would find her way back.

I caught sight of the boater on my bed. I swiftly picked it up, opened my cupboard door and placed the boater on the top shelf safely out of the way. I closed the cupboard door again.

Devon watched curiously but didn't say anything.

'Remember what I said, Devon,' I warned.

He paced nervously on the spot from left to right, his caramel-coloured legs trembling as if in a spasm. 'I don't care about your damn hat. Your friend's gone missing! Is that all you can think about?'

'I told you to not mess about with it. If you didn't play your stupid game of *catch*, then Lauren wouldn't have run off with it. Now, she's gone!' I argued.

'So, it's *my* fault, is it?' Devon blurted, raising his voice.

'I didn't say it was *your* fault... No... I... I...'

I couldn't even continue my sentence. Running to the window, I drew the curtain to the side and leant onto the windowsill; my head rested on my folded arms. I felt Devon place his hand on my shoulder and I instinctively turned to face him. His arms reached out and cradled me. It was probably the first time my brother and I had embraced. He reassured me that Lauren would be back in no time and that he didn't mean to shout. But his act of kindness and words of solace made me weep even more. With my head buried in Devon's chest, I thought about Lauren, retracing the steps leading up to her running out of the house. I remembered the Kray boy staring out into the distance...

The sound of hurried footsteps scuttling along the balcony outside caused Devon and I to break our embrace and simultaneously poke our heads out the bedroom window. Mum and her chain-smoking helpers dashed along the concrete balcony and stopped for a moment, panting on the doorstep.

'She's not here!' Mum despaired as she craned her head up at our weary faces peeking through the gap in the window.

Mum then darted to the top of the stairs where Devon and I stood. She grabbed the telephone receiver from the wall and frantically dialled 999, whilst ordering Devon to alert Dad about Lauren's disappearance. Mum's hand shook as she dialled the numbers and confirmed *police, please*. She managed to pull the telephone wire around the corner into her bedroom and closed the door to filter out the background noise, allowing a small gap for the telephone wire to peek through. The music from downstairs turned into a hubbub of loud chatter. Still trying to control her breath, Mum gave the police a description of what Lauren was wearing, her age, height and the circumstances (as Devon and I reported) and the approximate time when Lauren disappeared. Mum repeated several times when questioned that we lived on the estate off Demata Road and that Lauren was a friend. She repeatedly said we looked around the surrounding areas of the estate already several times and that it was over thirty minutes since Lauren had gone. I could hear Mum's growing frustrations as she gave details about the incident and confirmed that, *'Yes — she was officially reporting a missing child.'*

The conversation ended abruptly. Mum just stared blankly ahead of her. Her head then jolted as if remembering something. In a frenzy, Mum searched in her bedroom drawers and found her diary and frantically started dialling: '...0171... 654...'

Mrs Harrison's bright voice on the answer machine invited the caller to '...*leave a name and number and I'll get back in touch as soon as possible...*' Mum quickly pressed the receiver button down and hung up before the beats commenced.

Dad and most of the party searched the surrounding areas of the estate. From the living room windows, we could see groups of three or more party-goers huddled together, then roam around in the darkness, searching corners, wading across patches of grassland, crossing pathways, looking through gates of back gardens. Dark figures corresponded with others and chatted before going off in different directions and searching again. Mum, Aunt Cassy and couple of elderly adults and children congregated downstairs.

Aunt Cassy asked Devon to relay the sequence of events. After he finished, Aunt Cassy continued her onslaught, *'But that don't make sense. How old is she again, Sophia...? Perhaps she's done it before... or she's gone to visit a friend nearby,* ending with... *Well, you know how these* wh***...' but before Aunt Cassy could finish her sentence she was curtly cut short:

'That's enough, Cassy,' barked Mum.

Chapter 2

Dim The Lights

They all said how well I was coping under the circumstances — *they* — being school *and* the *social services*. The police interviewed Mum and Dad, and Devon and I numerous times as well as a host of family members/friends from the party. I even heard Mr Baldwin from school was interviewed, even though he had since left.

Devon and I recounted what happened on that night over and over again and wondered why the authorities kept asking us the same questions but in different ways. The police seemed perplexed by our 'story' and commented as to why fourteen and fifteen-year-olds would be playing such a juvenile game as *catch*. Mum interrupted, '*Well they are juveniles!*' and asked the police what they meant by their comment.

Two weeks had passed, and I remember the estate being littered with more police patrolling the area, making more house-to-house enquiries. I would give the sniffer dogs a wide berth upon leaving and returning home. I say *we* because Mum had to escort me to and from school. It was advised that I should not venture out alone given the circumstances.

The immediate area surrounding our house was cornered off after further leads led to more inspections of our local area. Posters went up on lamp posts, windows of local shops with some further afield — a constant reminder that Lauren wasn't here — hadn't been found. I remember Aunt Cassy saying it was amazing how the law enforcement only ramped up the missing persons investigation once they found out that it wasn't a girl from the estate that was missing.

'But *why didn't the police come straight away?*' she complained. *'They knew well what they were doing. Serves them right!' 'Perhaps if they came quicker Lauren would have been found!'* Aunt Cassy kept pointing out. I couldn't understand why Aunt Cassy was so vexed. Lauren was gone.

In the following months, life on estate continued to dwindle. A once neighbourly face was now filled with suspicion and awe. People seemed to hurry past us — their heads would look in the other direction, with others taking the opportunity to dart across over the road when they'd spot us in the distance.

'*Child disappears after party on South London estate*': *'A fourteen-year-old white girl inexplicably goes missing under the care of partying 'religious' black family on notorious South London estate',* shamed one of the local newspapers.

The paper even detailed witness reports (next-door neighbours) saying that they heard children's raised voices coming from our house, sounding like we were having an argument — with calls for the person in question to, *'Get out of the house!'* Dad said he didn't know how much the 'witnesses' were paid, but people were *the wickedest of beasts*. Another 'close source' apparently reported that someone at the party planned Lauren's abduction and that it was a perfect opportunity for Lauren to be taken, sold off and trafficked (to another country).

Some papers even suggested that Lauren's disappearance was the result of entanglements with our family's ancient voodoo traditions, ending in the *'sorrowful, traumatic event'*. *'How can they call themselves Catholics when they allowed something like that to happen right under their noses?'* *'Eventually the evil perpetrators will be brought to justice'* were other circulating comments.

The only constant friendly face on the estate was the lady at No. 24. She would often come to the front door to just say hello and ask if there was anything she could do. Her usual bellowing voice was now reduced to near-normal conversational level, especially as *the Old Bill* was in the vicinity.

But more harrowingly, apart from my loss, nothing could be worse than the anguish and despair encountered by Mr and Mrs Harrison. They were completely heartbroken. I overheard girls hushed voices at school saying that Lauren's parents couldn't forgive themselves for letting Lauren come to our party. They desperately mourned their only child.

Even years later, they still held onto hope that Lauren would someday return. I couldn't help but feel responsible for their loss… our loss.

At first, Tina and Sarah made the effort to talk to me at school. Shortly after Lauren's disappearance, they sat next to me at lunchtime and asked about the chain of events and seemed really sympathetic about what happened. And that if ever I wanted to talk to them I could. But by the next day the girls never as much as gazed my way in the lunch hall. When I clasped eyes on them, they'd quickly look away, pretending they couldn't see me. I fixated on their sharp-tongues wagging — filling their friends in with my 'version of events', I presumed.

Lauren was officially a *long-term missing person* as a month had now passed. And as the weeks and months went on, I felt the school walls closing in on me. I became withdrawn, suspicious — it seemed nothing could save me from feelings of loneliness and isolation.

Conversations with fellow students became shorter in duration and less frequent. Fixated smiles borne out of pity turned to disdain. The empty seat next to me during lunchtimes and at the school desk became the norm again. Perhaps everyone read the local papers and believed in the rumours too. Perhaps pupils' parents had warned their children not to go near me in case some malevolence might rub off on them too or something ominous might happen

— like it had to Lauren. Some teachers would offer a friendly ear. But I didn't want or need *adult* conversation. I just craved someone my own age to throw me an olive branch; hold out their hand; let me into their circle; help me understand what was going on around me.

Autumn turned to winter then to spring. The ostracization I felt at school routinely continued together with the video player in my head replaying Lauren running off into the darkness on the estate — echoes of her laughter ringing out in my ears and dying out in the distance.

Without fail, every night the sequence of events played out in my head. The repetitious sound blended in with sounds of incessant cries of a child faintly circulating in the night air.

I would drift off to recollections of Lauren and I singing in her bedroom; writing her love letter to Mr Baldwin; re-enacting scenes from *Fiddler on the Roof* and tap dancing in the hallways at school together. It was not until one night that the video playback commenced again — the sounds of Lauren's laughter and cries of a young child merged together, reverberating in my head. Then, it slowly diminished...

A gust of wind breezed through the opened window causing my bedroom curtains to flap gently against the wall. The incoming mist created cloud-like shapes. I bolted upright in bed trying to comprehend the sight before me. The mist kept forming and reforming its shape with a blurred image of a young girl appearing. I kept blinking my eyes trying to adjust my vision to get a clearer view of the figure in the darkness. Although unnerved, I felt unafraid by the presence. The hazy image lingered for a while, then dissipated...

Chapter 3

'Oi… you girl'

Looking back, I wasn't the sort of person who'd find pleasure in doing high kicks and wearing fish net tights for a living. I could have been described as the shiest most introverted person that you'd ever come across. Certain family members would always bully me into squealing at the top of my voice at nearly every family gathering; be it birthdays, communions, deaths, and 'getting through to the end of the week' parties. Or any other excuse for a party you could care to think of. But I had it seemed no choice but to wail at every request.

My family loved a good party though. By which I mean extended family. They always enjoyed weekly get-togethers. It didn't matter the occasion, just any excuse to have a jump up (that's lots of dancing that includes anything from hoisting bums in the air and waving hands ferociously to the music) to the 'snake dance' — a chain of people dancing calypso in a conga line. This would always exhaust itself by the time the 'snake's head' darted back to its origins in the front room, having weaved its way through every corner of the poor host's house and demolishing every precious china ornament in sight! If you refused to join in this ritual, you were certain to be dragged into line if you hadn't already pre-empted your 'get-out clause' and locked yourself in the bathroom to escape the commotion. An old Calypso favourite was playing and everyone joined in singing,

> '...*Bills bills everyday*
> *Bills bills ma-ka-pay...*
> *Water bills... TO PAY*
> *Gas bill... TO PAY*
> *............ TO PAY*
> *............ TO PAY*
> *Woy-yo woy-yo I'm going crazy*
> *so much bills TO PAY*
> *Woy-yo woy-yo I'm going crazy*
> *so much bills TO PAY!'*

I cocked my ear to the bathroom door and waited until the last of the footsteps made their way back down the stairs.

'Where's Sophia?' sang Mum. She still had traces of her lovely Caribbean accent.

Thankfully all was not lost at sea on her journey to England.

'She must be in her room, you no see her?' I could hear Aunt Cassy saying.

'I neva see her,' Mum sang back. 'Eh eh, where is she? Sophiaaaa... Sophia, you in the toilet?' Mum called up the stairs above the din.

I sheepishly made my way down the stairs and could hear my aunt's cackles getter louder.

'Kek kek kek kek kek kek kek kek kek… you been in the toilet, Sophie?!'

Aunt Cassy spoke loudly enabling everyone to hear. Her laughter caused her head to fall back as she grabbed my arm, pulling me into the conga line. The whole room erupted as, 'BILLS BILLS' came to a climax with everyone singing at the top of their voices. The thumping beats were heightened by the continued cackles emanating from my beloved aunt's mouth. She was famous for her laughing at any little thing that tickled her fancy. It's amazing to witness someone who can genuinely laugh at… anything. This hilarity would be joined in by onlookers, delighted at her high-pitched squawking, which would even give the most miserable of party-poopers a teeny-weeny bit of pleasure.

Next time, it was Mum's cock-headed dance movement that set aunty off. The bellowing music could be heard streets away. Childhood days were times when hardly any neighbour complained after a night of loud music seeping through their adjoining walls, hearing different voices out-do the other during speakers' mike-hogging time. Neighbours on our estate who weren't invited were probably dancing to the music in the middle of their front rooms, or rocking in the comfort of their beds, especially if Lovers' Rock was playing. You couldn't find any sweeter music for lovemaking. One could imagine couples hypnotically rolling around on their satin sheets. It would only be a matter of hours before they'd swiftly snap out of their unconscious worlds, with tugs from their offspring pulling at their parents' feet protruding from under double duvets.

Back then, no reports were made to the environmental health committee for 'noise pollution'.

No neighbour was eager to smugly set their 'noise logger' devices ready to monitor the din of the music, whilst grinning with delight when their devices measured 'over and beyond' the required readings for a healthy neighbourhood. Party hosts could sleep guiltlessly at the end of the night when their loud voices slowly diminished giving rise to daylight. No. Final readings for the Noise Pollutants Local Council Complaints Committee would be savoured for the forthcoming 'Health and Safety' generation.

As the night progressed, the music slowly fizzled out. A conveyor belt of well-wishers would try to out-do the previous speaker with an even longer and well-intentioned speech. People who didn't need a mike insisted on using one anyway. Their lips firmly locked to the mike, showing more intimacy with the metal object I'd imagine, than they would have done all night with their bed partners.

When Mum found a chair and sat down, you knew the party was over and we were in for a long speech. Nothing could stop her dancing, as she'd find the beat in anyone's speech and wriggle her hips in time to the rhythm. But this speech was painstaking slow and long and ended with

'...anyway congratulations on moving out of your niece's room and finding your own place to stay!'

'Kek, kek, kek kek, kek, kek, kek,' squawked Aunt Cassy.

A final call was made for any stragglers or LIPS (Least Important People to Speak) as aunty secretly nicknamed them. 'Where are the LIPS?' aunty would say, whilst pouting her lips like a fish and making sucking noises, and then breaking out into laughter again. This meant only one thing. It was time for the Stage School girl to stand like a lamb to the slaughter ready to cry out to her devilishly expectant prey. I couldn't get out of this one. *We* were the hosts. And it was *my* room that aunty was moving out of. I always opted (somewhat reluctantly) to warble some old show tune or jazz standard from yesteryear as the old timers usually appreciated it. And they were the ones I needed to please the most. More importantly, I didn't want to let my parents down. After all they *did* sacrifice everything to send me to private school, and 'they' needed proof that my parents' investment wasn't all in vain.

Well, at least not yet anyway. Creases would deepen in my forehead, and I'd begin to look much older than my eleven years.

Then, someone from the crowd cried out. 'What you singin' for us, Sophia?'

I gulped and tried to compose myself, looking to Mum for encouragement. 'Erm, I'm going to sing Blue Moon?'

'Aww, ain't that lovely. You sing it girl!' the crowd crier replied.

The song was followed by a rapturous round of applause: I smiled at a sea of delighted faces. Had it not gone down too well, I'm sure the smiles would have become very stilted and fixed. I could see my brother Neville's white teeth gleaming as his head poked out from behind the living room door.

He tilted his head and then let out an almighty cry, 'Bluuueeee moooooo... oon ooo ooooo ooo,' howling like a wolf and laughing uncontrollably whilst clutching both hands to his stomach.

My other brother Devon couldn't resist the opportunity and picked up where Neville left off. He flashed his teeth and clawed his hands as if howling at the moon. 'Blue moooo... oooo... oooooo... Scooby Dooby Dooby Doo..ooo.'

The room erupted.

'Kekk kek kek kek kek kek!' Aunty's cry was loud enough to wake the sleeping drunk in the corner of the room. I watched a room full of bodies doubling over with their heads rolling back and forth. It was my brother's antics and not my singing that set the party alight, and aunty's cackling made it just that much worse.

I caught Neville's eye and bolted after him up the stairs. He quickly locked himself in the toilet before I could get to him whilst wailing in fits of hysteria.

'I'll get you back, Neville. You devil!' I wept as I ran off to my room, feeling sorry for myself. It simply made him laugh even harder.

A new school week was upon us. Most mornings, I'd wake up before the alarm went off. My neatly pressed blue kilt skirt shined from over-ironing. This, together with my light blue shirt, V-necked jumper, tie and blazer, were neatly suspended from a skewed metal hanger on the knob of my bedroom cupboard door.

I usually escaped the house before the early morning groans of my brothers who were fortunate enough to literally roll out of bed and into their all-boys secondary school an hour later which was located only a stone's throw away from our maisonette. Tulsen Boys was as rough as it comes. My brothers would tell me stories of nervous teachers locking themselves in the toilets to avoid hurls of teenage boys storming through the corridors during break and lunch times. How they'd survived that school was anyone's guess.

Just as I was ready to leave home, Mum would appear from nowhere and hand me my blue boater that was left dangling from the tall white plastic coat stand in the hallway.

'I paid enough money for that, you know, make sure you wear it!' Mum demanded, whilst thrusting the hat under my nose. Without objection, I'd take the smart-looking hat, prop it on my head and smile at Mum as if to say, 'thanks for reminding me'.

Mum was going to make sure I wore that bleeding hat if it killed her. Once, she even followed me half-way out of the estate in her nightie waving my hat around like 'someone who'd just been let out into the community', or like I'd forgotten to put on my undies or something. She didn't know of the disapproving looks I'd get from local schoolgirls for owning such a thing. Yes, my parents had paid dearly for that hat, along with the extortionate school fees, and I was made to wear it religiously from Autumn through to Spring.

Thankfully, the school's Summer straw hat was a tenner too far.

As I crept off into the darkness to catch the early morning bus to school, I'd look out for peeping toms or any other creatures that might surface from well-known corners on our estate. Sotch, a big black ferocious dog with red eyes that lived on Demata Road, had the tendency to jump on children and have a way with them. Devon had told me all about it, even though I didn't completely understand what having a way quite meant. As soon as we'd hear Sotch's bellowing bark, we'd run like headless chickens to the safety of the playground on our estate. Along with the other kids, my brothers and I would climb to the highest point of the climbing frame to escape him. Yet still, Sotch would growl and jump up as he'd try to catch the end of a girl's skirt or a dangling brown leg as a source of food. Devon said he was sure that the owner (a skinny Jamaican guy who lived with his mum) was intoxicating the dog with his fumes which would send the dog into a frenzy.

Once out of the estate, I'd remove my boater and squeeze the soft felt of its brim between my thumb and forefinger so as not to lose it on my way. Either that or a gust of autumn wind might threaten to take its hold. Other potential thief takers could be the South London gyals who I imagined might try and grab hold of it and mock me for having such a posh accessory to my already 'outstanding' uniform. I had to ensure that my precious hat bought from an exclusive outfitters' shop in Liverpool Street station (as Mum would remind me) didn't fall into the hands of those South London preying-mantises. Mum would surely have been on the warpath and hunted those girls down if any harm had come to my hat, or indeed to me.

I could see the red double-decker bus swooning around the corner as it brushed past the over-hanging shrubs that took up half the pavement. I picked up the pace and darted across the road at High Trees. Two familiar morning faces welcomed me at the bus stop. But the prospect of catching up with the local gyals with their vicious peering eyes sizing me up and down was something I always dreaded.

As the bus approached, I could see some girls striding round the bend, but I couldn't quite make them out. Thankfully I got on the bus before they reached the bus stop. Once inside, the conductor looked up in the mirror placed in the corner of the top deck and called out for any persons standing to 'come downstairs otherwise the bus wouldn't be going nowhere.' 'Anywhere,' I corrected the conductor in my head.

I had two elocution lessons per week at school taught by a hair-flicking elderly gent called Mr Hodge, and I could imagine him proudly nodding in approval. Signs clearly stated: **No standing on the top deck**, although some conductors didn't always enforce this ruling.

When the bus engine was abruptly switched off, mutterings and tuts spilt out of passengers' morning breaths. A lady in fake fur with a feather protruding from her hat began to squirm in her seat as if trying to release some obnoxious gas. She must have boarded from somewhere like Crystal Palace looking like that — not from around here! People started checking their watches for the continuing delay to their journey. Finally, a few passengers reluctantly made their descent onto the lower deck, much to other passengers' delight and the engine was revved up and the bus was on the move again.

The 2B bus route went all the way from Crystal Palace to as far as Baker Street in Central London. The old route masters with the open 'hop on and hop off' platforms were met with a large step up onto the lower deck with seats spread across for four passengers on opposite sides. I could feel the unwanted gaze from a bald-headed man wearing a beige trench coat sat with his briefcase upright on his lap. As usual I didn't want to show that he bothered me in any way as I regularly saw him on the bus to school. But he continued to sit there, smiling, like he knew that his unwanted attention was a cause of irritation for me. Even at the age of eleven, this man's look indicated that there was something else going on behind his 'kind eyes' and 'pleasant' smile.

Our school grounds, set in a pre-dominantly 'black area' in Clapham, were dominated by white faces. I was the only black girl there. School days were full on and crammed with academic and vocational lessons. Lunch was nothing like what we saw on our weekly televised edition of *Fame*.

I'd intriguingly listen to girls' conversations about who was staying over at who's house that weekend and overhear stories of elaborate dinner parties and weekend trips to Marbella: a world away from mine.

I wondered what the Covino Kids would think of our 'jump ups' on the estate? I felt different: from a different culture, a different world. But *their* world appeared much less complex than mine and absent of grief.

The daily disturbances between our school and the local comprehensive at Clapham North tube station was unnerving though. The station was regularly peppered with bobbies on the beat on hand to settle any minor scuffles between their Public and our Private. Kids from my school thought I was crazy braving the streets of South London by turning right instead of left out of the grand school doors that secured the Academy. Turning right was a no-go area for our pupils. Heads from our school didn't even so much as look that way. Although pupils turning left out of our school were at risk from 'attack' from neighbouring warring schools, I suppose it was safety in numbers. It was also as if they knew something *I* didn't.

But I remained blissfully ignorant, and at the end of each day, I would walk purposefully to the bus stop in

Stockwell going homeward bound with 'the locals'. I felt proud that I didn't encounter any incidents walking home alone directly from school. It was closer to home where I had to be on guard. I could hear footsteps rapidly getting louder from behind.

'Oi. You girl.' A girl with thick jet-black hair pulled back so tight in a ponytail that you could barely see her eyes continued speaking, 'Where you rushin' to?'

I turned around to face a group of girls panting as they made their way towards me.

'Nowhere.' I tried hard to appear as though I wasn't fazed by their presence.

'What's your name?'

'Sophia?' I replied in a higher-pitched voice than normal.

'What school d'ya go to?'

'It's in Clapham,' I replied, not wanting to give the name of the school away.

'Oh, right.' The lead gyal looked at her friends and was satisfied with my answer. 'I like your uniform,' she lied.

'Innit, its nice, innit.' A weedy voice came out of a small round girl loaded down with lots of school bags. The lead gyal looked down at my hat as I slowly attempted to move it behind my back. But before I could hide it, she piped up.

'Does everyone have to wear one of those?' A couple of girls sniggered making snotty noises. I nodded my head in agreement. But honestly, I'd never seen anyone else wearing a hat to school. And I wasn't about to tell them.

'Can I try it on?' the lead gyal asked teasingly. 'I neva tried one o' dem on before.'

I looked down at my boater and a vision of my mum flashed before me. I thought it'd be best to comply and hand the hat over to the gyal. Her face lit up. She plonked her school bag onto her friend, adding to the poor round girl's mounting collection. Then she plopped my hat onto her head and struck a pose.

'I look good, innit!' she boasted whilst turning to look at her friends. They all cracked up laughing as she began to use the alleyway for a catwalk — parading up and down and revelling in all the girlish attention. 'Are you meant to walk like dis?'

Her poker-face mocked deep concentration and the entertainment continued as she placed one foot purposely in front of the other, as if walking on a tight-rope whilst balancing my *Complete Works of Shakespeare* on her head.

'I better go home now.' A small voice finally ventured out of my heated body.

'Ah. Sorry, Sophia, mummy must be wondrin' where you are.' Her voice dripped in sarcasm. They all burst out laughing. And with that my boater came hurtling towards me at high speed and the girls made off.

'Run along now.' A voice rang out in the distance. 'See you again, Sophia.'

I gripped my boater tightly in my hand and breathed a sigh of relief that the interrogation was finally over. The hat was so secure on my head that its brim nearly touched my eyebrows.

When I got home, I was glad to see Mum and I hugged her tighter and longer than usual.

'You okay?' she asked, sensing something was up.

'I'm fine.'

Her eyes scanned my head — delighted upon seeing my hat upon my head. If only she knew.

Despite my encounter with the local gyals, coming home was a great comfort.

Everyone was fairly friendly on the estate. We were all in it together. Even though some taxi drivers refused to go down to the other end because a cabbie met his fateful end there; it didn't seem so bad. Demata Estate didn't have the worst rep as estates go. But it didn't stop everyone secretly hoping that one day they'd finally get out.

Chapter 4

From Public to Private

Hearty meals and regular squabbles with my brothers at home were a great source of comfort. Sometimes though, I'd look out of my bedroom window and onto the fields of my local secondary girls' school and view the vast grounds and tennis courts that belonged there.

The screams and caterwauling from the girls convinced me that they were always having a blast, letting out cautions to the wind and feeling free. I imagined what it would have been like if I decided to go to the 'free' school instead.

St Saviours was my second choice for Secondary Education. Would I have been happier there? I was desperate to get rid of this feeling of not fitting in all the time. Hearing the laughs and shrieks from the girls at after-school tennis sounded so much more refreshing and less pretentious in comparison to the girls at my school. Also, had I gone there, I wouldn't have had to dodge the South London gyals because I'd be *one of them*. In contrast, our school of performing arts was securely closed to the outdoor air. No playgrounds for us.

Covinos was full of rich kids talking about mummy and daddykins, with posh girls showing oral displays of wealth dripping and spewing forth from fashionably lispy tongues. Some spoke with Sloaney drawls, and others sounded like they had a couple of plums stuck firmly in their throats.

It was the summer of '83 and even our estate in Tulse Hill looked pretty in the morning sunshine. The brickwork was terracotta with the usual slated roofs. The driveway circled our enclosure like a grand prix circuit track, ready to guide any lost souls in Cortinas safely out of the estate at night. The circuit gave rise to a number of sleeping policemen along its track, which provided lots of fun for boy racers. But not much fun for car suspensions. You'd never know when foreigners to our estate needed to make a speedy exit when darkness fell.

A block of old people's homes was used to separate the two parts of the estate, with warnings of *Keep off the grass* and *No Ball Games* posted to deter us kids from *looking at* much less entering the 'protected zones'. We were lucky that no occupants had to climb any further than three storeys high to reach the safety of their homes; unlike the unfortunate people stacked one on top of each other in the twenty-storey blocks at Norwood Heights only a couple miles up the road.

I remember we had the pleasure of grandma looking after us for most of the Summer.

She lived in the Caribbean and rarely made visits to England. So, as Mum repeatedly impressed upon us, we would finally get the chance to spend some quality time with her. I remember grandma's ease at singing hymns. It was as if a beacon of light would shine down on her every time she let out, *'Oh let me walk, oh let me walk, so close to thee... eee'*. Aside from her heart-warming songs of praise which gave my brothers and I something to joke about, grandma's daily preachy mantras and religious quotes from the bible appeared to be as much for her own sake than for anyone else who cared to hear, but not listen. In her heart of hearts, the *Christ Church's Way* was the only way. And didn't we know it!

Mum and Dad were always busy at work. Mum was probably on her second job of the day by the time I surfaced from slumber. I could hear my brothers excitedly playing downstairs, glad that the start of the six week's holiday was finally upon us. Surely even the bully boys at Tulsen School would be glad for a well-earned break from having to keep up the tediousness of their own bullying.

There was a knock on the door.

'Hi. Is Sophia coming out?' a girl blasted assuredly.

'Halloo. Good morning,' grandma said to the stranger cheerfully. 'Sophia?' she quizzed, as if wondering who she was referring to. 'Oh, oh, yes she still sleeping.' Grandma's Caribbean lilt lingered in the breezy air. 'What's yer name?' she enquired.

Carmelle continued in her cockney accent. 'I'm Carmelle. Sophia told me to knock for her. Is she playin' out today?'

Grandma hesitated and then: 'Soophiyah.' Silence. 'Sophia, yer up yet?'

Grandma's voice rang out, finding its way up the stairs to my bedroom and under the duvet. I tried to keep still under the covers. I didn't stir and held my breath. After a short pause grandma continued. 'Don't worry errr… um, what's ya name agen?'

'Carmelle,' said Carmelle flatly.

'Don't worry Carmelle, I'll tell her yer called. Oohkeh?'

And with that the front door slammed shut. I could just imagine Carmelle pushing out her bottom lip, rolling her eyes and slinking around the corner, peeved that she'd be returning home once again without me in tow.

I drew a sigh of relief and rolled onto my back to face the naked bulb that decorated the ceiling. Thank God I had escaped the wrath of Carmelle. Don't get me wrong, she was a nice enough girl and from a loving family. But she could be a little overbearing at times. She was the complete opposite to me. She talked ten to the dozen and loved the sound of her own voice. It was good though I suppose to have a friend who qualified as a true south London gyal. She wasn't like the others. She liked me. Our parting after local primary school sent her off to the all-girls school up in Norwood. She had to be tough to have survived a year there.

Girls in the area didn't mess with her as she could hold her own. Being seen with Carmelle also showed that I hadn't completely neglected my South London roots even though my school uniform would suggest otherwise.

We'd exchange homes for girly chats, and I enjoyed being in her company. Her house was usually a no-go zone though. On the rare occasion that I plucked up the courage to pay her a visit, I would always fantasize that her Alsatian bitch would claw its way through the locked backdoor of her garden, smell me out, and with a pent-up passion penetrate my skin with her gnashers and crunch her jagged teeth into my tender, succulent bones. At hers, one ear was always firmly attached to the garden door, with both eyes transfixed by Carmelle's lips which moved as quickly as I would run if that bitch had the audacity to escape.

Our long summer with grandma was blissfully interrupted with visits to Brockwell Park lido, coach trips to museums, zoos and amusement parks. Days out on the Blunder bus (a re-painted graffiti-styled old route-master bus that had all sorts of children's activities on board) sat stationary on Demata Road. This was fun enough and wasn't an activity that would cost my parents and arm and a leg, but you'd soon get bored after your third trip 'on board'.

There was only so much a kid could take of the same adult dressed-up in a pirate's costume with a parrot on his shoulder shouting, *'ooh ahh, ooh ahh'* as he welcomed you onto the bus.

The only trouble was, the Blunderbus was positioned right outside Sotch's house on Demata Road. My brothers and I would check from the safety of our maisonette balcony to see if the coast was clear. Then, with a unified nod we'd make a run for it. Dogs it seemed was the bane of my life and forever plagued my childhood. But creatures (my dad would always warn) come in many different forms and guises.

The trip to Woburn Abbey was a favourite of mine. Our car journeying the streets of London in the sweltering heat was as much fun as the destination itself. Mum made sure she'd slip in our favourite snacks of iced gems and French fancies and litter our picnics with ham and cucumber sandwiches with cans of ginger beer to keep us sugared up along the way.

Musical Youth blared out from the car radio, and we all sang along whilst bobbing our heads to the steady reggae beat:

'Pass de dutchie pon de lef hand side
Pass de dutchie pon de lef hand side
It ah go bu'n
(give me de music let me jump and prance)
It ah go bu'n
(give me de music let me rock ina de dance).'

My brothers and I would blast out the chorus every time it came up and hum along to parts we didn't know the words for. Madness' *Baggy Trousers* was also still popular and every time we'd hear the song, we'd challenge each other to see if we could remember all the words.

'Lemme do it this time,' pleaded Devon.

'Nah you did it last time,' stropped Neville, 'it's not fair.'

'Aw go on den, go on den,' Devon relented. 'You won't do it better than me anyway. I am the master blaster... innit.'

Neville sang the song word perfect all the way through to the end. We complemented him by doing the Madness Dance on the back seat together with dead-pan facial expressions. When the song had finished, Neville nodded his head like an old schoolteacher showing admiration for a class full of obedient pupils.

'Tssst ah,' he boasted whilst blowing onto his knuckles and rubbing it against his chest in a self-congratulatory fashion.

'You see it deh. I... am... de best... oh yesss... so ressss',' Neville persisted.

Devon and I had to endure his 'victory' all day long.

On the way home, I'd escape their boyish banter by studying the street names of London. Thanks to Dad, I now knew most of London on the back of my hand and would've surely passed the Knowledge (Test) for black cabbies had I been old enough. Because we didn't have a garden Dad also decided to get an allotment. We spent many a summer day there pretending to grow vegetables but spent most of the time drinking lemonade from plastic cups, laughing, weeding and playing in the sun.

Night-time on the estate was a different animal. Sometimes power cuts kept us in the dark for hours at a time. Occupants of our estate would rush home with keys at the ready to unlock their front doors, breathing a sigh of relief once the door was locked firmly behind them. Overweight workers on the late-night shift quickly found a new pace, fleeing home like cockroaches scuttling to find refuge in hidden corners of a kitchen when the lights are turned on. Most nights were eerily quiet. Apart from the grave incident that took place down the other end of our estate which was not really talked about, and unless we were having one of our parties, it was quite quiet. But there was always a sense of unease. Cars didn't frequent as much as in the day.

When Mum wasn't on the night shift, my parents would stay up to watch late-night films. They loved *Hammer House of Horror,* and sometimes my brothers and I would be allowed to stay up and catch a glimpse of it with eyes peering out from behind fluffy cushions. It wouldn't be long before we'd be sent to bed though. Devon often had nightmares and I'd find comfort in telling him funny stories until the lids of his eyes finally found their resting place. I cared deeply about him and even though I was younger, I felt it was my duty to look after him and protect him from his night terrors. Once he was asleep, I'd slip away to my room.

I always noticed a black car that used to hum outside which was in direct view of my bedroom window. I often wondered what the driver could be doing for so long in his car, if indeed it was a 'him'. Sometimes I'd creep out of my bed and peek through my curtain to catch a glimpse of the offender. But would quickly lose courage and pull back from view in case the person could see me. Moments later, I'd hear the sound of a front door being closed a few doors down. It sounded as if it came from the other end of our balcony.

I'd slowly tiptoe back into bed, pull the covers over my head and stick my fingers in my ears to shut out any more normal yet intrusive noises.

Another Summer had passed, and grandma was on route back to the Caribbean. Trips to the airport were usually a family day out, and by that I mean our whole extended family.

The equivalent of say a family day out to IKEA; pointless but essential. Being tossed around in the back of an HGV with ten other members of your family was not only against the law, and painful, yet exciting. Of course, my aunt could be heard squawking in the back of the van whilst rolling around in fits of hysteria whilst the driver made another sharp bend without warning.

'Eh, how you getting on with the Hooray Henry's at school?' my dad's cousin twice removed asked.

'It's good,' I replied, trying to keep the conversation short.

'And do you do ballet — lots of prancing around and that?' he asked in his Caribbean come Cockney twang.

Trying to remain upbeat I said, 'Yeah, we do lots of different styles like…'

But before I could start listing them he blurted, 'But aren't you too fat to be a ballet dancer?'

Everyone laughed. Even I saw the funny side of it. It was the usual banter within the family.

Everyone got ribbed in some way or another — no age discrimination here. I *was* admittedly a little weighty, but I was a child. And I seemed to be getting jibes from all directions and on a more regular basis. What the heck, I thought, and I reached for a chocolate digestive from the bag of goodies hanging behind the drivers' seat.

Mum changed the subject. 'Oh. I wish I was going to the Caribbean. Could do with some sunshine,' she complained.

'Yeah, well ya should have bloody stayed where you was, innit. Who tol' ya to bloody come here?' the driver joked, in his broad Caribbean cockney accent. 'Bloody pissin' weava!' He swerved another corner. More laughter and cackling followed, and we finally arrived at the airport.

After five hours of milling around the airport and eating our snacks, it was time for grandma's departure. She religiously left us with a recital of a psalm from the *Gospel according to Luke Chapter 2 v 15*; whilst frenetically waving goodbye as she disappeared through the departure gates at Heathrow. We all turned to walk back out of the airport terminal. Some relatives wiped away tears and hugged each other, with others turning back to see if grandma was still in sight. Dad's cousin twice removed shook his head and said, 'Thank bloody God for that!'

The new academic year was approaching, and it was nearly time for my boater to make another unwelcome appearance. Don't get me wrong, I liked school; liked my teachers; and liked the lessons. It was just my loneliness within those grand walls that thwarted me. I still hadn't managed to find someone I could call a friend. A year had gone by and by the end of the Summer term it still felt like I was on the periphery; like I was attending a big party to which I was never really invited.

Letters had arrived informing my parents of what I needed for the new term.

Jockstraps (for boys), character shoes, tap shoes, jazz shoes, black leg warmers, a girdle to be worn under your leotard to hold in your waist, and pink tights were amongst other requirements and made for financially heavy reading. I was always excited by letters that came through the post from school, introducing our family to a new school year. Mum asked Devon and Neville if they wanted to do part-time ballet on a Saturday at my school. They looked at each other and burst out laughing and asked Mum if she'd lost the plot. They said ballet was only for nancy boys and wouldn't be seen dead in a jockstrap and a pair of tights. I was determined to make this new year like a new beginning. Surely it wouldn't be as daunting or lonesome as the first and I'd pluck up the courage to make a friend.

Afternoons were filled with learning an assortment of facts from the compounds of subcutaneous rock to the functions of the pituitary gland. I always had my head down and immersed myself in books and schoolwork to the point where my teachers once called my parents in for a meeting, because they were concerned that I was way too serious for a twelve-year-old. They thought something was troubling me which the school needed to know about.

Hmm, well I could list a few. But my parents weren't overly concerned as my behaviour at home hadn't changed. It was just the way that I was. I was just a bit serious I guess for my tender years and found it difficult to make friends. If something was bugging me though, I wouldn't dream of burdening my parents with my childish woes. They had enough to worry about with keeping a roof over our heads, keeping food on the table and wolves from the door. Needless to say, the stress of mounting school fees was a continual pressure. I felt I had to help out in some way and many an evening sat down with my dad to write to the *Manpower Services Commission, GLC, ILEA* (that's Greater London Council and Inner London Education Authority) along with any other elected service we could find in the Yellow Pages to ask for sponsorship.

Unfortunately, the suggestion by my primary school teachers to apply for a place at the prestigious private school came too late, as I'd just missed the auditions for grants and funding by a matter of weeks. Most mornings I'd anxiously linger for the postman in the hope we'd get a response from the various financial institutions we applied to for help. We got some. But that was just to say they couldn't assist us in any way, but good luck for the future!

School fulfilled a personal void though. There was something that I loved about losing myself in the world of make believe. I wasn't your typical showbizzy type, but I loved dance, drama and singing for the joy that it gave me. Attending stage school was just a way of getting as far away from me as possible. Our School's Agency encouraged kids to wow them with lots of personality, and it didn't take long before kids found stints in television's Grange Hill or every production of Bugsy Malone that was going at the time.

A new girl had moved up into our year group. The teachers said it was because she was bright for her age, but we all knew it was because some girls in her class were bullying her. My blue plastic briefcase along with my rucksack bulging with tap shoes wrapped in leg warmers was always used to occupy the seat next to me during academic lessons. I was determined to get as close to 100% in my tests and no one was going to get in the way of my mission.

'Is anyone sitting there?' the new girl asked. I shook my head whilst smiling apologetically and continued with my work. It seemed I was my own worst enemy and missed out an opportunity on making a friend.

'Did you see that?' observed a girl from the desk behind me. 'Sophia wouldn't even let the new girl sit next to her.'

'I know. What a boffin!' her companion quipped, thinking I couldn't hear.

The next morning, Dad was still asleep along with my brothers who were to surface as usual way after I'd left for school. I could hear the sound of letters descending onto the front door mat with a slap, giving it its morning greeting. Excitedly, I ran out from the kitchen and sieved through the letters, checking the postmarks for signs from the financial institutions we had written to. Mostly bills with hints of pink and red peeped through the transparent rectangular boxes. I placed the offending letters on the sill near the front door so as not to alarm Mum with RED WARNINGS so early in the morning. One letter with no window had the school's stamp on it. I was curious as to what it could be about. We had already received welcoming and introductory letters from school, and any other letters would be handed to us directly at school since we were back.

'Mmm… Mmmum', I called out in a staged whisper so as not to wake the others. 'There's a letter from school. Shall I open it?'

My faked pleasant tones tried hard to cover my pessimism. Mum popped her head over the banister at the top of the stairs, her afro hair forming a lovely Mohican from a night of tossing and turning. She rubbed the corner of her right eye allowing her eyelashes to come unstuck and told me to wait a minute. The sound of the toilet flushing and the creak of the floorboards were followed by the sound of the water swirling down the plug hole and along the pipes. Maybe they were moving me into a different class same as they'd done with the bullied girl? Or perhaps they still thought my isolation was a cause for concern and needed a follow-up meeting to recommend a more 'appropriate' school? Worse still, maybe they were simply writing to say I'd be thrown out very soon if their demands for school fee payments weren't paid in FULL AND FINAL SETTLEMENT.

'Lemme see,' Mum croaked with her eyes narrowing as she approached me at the bottom of the stairs. I handed her the letter and slowly retreated so as not to get the full effects of the blow. A flash of blue skimmed along the seal as mum swiftly opened it.

'Eh eh... hold on... what... what's this?'

Mum slowly sat down on the bottom of the steps and pulled back her head to read.

'What is it, Mum?' my voice clearly shaken.

'You didn't tell me,' said Mum in confusion.

'Tell you what? What's the matter, Mum?' I asked, crazed at the way she left me dangling in suspense. Mum's expression changed. She cleared her throat and then proceeded to put on what we'd call her posh telephone voice. It read:

'Dear Mr and Mrs Healey,

We are pleased to inform you that your daughter has been selected to appear in our school production of *Fiddler on the Roof* which will be staged at London's prestigious Shaw Theatre. We will contact you further in the near future about what will be required for your daughter's involvement in the production, but just need your consent for her participation at this stage.

Congratulations Sophia!

Please sign the consent form below...'

***

Mum didn't bother reading to the end. Instead, she pulled up her long cotton nightie to knee-height and shook her hips from side to side finding rhythm in the early morning bird songs and then squeezed me tightly.

'Ahhh. Well done, Sophia,' Mum finally blurted out with tears of joy. 'You kept that quiet.'

'I never knew, Mum!' I replied with shocked delight. 'They must have picked us when they were doing their walk around the school'. 'They' being the Principal and Heads of Department. Anyway, I wasn't about to question it. I excitedly read the letter just to see the good news for myself and squeezed Mum back, pressing my cheek against hers. She was ecstatic. Not only for the obvious reason that her daughter had been chosen to appear in her first production, but more importantly all her anxieties about my struggles at school was hopefully to be a thing of the past.

I picked up my school belongings and headed for the front door. Just as I was about to pull the door handle, I could feel Mum's eyes protruding through the back of my head.

Without further hesitation, I reached my arm up and grabbed hold of my boater from the curve of the coat stand. I flashed Mum a smile and flew out the door. As I gave my final farewell, a deep voice squeezed its way through the wooden door frame before it shut.

'Eh eh, what's going on down there?'

Rehearsals for *Fiddler* were well under way and I'd never heard such magnificent music.

'Tradi-sharrrrrrrrn... Tradition (bah dah dah dah dah dah dum) Tradition.' Then, even louder and in a key higher key: *'Tradi-sharrrrrrn... Tra-di-tion (bah dah dah dah dah dah dum) TRA-DI-TION!'*

The swelling of voices: sopranos, tenors, altos, basses, and all those in between combined to produce a glorious sound to rival any first-rate production in London's West End! The sound reverberated around the rehearsal room bouncing off the walls and spilling out onto the grubby streets of South London. Mr Murphy would always catch the person who dared to linger a tad longer after his abrupt musical cut-off. And then give them a cut-eye as if to dare them to do it again.

Mr Murphy was our well-respected music teacher who acted as a pianist, conductor and crowd-controller all in one. He had piercing blue eyes and when he spoke, we listened.

No one dared answer Mr Murphy back. But to me, the glint in his eye and his pursed lips that sometimes curled up to one side betrayed his façade. He was just pretending to frighten us into sounding like real pros. When he'd flick up the collars of his light-blue denim shirt we knew the maestro was ready to begin. He appeared like a God from behind the Steinway and we stood as his congregation before him.

Mr Murphy came from Sheffield but often spoke in an Italian accent. He'd interject his lectures about attaining musical excellence with Italian phrases in his determination to whip us musical theatre wannabes into shape. Most were impressed. But I'm sure his Italian didn't even extend beyond the first quartile of an Italian dictionary. But he had most people fooled. And scared shitless. But I liked him, and I think he had a soft spot for me.

He would scan the rehearsal room as if he was going to name and shame the warbling straggler. Everyone froze so as not to attract his attention. I wondered if he'd secretly laughed to himself as he viewed a roomful of puppy dog eyes that cried *please don't pick on me*.

'Tut. It has to be pianissimo at bar 34 tenors.' Then his Italian accent kicked in. 'It hassa-to be- a-like-you-caressin'-a-cryin' baby... pianissimo... pianissimo. .'

He stared ahead as if he was in a trance-like state which was void of bodily contortions. Then he closed his eyes. The whole room was motionless: fixated on him. He then opened his eyes again and searched the room. He found a girl with big boobs and red hair and paused for a moment. He raised an eyebrow and searched the room again. He found me and I stood there in fear, not knowing if I was *the chosen one* that day. But a soft voice emerged from his pursed lips, 'Sophiahh.' He then proceeded to sing my name to the tune of 'Maria' from West Side Story:

'...So-ph-ia, So-ph-ia, So—ph-iaaaahhh,
I've just met a girl named So-ph-iaaaahhhh.'
'Hmm hmm hmm hmm hmm hmm
Hmm hmm hmm hmm hmm hmm
Hmm hmmmm.'

Mr Murphy got lost in his own passion building up to a crescendo in the song and swaying to the music. Then, he shook his head as if awakening from his own spell and placed his Italian lips into position.

'You-hava-to-feela-ze-mo-ment a...Colla voce — Freedom of the voice.' He turned to look at me.

'You a-gree-a, Sophia?' Mr Murphy teased.

I smiled and nodded in agreement. Then it was back to business as usual – back to *Fiddler* – as if his dramatic episode had never happened.

'Sops (sopranos) you sounded fantastic,' he concluded in his Northern accent. Everyone's tape recorders were set and ready for a final blast of *'Tradition'*.

Singing made me feel free but with no playground and no outdoor space, school could get a little claustrophobic. The openness of our estate gave me a sense of freedom and release. So, before I'd settle down to homework, my brothers and I would glide along our balcony on our roller skates and skateboards. My older brother was a whiz on his skates, and I'd always envied the way he moved so elegantly on his wheels. I just rolled along clumsily transferring my weight from one foot to the other and never gaining momentum or developing any sense of style or grace.

We'd wheel to the end of our balcony much to the annoyance of the older white couple at Number 23. Sometimes they'd bring out their bucket of water and a hard broom, pretending it was necessary to start cleaning the concrete balcony floor with disinfectant.

Once 'The Miseries' as Neville called them had finished 'cleaning', we'd resume skating again and swiftly pass their door next to our friends at No. 24.

The African lady who lived there with her two sons always had her door wide open, ready to welcome guests at the drop of a boater. She had two sons: one was stunted in growth and the other made inaudible noises and didn't speak much.

Her front room was turned into a hair salon with carpets replaced with lino and hair dryers for heaters which neatly lined the perimeter of the room. Her pay dial-a-telephone hung on the wall next to her kitchen (which was twice the size of a store cupboard). Our telephone hung in a red box next to our local sweet shop.

'How are you? You okay?' asked the African lady from No. 24 as I poked my head round. 'How's Mum?'

Considering we lived only six doors away she could have easily found out for herself.

But I guess she always just asked out of politeness. It was a conversation starter. She always had a smile to greet us and would often offer my brothers and I ice-cream on square cones if we happened to peer through her front door. Her clients would sit like statues under their hair dryers whilst reading the latest edition of *Black hair and Beauty* to break the monotony. We never lingered too long as the stench of peroxide and oils would poison the air, and kindly accept her offer of ice cream with one hand whilst holding our noses with the other.

Evenings were growing darker and after watching my daily dose of Blockbusters with dad jokingly saying, 'Can I have a 'p' please Bob?' for the umpteenth time, I'd go upstairs to my bedroom. Most evenings were spent sitting at home at my desk, burying my head in a book. It wouldn't be long before I'd smell the aroma of Mum's Caribbean cooking. With a twitch the nostrils and an intake of air I often felt full before I'd even eaten. Home was safe and warm. Nothing could invade our peace — our sanctuary. Or so I thought.

Chapter 5

Don't Look Down

It was half-way into term and rehearsals for the production were coming on nicely.

Normal lessons resumed, and preparations were being made for our entrance into our RAD (Royal Academy of Dance) exams. Ballet classes were mainly held on the ground floor in the large hall with a ceiling as tall as the sky. Girls with pink tights, black leotards and thin bands to secure their delicate waists held one hand lightly on the barre, with the other in 'first position'. As we listened to the two-barre piano introduction, ballet arms would move in unison, up and down to the music (known in ballet terms as 'breathing'). Mrs Court would begin to count using her singy-songy voice to complement the music, 'Plie and a one... two... three and a four, rond de jambe six seven close eight.'

Pull up from the waist, stretch your toes and *don't look down* were some of the regular phrases used to keep us dreamer ballerinas in check. Barre work would be followed by centre work, which were sequences danced (as the name suggests) in the centre of the room. I loved the dramatic music that accompanied our glissards and grand jetés across the sprung-wooden floor. Half an hour of the barre was enough to send even our prima ballerinas to sleep.

Mrs Court would split the class in groups, so that she could walk around and concentrate on correcting individuals' ballet positions. My group was the first to perform our ballet sequence. Some of the girls sat watching on the floor in crossed legged or stretching positions, with others resting on the huge stage with legs dangling whilst patiently awaiting their turn. Mrs Court came around and did her usual adjustments to girls' out of place arms and legs. As I lifted my leg to retiré (that involves standing on one foot and sliding the other foot up the side of your supporting leg with your big toe meeting the side of your supporting knee!) I'd try to keep my balance. Then, with my thigh held in place I'd extend my lower leg out so both legs made a right angle. Obtuse angles were made by your more flexible ballerina, but no one came close to 180 degrees.

As I lowered my leg, I noticed one of the girls who sat on the stage trying to stifle a laugh whilst sneakily elbowing the girl next to her. The nudged girl followed the direction of her friend's eyes which appeared to be staring straight at my crotch. I could feel my cheeks tingling but was unsure why. Anyhow, I carried on dancing in time to the classical piano playing.

It was time for groups to swap. I told myself to forget the girls' stares, but as I was about to walk towards the stage to rest Mrs Court's voice rang out. Her instructions came with a tilt of the head and a raise of the eyebrows.

'Sophia, Lucy and Kendra, can you go again with the next group please, and this time think about your corrections?'

With my cheeks still flushed from the attention I had gathered, a girl from behind me brushed past my shoulder on her way to being seated. I looked around to see what could be wrong, searching for a reassuring glance to help me feel at ease. Conspiratorial whispers waged around me. I couldn't escape. I had to dance again.

As the music swelled a repeat of more stifled laughter and eyes bouncing on and off my crotch filled me with panic. My legs shook fervently, and I wobbled on one foot like an anxious-ridden trembling patient newly-diagnosed with a neurological disorder.

At last, the music stopped.

I slowly lowered my head and looked down between my legs and was filled with sheer horror. My leotard had bunched up to form a lovely bulge like an undulating hill. My sanitary towel had been wedged out of place from all the pirouetting and jetés that I'd done, and it looked like I'd stuck two pairs of thick woollen socks underneath my leotard.

I slowly raised my head, and as if in slow motion looked around the room for help, pleading for a pitiful smile to comfort me and say there was nothing to be ashamed about. But nothing came.

An eruption of laughter was cut short by Mrs Court. She dismissed the class and warned everyone to come to class with a more mature attitude next time. Still searching, I stood alone, trying to catch a friendly eye. Instead, girls in ballet buns dispersed from all around me like flies escaping faeces when footsteps come near.

I didn't tell Mum about the incident when I got home from school. I brushed it under the carpet, together with the book I'd hidden under my bed about menstruation. It had a blue front cover with its title written in white and a red blob for the dot of the 'i' in the word 'Period'.

My humiliation at school was bad enough. If my brothers got hold of the book, there would be no end to their teasing.

Still distraught from the incident at school, I asked Mum if I could go and knock for Carmelle. Carmelle loved talking and I was sure she could comfort me with her kind words.

Mum said it was fine and said not to be longer than half an hour. I hurried out of the estate and made my way towards Carmelle's house, praying that her garden door was firmly bolted from the inside with her dog Proctor on the other.

I told Carmelle about the whole embarrassing episode. I told her how no one had come to my rescue and how I couldn't even tell my mum about it. She listened intently and was very sweet. And kept repeating phrases like, 'don't worry' and 'it's nothing to be ashamed about' and 'they're probably just jealous'. Even though I *did* worry, and I *was* ashamed, and they probably *weren't* jealous, but talking to someone about it made me feel better.

It was soon approaching technical rehearsals for *Fiddler* at Shaw theatre. My aunt had put the finishing touches to my costume. That was one of the requirements for taking part: you had to provide your own costume! My long brown woollen skirt spun out nicely when I twirled around, and my matching headscarf tamed my waves of curly afro hair. My light caramel-coloured skin was drained of any colour once under the bright stage lights, which afforded me the ability to 'blend in nicely with the other chorus girls,' so I had been told.

Us children of *'Anatevka'* danced as children would in happy musical numbers; smiling, holding hands and weaving in and out of street scenes. Mournful songs gave rise to beautiful childish voices and sorrowful grown-up cries of woe. All manner of assorted props including candles, tankards, wooden benches, carts, heavy cloths and delicately embroidered lace adorned the stage. *Anatevka*, a number about *belonging* and *home* was one of my favourites.

Italian phrases like 'pianissimo, legato and staccato' could be heard from a voice screaming out from the orchestra pit!

Our first night was buzzing with pre-show nerves and healthy doses of adrenaline.

Company members would practise choreographed dance routines, whilst others huddled in corridor corners, practising harmonies with one hand cupped over one ear and hand-waving like a frenetic conductor with the other. The Curtain went up and came down three hours later.

'Well done, sis,' mocked Neville, who then proceeded to mime using a skirt and twirling around on the pavement, trying hard to sound like a baritone when his voice hadn't even dropped yet.
'Tra-di-sharrrrrrrrn... Tra-di-tion... bah dah dah dah dah dum. Tra-di-tion.'
Devon took over, *'Tradi sharrrrrrn... Tra-di-tion... bah dah dah dah dah dum... Tra-di-tion!'* as he stamped his feet to a steady four/four, then bursting into fits of laughter.

I looked at them both and shook my head. *They* were the ones who should have been on stage I thought! Although I had to endure listening to Neville's rendition of TRADITION over and over again in the back of the car, I was on top of the world, and no one was going to burst my bubble.

Mum and Dad were jubilant and reminisced about the original film with Topov, and agreed to disagree about other films he may or may not have appeared in. Mum was always keen to display her knowledge of the old films. She was a sucker for thrillers and weepies and never ceased to amaze us with her broad knowledge of the celluloid kind. She would discuss many films in detail and analyse characters — intrigued by their scheming behaviour and motives.

After my brothers' teasing wore thin, I decided to brush up on my Knowledge. I clocked Dad's route carefully from Euston all the way through to Brixton, memorising street names and different points of interest. Luckily, we made it in time for last orders at our local Chinese restaurant for a celebratory meal to mark my debut performance in *Fiddler*. Dad ordered his usual helpings of fish, chips and peas, whilst we tucked into our won ton soups and more of the traditional Chinese food! It was a perfect end to a perfect night.

The next day, everyone at school said how great the production was, and the principal reviewed the show as a resounding success. The director warned us about the curse of the second show, but just said 'remember to enjoy it' because the run would be over before the *over-sized Jewish lady could sing*.

There were lots of arms flailing around, and students and pupils giving each other congratulatory hugs and lots of kissing of the air. This continued it seemed for most part of the morning. In the afternoon, we received our director's notes and rehearsed a few scenes that needed tidying before we made our way to the theatre for 7:30pm start.

The second night went well (even better than the first some thought) and I looked forward to telling my dad all about it at 'Curtain down'.

When Dad met me at the stage door I noticed that didn't seem his usual cheery self.

'Hi, Dad', I said with a smile. 'We had so much fun tonight! One of the boys tried to make us laugh during the death scene!'

My voice half-petered out. Dad's expression was vacant.

'That's good, Sophie. I'm glad you enjoyed it.'

He kissed me on the cheek and took my hand and led me a few streets away to our ride home. Dad let out a huge sigh as he placed his hands on the steering wheel and turned to face me. He thoughtfully asked, 'Are you hungry, Sophia? We could pick up something on the way home if you want?'

'It's okay, Dad, I don't mind finding something at home. I'm not that hungry really.'

Dad turned the radio on for company and I studied our route back home, checking if I could remember the streets off-by-heart from yesterday. When we got to Brixton, Dad stopped and picked up some chips and sausage in batter from the late-night kebab shop. I quietly munched away.

As we turned into the estate Dad slowed down before he approached the sleeping policeman, and he cleared his throat.

'You know… grandma isn't too well… I may have to take a trip and go see her in Dominica. So… I may not be able to see your last show on Saturday. Okay?'

I wasn't concerned about Dad missing the final show. I was more concerned about him and worried about poor grandma. I wanted to ask what was wrong but didn't.

'Don't worry, Dad. I hope grandma'll be okay.'

I visualised grandma with the beacon of light shining down on her. Her hymn hauntingly rang in my ears, *'Ooh let me walk, let me walk, so close to thee.'* I said a prayer. Then made a sign of the cross and fell asleep.

Dad was up unusually early and told me he'd see me later after the show. I gathered my belongings and made my way to the bus stop. As I exited the estate, a route master bus whizzed past me on the other side. I looked in the opposite direction to see if I was lucky enough for another to follow behind. Just as I crossed the road to the bus stop I could just make out the South London gyals headed in my direction. I looked back at the estate and back at the girls again, remembering what happened last time. With thoughts of Dad and grandma, I wasn't up to another repeat performance, but it was too late to turn back.

I could see a gangly girl with hair pulled back off her face gaining pace as she balled out my name. As she approached, she bent over whilst trying to catch her breath, as if recovering from a half-marathon.

'So… so… how's posh school going?' she asked whilst panting. 'I heard… I heard… you're doing a show?' She grimaced whilst clutching her stitch. I looked around hoping that some willing stranger would join me at the bus stop.

'Yeah, it's fine, thanks,' I replied smiling nervously.

'What's the show called?' she enquired, whilst finally regaining her composure.

'Fiddler,' I said.

'FIDDLA…? What kin' of name's that?'

Her entourage joined in laughing.

'It's called *Fiddler on the Roof*. It's a musical,' I informed.

'I ain't never heard of a… fiddler on a roof before… he best get down 'fore he hurt 'imself, innit.'

I tittered, pretending to find the joke amusing, joining in with the catty chorus. Lead gyal glared at me.

'You think it's funny?' Her tone was serious; her face contorted. My eyes glazed over and widened slightly. Then she flashed me a smile saying, 'Only kidding, Sophs. A joke me a-tell.'

I hesitated, thinking this might be a trap. Then as her friends began to crack up, I sensed it was safe to crack a fake smile too. I watched as cars and passengers raced by, praying for a rescuer. Lead gyal didn't let up though. She was on a roll. She thought for a moment and then her eyes sparkled.

'I hear you do lots of dancing and ballet. Is that right?' She looked around as if to say now watch this one. I nodded tentatively. First, she started pirouetting on her toes and was lapping up the laughter all around her. Then, she started again. 'Do you have to wear… what are they called again… errr … jock… urm dat's it… a jockstrap?'

A voice piped up from behind, 'Dat's what boys wear, you dufus. To hold their tings in.' There was a roar of laughter.

'Nah, nah nah nah… wait a minute.' She went in for the kill. 'But I heard that in ballet you have to wear like…

errr, what is it?... urrm... like... bulky tings between your legs!! Is that right?!'

My face turned a bloody-red colour.

'AHHHHH, shame guy!' wailed the small round girl at the back, carrying three school bags that were strangling her neck.

And with that they ran off laughing and screaming along the road until out of sight.

'Have a good day, Sophie...!' lingered a voice in the air.

I froze, transfixed on the diminishing figures in the distance. I turned away from the passing traffic, bent over and balled my eyes out. I thought about grandma. Thought about school. I thought about those horrid girls. But worst of all I thought about Carmelle. She betrayed me. How could she be so cruel?

Chapter 6

Sell Out!

A few days had passed and the excitement of performing the show every night was swiftly dampened by the troubles overshadowing me closer to home. Dad tried to put on a brave face, but I knew he was hurting deep inside. When grandma spent the Summer with us, I noticed that they didn't spend much time together. Their daily communication was more reminiscent of a handover at a workplace. Grandma would help us to get ready for the day ahead: organising early morning duties, cooking breakfast and then making sure all Mum's snacks were packed and ready to go and not short of an Idris (ginger beer) or two. Grandma mainly stayed at home when trips were made further afield. She was spared the long car journeys with all its rowdy noise and back-seat banter. After fun days out with Dad, grandma would then resume the evening shift, cooking us Caribbean dishes in Mum's absence and getting us ready for bed.

    That week, Mum's shifts were doubling in number and she was working even more hours that God could send. Her main job at the Residential Care Home was in neighbouring Streatham. I couldn't tell you how many other jobs Mum had on the go, but I'd never forget the one that involved my brothers and I neatly folding office furniture leaflets together with order forms and stuffing them into envelopes. We had a good system going and in factory-like precision we would seal the freepost envelopes and swiftly add them to the finished pile. The mountain of envelopes would stack to over four feet high in the middle of our living-room floor. However, the quicker we got through one box of letter stuffing, the sooner it'd be replaced with a new one.

When I got home from the evening shows, my brothers would relay what had been happening on the estate. Whilst I had been *prancing about on stage* as they'd put it, they said that the lady from No. 24 was becoming a regular visitor to our doorstep. They told me how Mum had confided in her after she caught Mum rushing in from work one evening looking stressed and fatigued. Mum told her about our ailing grandma and our rising struggles with mounting debts. Mum wasn't the sort to tell anyone her business as it were, but she was near breaking-point and needed an outlet, otherwise it wouldn't just be grandma on the verge of walking 'up close and personal' to thee. My brothers overheard the lady from No. 24 mentioning that *if there was anything she could do to help that Mum should just let her know.*

Dad worked his usual shift at the Skill Centre and when he got home, he continued his ritual of greeting my brothers with *the* best scrambled eggs and slices of white bread with a mars bar placed in the centre of the table as a treat for Afters. Although I had missed this daily ritual for a whole week, my brothers soon huffed and puffed when they'd discover remnants of fish and chip wrappings in the bin the next morning, following my post-show late night feasts!

Dad told his work about grandma's illness and asked for an advance payment. His manager at work sympathetically gave him the money so Dad could fly out to the Caribbean as a matter of urgency. My brothers and I weren't aware of grandma's health issues when she spent the Summer with us. We hadn't noticed anything that suggested she was suffering in any way.

But I did catch sight of grandma rotating her wrists and exercising her finger joints every so often; and letting out a woeful sigh at the end of her routine. Dad booked a standby ticket to Dominica for the coming Saturday which was to be the first Saturday of October and in between Mum's busy work pattern and homely duties, she'd help him pack his suitcase. This was the trip Dad dreaded but knew he'd eventually have to make, Mum said. Dad and grandma's distance still baffled me though. Perhaps it had something to do with the *sanctimonious drivel that spouted from grandma's mouth* as I once overheard Dad saying to Mum.

Luckily, I hadn't seen the man on the bus or bumped into those ghastly gyals for a few days on my travels to school. God must have been looking down on me and acknowledged that I deserved some respite.

Saturday finally arrived, and it was the last day of performances for *Fiddler on the Roof*. I was already mourning the fact that the show was coming to an end, as I'd be on such a high all week. Being in the bubble of the show helped me to forget about my anxieties if only temporarily. Dad said his goodbyes; we all shed a few tears and he made his way to the airport early in the morning. On this occasion, Dad's journey to the airport wouldn't consist of a shed load of family members squawking from the back of a van to add weight to his load.

Instead, he travelled to Heathrow from Brixton station, courtesy of public transport — changing to the Piccadilly line at Green Park underground station together with I'd expect camera-flashing Japanese tourists and West End shoppers eager to clinch the latest *must haves* in the form of the latest 24" televisions with built-in Ceefax.

In light of our father's absence, it was a comfort to know communication with the outside world was now only six doors away. Our neighbour (the lady from No. 24) proposed that Mum was very welcome to give out her home telephone number to persons who might want to contact us in an emergency. Mum opted to use No. 24's telephone for less private conversations, but still had a preference for using the telephone in the red box next to our local sweet shop for conversations of a more intimate kind. Shortly after Dad left, the click clack of sandals along the concrete balcony floor could be heard getting louder until they suddenly came to a halt outside our front door.

'Mrs Healey, you deh?'

The lady from No.24 shouted through the letter box. This was followed by a loud knock, as if her booming voice wasn't enough to warrant a swift answer to the door. And doing things quietly I later discovered was something our neighbour wouldn't even preserve for night-times. The lady from No. 24 was hell bent on making sure our neighbours knew she was in the vicinity.

'I jus' got a call from your wo'k, and deh want to know if you kyan do an extra shif' todeh.'

Mum opened the front door and lowered her voice hoping that she'd follow suit.

'My work just called you?' Mum asked quietly conspiring. 'I'll have to let them know I can't do it. Sophia has her last show tonight and I have to pick her up. Can I use your phone please?' Mum grabbed her purse before she could answer and searched for coins.

'Eh eh. Well of course you can use the phone, Jean,' the lady from No.24 replied in her same loud voice.

'You know, Solly left this morning. He got a stand-by flight to go back home. I don't know…' sighed mum heavily.

'Oh, he got de flight.' Her voice inflected. 'That's sad… I mean it's good he was able to go, but his mudda… dat's sad. I hope it will wo'k out okay. Eh eh. Don't you worry, Jean.'

Mum stood motionless on the doorstep staring up into the sky as an airplane thundered timely overhead.

'Hold on. What time you need to pick Sophia up?' the lady from No. 24 enquired.

'Well, the show finishes about ten o'clock. Solly usually picks her up in the car,' Mum said resignedly. 'I'll have to get the bus to meet her with the boys.'

'Hey, you know wha'. Don't worry yo'self. I can pick Sophia up with de boys if you want. Then you c'yan do your shift,' the lady from No. 24 proposed.

'That's really kind, but I really don't want to bother you with…'

'…ah come on. It's no bodda at all. Really. I did ask if there's anything I c'yan do. They can stay at mine. Your boys can share one room with my boys and Sophia can have de other. It's really no trouble at all. I know its ha'd for you all at de moment.'

Mum was grateful for the kind offer and surrendered to her pangs of guilt by accepting. Her 'sleeping-over' payment at the residential home would cover at least a week's shopping. Mum had already thought of ways she could return the favour to the lady from No. 24. She even thought about braving the peroxide atmosphere by promising to have her hair done at the 'living-room-come-hair-salon' when things got better as a way of repayment.

Mum was a braver woman than I thought!

That Saturday, two bus journeys later, I arrived at the theatre in Euston just after 1 pm.

My knowledge of London was a great help in my solitary quest to find the theatre.

Previously, we had travelled to the Shaw theatre in a group directly from school. But today, 'artistes' (as we were termed) would be making our way from home for our first matinee and final show of the week. With my colourless A-Z in tow, I navigated my way from the no. 38 bus stop on Euston Road to the theatre.

When I arrived, the Stage Door keeper handed me an envelope addressed to me and I studied the post mark and writing. The envelope stamp revealed it came from South London, but the fancy grown-up writing was unfamiliar. On my way up to the children's dressing room, I ripped the envelope open in my eagerness to read the words of encouragement and support from Mum and Dad.

It read, *'Sophia, hope you enjoy your final show. Your smile lights up the darkest of clouds. Stay sweet, x.'*

The card had a puppy dog on the front with the saddest puppy dog eyes. Even though four-legged creatures weren't my favourite of friends, the photo *was* kind of cute. The only thing that puzzled me was that the card wasn't signed by Mum or Dad, plus they knew I couldn't stand the sight of a dog, even on paper!

Maybe the anonymous card was sent by someone in the Company or from a pupil at school. I was flattered that someone had thought of such a kind gesture but was more astonished that I might have an admirer in my midst! I never thought anyone really noticed me.

I visualised all the grinning boys in the show and marked them off one by one in my head... until I got to Tim. Tim was always cheery around me, and he *did* try to make me laugh on stage in the middle of a scene the other day. I noticed that he regularly made an effort to say 'hello' and 'goodbye' to me, unlike the others. Maybe the card was his way of telling me that he more than just liked me. He must have got one of his parents to write it for him and post it from school. I imagined that this was what it felt like to receive a Valentines card.

Last Valentine's Day, I remember girls in my class bragging about the number of poetic messages they'd received from swooning sweethearts. Now *I* had first-hand experience of the excitement of playing detective and searching for clues to find my admirer.

At every opportunity backstage, I'd search for someone to give me a sign and surrender to their anonymity. I was too shy to approach Tim, but the more I caught a sneaky glance at him on-stage, the more he smiled back. It had to be him. How sweet! It would remain our little (wink wink) secret.

The matinee was full of customary pranks, which I soon learned was a theatrical tradition carried out on the last matinee of a Show's run. I even heard real beer was put into tankards, which the leading actor playing Tevye drank out of and then spat out immediately on-stage during the *Wedding Scene*. The Company Manager reprimanded the offending culprit by giving him a firm talking to in-between shows.

The acting company were mainly students, so *were* legally able to drink alcohol, but *the powers that be* didn't see the funny side of it or perhaps didn't want to be seen condoning such irresponsible behaviour! In the workplace, adults were always full of contradictions as I remember seeing bottles of wine on the table in the staff room once when I had to speak to one of the teachers after school and caught a sneaky glance of them lapping up their alcoholic indulgences behind closed doors.

With pranks still in full flow, one of the chorus boys stuck on a moustache which looked like it belonged to Agatha Christie's Monsieur Poirot. Everyone on stage in the *Dream* scene tried hard not to laugh. But titters coming from the audience made it impossible not to embrace the traditional spirit, and we all ended up 'corpse-ing' onstage (that means laughing onstage when you shouldn't!). On the contrary, the graveness of the scene turned more into a scene from a pantomime, but all in good humour.

The evening show was a sell-out and the audience gave us a standing ovation. With the house lights turned on full, the Fiddler company joined hands to bow proudly to our captive audience. The electrifying atmosphere gave rise to a well-received speech by the School's Principal, who thanked everyone for all their help and support for making the show a resounding success.

When we signalled for the band to take their Curtain Call, the main spotlight honed-in on a bald head shining from the orchestra pit. It also illuminated his set of white teeth which gleamed as brightly under the lights. In contrast to our fears of being on the receiving end of Mr Murphy's glare and being guillotined with just one look for singing a beat after his musical cut off, the audience had the privilege of witnessing his proud orchestral prowess and winning smile. That was probably the first and last time I caught sight of Mr Murphy's perfect gnashers! They only came out on special occasions — and this certainly was a special occasion.

Faint strips of white made their appearance down made-up rosy cheeks. Tears cascaded down cast members' faces caught up in the emotion of it all. I leant forward to catch a glimpse of Tim who was about three hands down the line from me. My mind flashed on my card with the cute puppy dog on the front. When he smiled back at me my cheeks flushed, and I turned my head back quickly to face the audience whilst simultaneously feeling a tingly sensation down below.

At the end of the show, we all said our goodbyes and did lots of kissing of the air and hugging as if it was the end of term and wouldn't be seeing each other for a while. But it'd only be a day before we were back at school again. Tim said goodbye to me on his way out of the Stage Door and I gave him a long lingering look and a knowing (wink wink) smile.

The minute hand was now firmly on the 'six' with the hour hand half-way between ten and eleven. Most of the company had already left the building and I sat patiently watching the minute-hand on the clock.

'It looks like you'll be sleeping with the theatre ghost!' joked our lovely stage door keeper Gillian.

I winced at the thought and suddenly missed Dad even more. Dad was always prompt. My mind ran on Tim again and I decided to take a peek at my card from the inside of my bag to distract from the lady from No.24's increasing lateness. I secretively read the words again.

Did the 'x' mean he wanted to kiss me? I smiled childishly to myself thinking I was alone with my thoughts.

'You got a fan then?' asked Gillian. I quickly closed my bag and stared straight ahead like I *had* seen the theatre ghost.

'It's from Mum and Dad to say good luck for the last show. They couldn't come tonight,' I blurted, trying to cover my deceit whilst furtively closing my bag.

'Ah, that's nice…' replied Gillian, stifling a smile. Gillian glanced at the clock on the wall then at her watch again and blew steadily into the air.

What could be the hold up? Mum made all the necessary arrangements before she set off to work, even to the point of clearly defining the route for the lady to follow, with a pen drawn on the map from 'home to the theatre' on our larger A-Z. I was wondering whether this might have been more of a hindrance than a help, as Mum wasn't a driver and her attempts as navigator always ended up with Mum and Dad arguing on route to every new destination we drove to after always getting lost.

Actually, coming to think of it, Mum's attempts at learning to drive were pretty dire, so her navigational skills couldn't have been much better. Most lessons consisted of

Mum exercising her voice rather than her manoeuvres. She may as well have just invited her driving instructor in for a cup of tea, biscuits and a chat. It would have been much more comfortable for them both and a far lot cheaper for Mum!

I remember Mum's attempt to pass her driving test, she'd spend most lessons in the same spot after two hours, having not moved an inch. Mum boasted that her driving instructor said she was one of her favourites, and at £18 an hour you could understand why!

Dad soon put a stop to it some months later. Co-incidentally, just before I started at the Academy.

At this rate my *pick-up* may well have ended somewhere in Shoreditch rather than the Shaw theatre with mum's skewed sense of direction.

Gillian made several calls to the lady from No.24's home number she had listed, but it just rang out. The stage door flung open so hard that the metal handle banged against the interior of the stage door wall; chipping off bits of paint work as it then crumbled to the floor.

'I'm so sorry, Sophia,' apologised the lady from No.24. 'I'm sorry to have kept you waiting,' she continued turning her head to address Gillian. 'I was waiting at the front of the theatre. I didn't kno' the artists had to come out of de back entrance! Eh eh!'

'Yes, we have a special entrance and exit for the artistes!' joked Gillian, managing to regain her sense of humour.

'A man at de front who saw me waitin' tol' me to come round here to the side door. Eh eh, that's no way to treat de artistes!' the lady quipped.

She sounded like she wanted to pull up a chair for a chat, completely oblivious to the fact that Gillian was now rummaging through her belongings, noisily rattling through her assortment of keys. 'Sorry, dah'ling,' laboured the lady from No.24 whilst opening her arms and squeezing me tightly.

As I got lost in her bosom a whiff of peroxide penetrated my nostrils which made me dizzy for a slight second. Once I regained my balance, I listened out for the sound of high-pitched voices that would trail behind her. But I didn't hear anything except for passing traffic outside whizzing by on Euston Road. The Stage Door was pulled open again by Gillian who kindly held it open for us. I think the lady from No. 24 finally got the hint and guided me out of the door with a smile. I crooked my head round the door to see where the boys were. Surely, I would have heard a rendition of Tevye's *Tradition* as homage to me by now!

'Where are the boys?' I asked, perplexed by their absence.

'Oh, they're at home. My fren' is looking after dem… Well, they were brushing their teef and getting ready for bed when I lef' them,' she laughed. 'Thank you agen miss and so sorry I was late.' And on that note, the lady from No. 24 nodded Gillian goodbye.

'Bye Gillian,' I waved as I departed the theatre, 'and thanks.'

Part of me wished my brothers *were* here. Despite their ritualistic mocking and shenanigans, it would have made the journey home much more bearable. For this was the first time I was alone with the lady from No. 24. What would we talk about? 'How's Mum?' and 'She's fine' was about the extent of our conversations. Luckily, my role as navigator would cover any potential awkward silences and possible prying questions from the lady as I directed her on the quickest route home with my knowledge of the Knowledge of the route home.

We got back to the estate in just under an hour after we eventually found her parked car.

Tonight, the familiar black vehicle was parked outside home somewhat earlier than usual. We walked along the balcony past our maisonette which was in complete darkness. It appeared lonely and dead to the world. As we entered No. 24 it would take me a few moments to get used to the air filled with its pungent mixture of smells. The atmosphere combined a heady mixture of the usual peroxides together with an undecipherable range of cooked meats.

Saturdays were the busiest days at the lady from No. 24's 'living-room-come-hair-salon.' The whole place was pitch-black, except for a bedside light which filtered through a door left ajar upstairs.

'You want something to…?'

I declined her offerings of food before the lady could finish her sentence and was led upstairs to a box room identical in size to mine — positioned at the front of the maisonette. Strangely, there weren't any noises coming from the other room where my brothers and her sons were sleeping. Perhaps the household fumes were so intoxicating it sent them all into a deep sleep from which they would never recover!

She turned the bed side lamp on in my room and hurriedly showed me the bathroom so I could get ready for bed. As I brushed my teeth, I heard the faint background noise of the television mixed with the whispering sounds of a deep raspy voice. I stopped brushing my teeth for a moment and cocked my ear to the wall. Intriguingly, up until that day, I had never seen or heard of *any* men frequenting No. 24, so I was curious to listen to their midnight chatter.

'You tol' me so much about her. It would be nice to meet Sophiaaaah,' coaxed the man with the raspy voice.

'It's late now. She's getting ready for bed. You'll meet her in de morning, baby,' she coaxed back.

'Hey, you know I can't stay de night, bebe, as much as I would love to... How was her las' show?' They exchanged kisses simultaneously, and they also exchanged rude words in between as the squelching sounds which grated on my ears. 'She missing her daddy?' he asked inquisitively in an accent not dissimilar to the lady's.

'Well, she doesn't really say much. She's shy,' the lady from No. 24 replied flirtatiously. 'Anyway, enough about her, what about me?' she giggled.

And on that note the door was gently closed — one... two... (shut). I shook off my disgust and made my way quietly back to the boy's bedroom. Her luring voice suggested she needed all the attention her visitors' hands and mouth could give.

With lights turned off, I stumbled across to the window to see the familiar black car still stationed outside. I climbed into bed, put my fingers in my ears and tried to block out the noises filtering through the gap underneath her bedroom door.

Chapter 7

I Confess

The next morning, I was awoken by the sun beaming through the window and the high-pitched sounds of my brothers playing on the balcony outside. Thankfully, my siblings had not lost all consciousness after spending Saturday night at 'the salon'. There was a knock on the door followed by a penetrating voice.

'Hello, Jean,' blasted the lady from No 24. 'So nice to see you. How was your shift?'

After Mum thanked the lady unreservedly for her kindness, my brothers and I made our way back home six doors along the balcony. We got washed and dressed and had our *'snap, crackle, and pop'* rice crispies before walking to church a couple of miles up the road.

St. Luke's Catholic Church was our local and we regularly attended Service on a Sunday, with the exception of course on days following our late-night parties!

Mum always encouraged my brothers and I to go to Confession before taking the Holy Communion. So, when the priest gave out the 'Body of Christ' (the host: an edible circular paper that's placed in your mouth like smarties to excitable children), I sometimes opted to go on my knees and *pray for forgiveness* instead. Most members of the congregation consumed the host on a weekly basis, which either dissolved on their tongues or you'd spend the rest of the service trying to prise it from the roof of your mouth with your tongue. Adult members of the congregation were fortunate enough to sip some free red wine as a treat, but only at Christmas and Easter.

During Confession, I often found that I didn't have much to confess about, so I sometimes just made things up (which was a sin in itself!). I always felt a little anxious about going into the Confessional Box and speaking to a man you unnervingly couldn't see but only hear. The priest's strong Northern Irish accent pierced through the black cloth causing it to flap about every time he bellowed. When asked by the priest to confess my sins, I'd say things like *please forgive me for hitting my brother and running off when mum called* or *sorry for telling tales on Devon* or *for taking three chocolate digestives instead of two*. At the tender age of twelve though, I did feel cleansed in some way after Confession. It felt like a weight had been lifted off my juvenile shoulders, even though I hadn't done anything gravely wrong.

Lamentably, who was to know at this tender age that airing my feelings to a *stranger* was something I'd have to endure for the rest of my life…

The church service began in its usual fashion with the congregation standing as the priest summoned *everyone to rise*. We always arrived at church just in time and therefore remained standing with the rest of the congregation. Our lateness would at least knock off at least a couple of minutes from the service. Fellow churchgoers welcomed our family with a smile and made room for us on their row. But by the end of the service smiles soon turned into grimaces and you'd often see members of the congregation moving from left to right in their wooden seats, releasing one bottom cheek and then the other to allow the blood flow to circulate again.

As I scanned the church for familiar faces, I recognised the back of a head that could only belong to one person I knew. It would be the first time I'd seen Carmelle since my run-ins with the gyals. Her short afro sides and curly top was a hair style rarely sported by the younger generation of the 80s. She sat right at the bottom left-hand corner of the church.

And whereas churchgoers beside her wriggled in their seats and turned to face the priest throughout the service and shake hands with those around them when directed to offer each other a *Sign of peace*, I noticed Carmelle just sitting there: motionless. Sitting beside her was her mum — who was just a bigger version of Carmelle, although barely two inches taller.

Carmelle's mum turned around and smiled when she saw us, but Carmelle looked as if she was wearing an invisible neck brace and couldn't move her head.

Although I was deeply upset about what happened, having licked my wounds I wanted to find out why Carmelle had betrayed me to those gyals and whether we could make up and be friends again. It took me a few weeks to pluck up the courage, and I tried several times to knock for her. I valued Carmelle's friendship as she was my only confidante in the neighbourhood, and I felt protected by having her as a friend on the South London streets.

Ironically, now that our friendship had been severed, I valued our 'friendship' even more.

However, every time I knocked for Carmelle, contrary to better belief, she was never in. I just couldn't understand why she didn't want to speak to me anymore. Surely, it was *my* feelings that had been hurt in her divulgence to the gyals about my bulging leotard episode.

For the first time though, I understood what it felt like to be in Carmelle's shoes. I got a taste of my own medicine, and now understood her disappointment when she came knocking for *me* and I never answered *her* calls.

Part of the church service where we received Communion meant that we were at least half-way through it. My brother Neville took the usual route down the central aisle to receive the host. He stood in front of the priest, stuck his tongue out and then in robot-like fashion made the sign of the cross — forehead, chest, left and then right shoulder. I watched him as he made his way back round to his seat.

Neville was definitely overdue a Confession, but Mum let him go up anyway. When he turned to head back to our row, he stopped in his tracks and stared in Carmelle's direction: his mouth gaping open and eyes flashing like twinkling Christmas tree lights. As he walked back to join us, Neville ended up standing at the end of the row as it was time for the congregation to rise... again.

As the priest continued another round of *Hail Marys*, all I could see was Devon and Neville frantically looking at each other, competing with one another to see whose eyes could widen the furthest. They exchanged smiles of mischievous delight and mouthed words devoid of sound.

Twenty stand ups later meant we were now nearing the end of the service — 'Thank God'. My stomach was beginning to make groaning sounds like the ghouls at the end of the film *Ghost*, when murderous Carl is finally taken to his rightful torturous resting place... to Hell!

Finally, the congregation was summoned by the priest to venture safely back into the big bad world (and what some churchgoers would describe as *hell on earth*). It would be at least seven days before the whole ceremony was repeated again, deplorably without much variation on the proceedings.

Neville whispered loudly as he made his way over to us. 'Have you seen Carmelle?' he chuckled.

'No. I haven't seen her in ages,' I replied not wanting him to know that we had a major falling out and hadn't spoken for weeks.

'I think she's auditioning for a job on the Blunderbus!' he spouted whilst trying to contain himself in the House of the Lord.

I looked at him and shook my head, wondering what had tickled his fancy *this* time. It was apparent that Neville had inherited my aunt's wicked sense of humour from a very young age, with Devon not following far in his bandy footsteps.

Mum led the way out of church. I could sense that Carmelle wanted to avoid me or anyone else for that matter, as she remained in her seat until most of the congregation had exited the church. Mum routinely dipped her fingers in the Holy Water which was kept in a hole in the wall and wet her forehead, chest, left and right shoulder and then mumbled something under her breath. I copied this ritual (minus the mumbles) and thought about Carmelle as I made the sign of the cross.

Devon and Neville were still up to no good on the other side of the church. I could see their shoulders shaking up and down with their bodies rocking forwards and backwards like they were on a playground swing. I tried to hurry Mum out of the church through to the foyer, as I hadn't told her about my encounters with the South London gyals or that of Carmelle's betrayal, but without success. Nor did Mum know anything about my mishap in ballet class. Just as we were about to reach the church's threshold, Mum's body swung back round to face the altar in order for her to make a final big-gestured Sign of the Cross. Instead, Carmelle's mum obscured her view, forcing Mum's voice to fill the entire church like a leading vocalist of St Luke's choir.

'Oh, hello, Ms Foster. How you doing?' Mum sung out, whilst motioning for the boys to join us. A gust of Autumnal air burst through the open church doors causing

Mum to sing even higher. 'Hi there Carmelle. How you doing? We haven't seen you for a while.'

Carmelle peeked her afro head from around the back of her mum to reveal a circular white patch taped across her left eye and a swollen bottom lip. My mouth replicated the shape of Carmelle's eye patch and hung agape for a while. Mum now progressed from a warbling soprano to just a piercing noise.

'Eh eh, wha' happen Carmelle?' Mum's voice wavered high into the stratosphere.

Carmelle stuck her head round a little further.

'I walked into a door, Mrs Healey,' Carmelle said flatly, still trying to keep her head in profile, whilst favouring her good eye.

Simultaneously, Mum and Ms Foster looked at each other, shook their heads and exhaled in unison; their groans plummeting dramatically to an 'e below middle c.'

Carmelle pushed out her bottom lip even further and Devon pushed my chin back up, so I was longer emulating a chorister at the climax of *The Lord My Shepherd*.

It all made sense now. Carmelle had a tough exterior, but when you're up against a posse of girls — you're simply outnumbered. Perhaps she had an altercation with the gyals after divulging my business as payback for being a friend with an outsider (me). She must have come to my defence and tried to protect me against those South London 'stray cats'. But why didn't she just tell me? I would have empathised with her if she was pummelled into 'dishing the dirt' and telling the gyals about my mishaps at posh school. I looked at Carmelle sympathetically for what she had to endure. But Carmelle, with her one patched eye still managed to cut the other eye after me. She obviously was still scarred mentally and physically from her ordeal. Both our parents exchanged head-shaking farewells and Carmelle trailed out of church like a lion cub trying to keep up with its mum.

It was no surprise that Neville and Devon were still finding pleasure in Carmelle's misadventure. Devon mockingly covered one eye whilst walking around in circles and tripping over his bandy feet, whilst Devon played role as director giving instructions: 'left, left left, right, right, keep going and STOOPPPPPPPPPPP!'

'What happened to Carmelle, Sophia?' asked Devon teasingly with a smile reminiscent of the Joker.

'She said she walked into a door. I don't know,' I retorted, shrugging my shoulders, knowing that it sounded ridiculous.

'That's the oldest one in the book! Hey, tell her she'd be great on the Blunderbus!'

Neville's squeaky voice imitated Carmelle's cockney twang, mixed in with tinges of Captain Bird's Eye from the television commercials. '*Ooh ahh, Captain. Welcome aboard my lovelies!*' Neville used his right hand as a beak, and looked more like he was emulating Rod Hull with his Emu than a Captain with his customary parrot.

Devon resumed Neville's role, pretending to bump into everything he came into contact with, as the boys fiendishly continued to fool around. Their ghastly laughs and mischievous play reached an almighty crescendo (which was grossly unfitting in a place of worship). Mum didn't say a word but simply raised her arm and pointed her index finger at them, signalling for the boys to stop their antics or face the consequences.

Sensing they had gone a step too far, Neville and Devon both froze, stared at each other and then made a run for it out of church towards the car park before Mum could lay her Holy-watered hands on them!

Chapter 8

Pink Tights and Ballet Buns

'...developé and a hold, point six, and a seven close eight. Hold your positions... and... relax.' Mrs Court's diminutive voice tailored off as she reached the end of her sentence and the harmonious piano chords drifted into the high ceilings of the vast ballet hall.

'Much better girls. But make sure you hold your positions to the very end!'

Mrs Court checked the room to make sure no tongue-wagging was going on in between exercises, and she firmly had her eye on Tina with her cheeky smile displaying a mouthful of metal train tracks.

'Now, for those of you taking your RAD Pre-Elementary Exam, we only have a couple of weeks left to prepare. So, if there's anything that you'd like to go over in the Syllabus please let me know and we can schedule it in. The rest of the class is dismissed.

'Erm, can you leave quietly, please?' Mrs Court concluded.

Our ballet teacher sat elegantly poised on her wooden chair beside the piano, her neck elongated with her hands choreographically placed on top of her knees, like she was ready in opening position to commence a Swan Lake solo.

'Now, are there any questions?'

Lauren's hand shot up.

'What about the digs, Mrs Court, when we go to Bradford? Where will we be staying?'

'Well, I'm glad you asked, Lauren. I'm pleased to say that Tina's mum has kindly offered for the three of you to stay at her house in Bradford for the duration. So, if it's okay with you all, we'll contact your parents to make sure this is a suitable and convenient arrangement for everyone.' Mrs Court scanned the four poised ballet-bun heads. 'Is everybody okay with that?'

Lauren, the new girl in our class with mousey-brown curly hair and blue eyes, stared straight ahead, expressionless. Her transition to our form group was working out well, even though like me she was an island. Lauren was a demure, respectable girl, admired by all the teachers, who were keen to make her transition into our higher set a smooth one.

Apart from Tina and her former elbowing-buddy, who now emulated an excitable nodding-dog, Lauren and I digested the information in silence — devoid of movement.

Tina's metal train tracks remained proudly on display until the end of the tête à tête.

With all too much enthusiasm, Tina took the baton from Mrs Court. Her confident performance included over-the-top hand gestures which attracted even more attention to herself (if that was at all possible) which kept going till she was well clear of the finish line.

Were her hand movements to form part of her grading for her ballet exam, she would surely have gained some extra marks for her audacious presentation.

Tina had a broad Yorkshire accent in contrast to her sharp features. Her undiluted tones didn't suit the grand ballet halls of Covinos, or match that of Mrs Court's perfectly demure RP voice. Tina was proud of her Northern roots, and if anything, she'd overemphasize her dialect and made sure her flattened 'a' and 'o' sounds perforated her listeners' ears.

'Yeah, me mom said you're all welcome to stay at mine.' (Hand gesture to chest with fingers spread). 'Sor, we can get the train down from Euston on the Tuesday marning.' (Point finger). 'Do the exam on't Wednesday.' (Point again in a circular motion). 'And come back to Lundon on't Thursday.' (Broad right arm stroke, signalling back like an air hostess during pre-flight safety instructions). 'Oh yeah, and mum said she'll meet uz at the station when we get to Bradford.' (Both hands upturned and gesturing out to signal 'the end of spectacular performance, ta very much'). Tina's mouthful of train tracks was now rounding the bend, signaling delight in her own performance.

Chisel-faced Tina held her finishing position for an opportune round of applause which never came. She waited... and waited, and then finally her voice inflected, 'And you can all meet me fam'ly!' with mouth wide open and eyes glistening. Da dah! Reminiscent of a hackneyed performance of Victoria Wood's *Kimberly*.

Lauren and I didn't flinch. Tina's elbowing buddy grinned from ear to ear, and Tina remained completely oblivious to the unenthusiastic 'response' from the two of us (Lauren and I).

'How's that sound then?' she grinned, still waiting for a reaction.

Err, like tumbleweed in an abandoned Detroit some might say?

Well at least *Tina* was pleased about leading our ballet quartet on an adventurous journey out of London to the 'friendly' North. Three whole days in the company of the laughing hyena with gnashers like Jaws from the James Bond films. Errgh. How was I going to cope? Tina hadn't even spoken to me *before* much less after her discovery of my *undulating hill* down below in ballet class. She hadn't uttered a word of regret for exposing my bulging ballet body; I was a mere pubescent pupil subjected to public pillory.

Mrs Court this time whipped her head in my direction, curious to witness my reaction.

I avoided eye contact by peering at Lauren for support. I sensed Lauren was just as 'elated' as I was!

I did wonder why Tina was being so 'nice' about inviting us to stay at hers in Bradford. Maybe she wanted to get into Mrs Court's good books again after the ballet incident? Maybe she was genuinely sorry about what happened, but didn't have the courage to say sorry to me face to face, and this was her way of making up for her wrong-doings?

Well, at least Lauren and I had an agreed unspoken sentiment about the arrangements.

'Well, if any of you do foresee any problems with this arrangement, please do come and see me,' Mrs Court suggested. And on that solemn note we all collected our belongings and headed to our next class.

'Thanks Tina,' mumbled Lauren out of politeness as she passed her out the hall door.

'Yes, say thanks to your mum. That's really kind of her,' I followed in pretense, not wanting to be left hanging.

'You're welcome,' Tina smiled.

We swiftly made our way to our Elocution lesson with Mr Hodge and apologised for our lateness. Mr Hodge accepted our apologies with a grimace and a stylised flick of his greasy, golden hair.

At lunchtime, I found a chair in the corner of the downstairs hall and placed my belongings on the seat next to me. The basement had windows with dark brown walls for a view — without a hint of daylight to brighten the atmosphere or lighten my depressing mood.

Resignedly, I practiced one of the breathing exercises we'd just gone over in Elocution and remembered our entrapment by 'agreeing' in theory to stay at Tina's in Bradford. I even wished that I hadn't applied to take the exam up North now, and the option of entering the exam in London seemed much more favourable.

Apparently, it was common knowledge that it was more difficult to pass the Royal Academy of Dance (RAD) ballet exams at *the* centre of excellence in London at the Royal Academy! And controversially examiners were notorious for failing ballet entrants at a far higher percentage in London in comparison to ballet entrants at other academic institutes across the country. Still, you were deemed lucky to be one of the few ballet entrants chosen, as teachers were *very* selective about who they entered for the exams. No teacher wanted a failing entrant; it may reflect badly on themselves and the Academy. But in my eyes now, however arduous it may have been, doing the ballet exam in London seemed a risk worth taking! Unfortunately, it was too late. Arrangements and bookings had already been finalized, and there would be a penalty for any changes (to which my parents could not afford the privilege).

Lauren entered the hall looking flushed and searched the room for a seat. She glanced over to where I was sitting, and I quickly removed my bag, welcoming her to sit down beside me.

'Oh thanks, Sophia. I'm absolutely knackered,' Lauren puffed, plonking herself down next to me. Lauren was a fabulous tapper and chose to do American tap with Mr Gregory on a Tuesday morning instead of Elocution.

'Was it good?' I enquired, trying to make conversation.

'He's brilliant Mr Gregory. His routine was so fast this week!' Lauren gasped in amazement. 'It was hard to keep up!'

'I'm sure you were great. I hear you did lots of tap before you came here. Is that true?' I continued, complimenting Lauren further.

'Yes, my mum's a tapper. She started me off early. Apparently, I came out with tap shoes on!' Lauren joked.

'Ah wow. Must have been torturous for your mum!' We genuinely had a good giggle and I felt comfortable in conversing some more. 'Hey, maybe I could get you to teach me a time-step or two. I never did tap before I came to Covinos.'

'Yeah, course. We could go over some basics together. Just let me catch my breath back first.'

'Oh, not now! I mean, sometime in the week — in the future,' I interrupted, not wanting to push her.

'Oh,' Lauren laughed, relieved at the latter prospect. 'No problem. That'd be cool. I need brushing up myself! You can never practise too much. Just let me know when then, Sophia,' Lauren willingly agreed.

We both ate our sandwiches and crisps in peaceful silence and washed it down with fizzy drinks: mine an Idris (ginger beer) and Lauren's a diet coke.

At the end of lunch break we made our way up to the cramped school rooms at the top of the building. Lauren resumed her seat at the back of the classroom, two rows behind me. I turned around during the lesson to check if she was ok sitting on her own. Heartily, she smiled back and looked fairly content.

It was pleasing to know that Lauren understood me and my ways. There's no better feeling than being accepted and understood. That's all I ever wanted. And for the first time at Covinos I felt a sense of ease and secure in the knowledge that I was to embark on a friendship and was valued by someone. Lauren was to be my saving grace.

Back at home though things were on a steady decline. Lamentably, grandma passed away in Dominica. We got an anguished call from the lady from No. 24, who shrieked in despair at the foot of our doorstep after she was given the arduous task of bearing the bad news to Mum. Dad wouldn't have wanted to burden the lady from No. 24 with relaying the sad news to us, but he didn't have enough minutes left to speak with Mum directly. The lady from No. 24 tried to console Dad on the phone in his grief-stricken state seconds before the telephone pips finally ended the long-distance call from the Caribbean. On hearing the pips, Dad urged the lady to tell us the news and to say that he loved and missed us all.

Mum ran out onto the balcony in her nightie and called Dad back immediately (to console him further being some 2,427 miles away). Even though Mum's stock of fifty pence pieces didn't give them much talk time, Dad was pleased to hear Mum's consoling voice. Dad also managed to send Mum a telegram detailing the proceedings in terms of funeral arrangements and other paraphernalia and formalities that comes with bringing you back to reality after drifting through the surreal haze of losing a loved one.

Our whole extended family flocked together and attended Nine Night, and sang hymns, conversed, and said prayers to commemorate our grandma's passing.

I warbled *Amazing Grace*, which was far from amazing, but my juvenile efforts were at least appreciated, given the sobering circumstances.

Some elder family members arranged flights to the Caribbean and others wore all black for the weeks leading up to and on the day of grandma's funeral. This would be the only time Devon and Neville would relieve me from being mocked for my wavering vocals.

A week had zoomed by and I took Lauren up on her offer.

'Shuffle hop step-shuffle-step, shuffle hop step-shuffle-step, shuffle hop step- shuffle- step, shuffle-step-shuffle ball change.' Lauren was going at lightning speed and tapped so skillfully and effortlessly.

'Shu-ffle hop… step… shuf… fle step,' I repeated laboriously whilst trying to marry the words with my feet. 'Shu-ffle… hop. What's next again?'

'You're repeating the sequence, but it's just on the other leg. So, it's the same sequence. Right leg, then left leg and then right leg again,' Lauren laughed, finding my difficulty at picking up the steps straight away incomprehensible. She spoke as if what she said was so logical. Tapping was second nature to Lauren, and I suppose she *did* say she came out with tap shoes on and not in a gender-identity-crisis-ed way!

'Don't worry, I'll be up there with the Sammy Davis Juniors of this world in no time!' I quipped. 'I'll practice my single time-steps for homework and show you what I got same time, same place next week!' I teased.

The small downstairs hall corridor with hard wooden floors became our regular weekly haunt for extra tap practice. Considering Lauren's high level, she was pretty patient with me as a novice, who was eager to tap out my woes through my leaden (heavy-footed) extremities. I looked forward to our timetabled get-togethers and we had fun sharing jokes in between a shuffle-step or two.

'I got drama with Miss Povey now. No doubt the theme's gonna be about some tragedy or another. Violence and death are her favourite topics!' I joked sarcastically.

'Oh great. So have I!' Lauren said with delight.

'Oh, that's good. Have you got a new timetable?' I asked. 'I haven't seen you in Miss Povey's class before.'

'The principal said I could swap some of my morning lessons around. You know, what with what happened with the girls in my year group and that…' Lauren's voice tailored off mid-flow and her eyes widened, and she stared straight ahead, realizing she should have kept her 'secret' under wraps. 'I mean, the principal said if I'd preferred to do more drama than dance, then I could change my timetable… You know what with me having done lots of dance before I came here and not so much drama and that. It'd be good to balance it out and that. You know…'

Lauren's muffled sentence ended in a heaped pile in her mouth, not dissimilar to me as a heap on the floor of the communal hallway after our tapping sessions. And for the first time Lauren sounded uncharacteristically incoherent and flustered and in a right flap. What had those girls done to her? And why was she bound to secrecy?

I decided not to probe Lauren about it. When she was good and ready to confide in me, I would be more than willing as Shakespeare would say, *'to lend her my ears.'* I completely understood what she was going through with my experience and fair share of gyal troubles.

Actually, I looked forward to the day when she would share her story with me, but not in a macabre way. I was always good at sorting out other people's problems far better than my own, and sharing would bring us closer together. That's what real friends do, confide in one another. Being advanced to another class didn't mean Lauren's problems miraculously drifted away. She was just 'relieved' from not being in such close proximity to her tormenters by not being confined to the same classroom as them. But *they* were still in the building. At least potential dealings with my *external* tormenters were a 'hit and miss' operation out on the streets of South London.

Downstairs in 'the dungeon', Miss Povey sat curled in her wooden rocking chair. Well, it wasn't a real rocking chair, but she made it appear like one. Another lot of momentous rocking movements would surely have landed her role in a remake of the highly acclaimed *One Flew*

Over the Cuckoo's Nest, but with women 'patients' instead. Miss Povey always had a bedraggled look about her, like she was pitifully worn down by life.

Even on special occasions, be it birthdays, Christmas, or end of term celebrations etc., her ruffled demeanor never changed. You could have told her her Number Bonds had come up and she would still introduce her lessons in the same drone-like fashion and get us to make up an improvisation around some form of violent act or social dispute. No magical, happy world of make-believe or sprinkle of showbiz here!

The 'world of glitz and glamour' was left to the buoyant and joyous nature of our other drama teacher Mrs Lloyd, whose brightly-coloured clothes and curly tousled hair instantly made you smile simply upon seeing her. Every lesson urged us to sway like *trees in the wind* or lie on our backs like *upturned ladybirds* and frantically kick our arms and legs in the air in excitement simply because us 'ladybirds' were seeing the world turned upside down!

Slunk in her chair, Miss Povey's withered voice and facial expression to match greeted everyone in the darkened room after her steady rock came to a halt. Drama students equally greeted her using her same uninflected tone. Although Miss Povey looked like she was frequently visited at night by a starved Dracula, she did get her drama students to produce some amazing improvisations! Stanislavski followers and method actors relished Miss Povey's classes and were sure to fine-tune their dramatic skills in this class.

Needless to say, the dramatics of the final group improvising the aftermaths of an aborted pregnancy and its effect on the family, left Miss Povey and some girls either gently rubbing their bellies in a circular motion or curling up into the foetal position with pained expressions on their faces by lunchtime.

Chapter 9

Stay Sweet x

It would be at least a couple of weeks before Dad would return from Dominica. His weekly telephone calls from overseas to No. 24 reassured us that he was coping okay. Mum tried to hide the fact that she was doing lots more shifts at her residential home — which included sleep overs, meaning the boys and I stayed at No. 24's overnight more frequently.

Dad would surely have objected to our increased slumbers at No. 24. He always held the principle that children should not be left anywhere but in the company of their parents. My newly-acquired position as *resident receptionist, tea maker and tidy-upperer* at No. 24's reception-cum-salon would also not have been favoured by Dad had he got wind of it. But earning three pounds a week Monday to Friday for after-school shifts and pocketing £5 for the weekend was an offer I could not resist, despite the stench of peroxide hair-straightening aromas filling my youthful nostrils. I just held my breath upon entering and exiting the room.

My earnings were certain to make me more popular with Devon and Neville (as well as our NHS dentist across the road in High Trees — ker-ching). I felt smug with the ability to bribe my brothers into being nicer to me by blackmailing them with my collection of sweets.

I'd buy a quarter of sweets in bulk at the end of the week, and then hide the tooth breakers in my old-fashion style mini wooden school desk in my bedroom. Late at night, I'd listen out for creaking floorboards outside my room in case the boys were planning on seeking out my sweetie storage place and pocketing some once I'd fallen asleep. Gently placing the lid down, I secured my prized possessions with the Complete works of Shakespeare and other bulky information books on top the desk in the event of a sweetie raid. Half-penny sweets included milk chocolate mice which Devon *loved*, jellies and sugary cola bottles which made your eyes water upon first taste. If the boys had been particularly kind to me (like not making fun of me for at least an hour), Devon and Neville were awarded with either dip dabs, a quarter of pink bon-bons, aniseed twists or cola cubes. However, the ultimate reward was the much sought-after candy cigarette sticks. Neville's ritual would consist of him delicately removing sticks from the slender cigarette box and then offering one to Devon which he would always graciously accept. Once they both assumed the position with said stick drooping out of the side of their mouths, they'd sit upright on their orange space hoppers and motion the 'fine art of smoking' whilst proceeding to converse about *the meaning of life* and *putting the world to rights.*

Winter was approaching — it was a Saturday morning and my shift at the peroxide-filled salon was due to start. Past-times such as playing knock-down ginger, telephoning random people selected from the phone directory books (if you were lucky enough to have a home phone) and then hanging up, youths huddling in groups on street corners to letting down random car tyres once in a while were probably the worst of the 'crimes' committed by restless and disenfranchised youths — that was the extent of the 80s concept of anti-social behaviour.

Clientele at the salon consisted mainly of women of Caribbean or African descent over the age of thirty, commonly dressed in long skirts with long-sleeved shirts to match.

They were pleasant enough. I always stood by the front door to greet customers and offer them cups of tea once they had undergone the arduous task of relaxing their hair. Relief came when they'd sit in rollers with pins dug securely into their scalps to hold the rollers in place under the hair dryer. They wouldn't complain about the scalp penetrations, they were just glad the worst of their ordeal (the relaxing process) was over. In those days there wasn't much prevention of scalp burns — it was the sacrifice you'd make in the pursuit of straight 'European-like' hair — that was a much-accepted part of the gruelling hair-straightening process. Sometimes scabs would form and weep like crying babies if the relaxant was left on the scalp for too long.

Hairs pins bearing the hallmarks of blood residue on its tips were soon wiped clean. Muted screams would get progressively louder if the lady from No.24 was tending to another client in the event of a crisis such as this. Then, and only then she would literally drop what she was doing and both her and the unfortunate scalded woman would run to the wash basin to rinse the white peroxide paste off her bruised head. The sufferance women endured was said to be the result of the brain-washed idea that black women should straighten their tight curls (every six to eight weeks) in order to aspire to the *European ideal of beauty* (a deplorable misguided cultural concept which many women of colour unwittingly bought into). The magazine editors would surely be hard-pressed to use a hair model with a natural afro hairstyle in their *Black Hair and Beauty* magazine. I even heard some hair salons refraining from blowing out women's natural afro hair. They had to be treated by a specific black hair stylist who dealt specifically with afro hair! Either that or have the less torturous curly perm which would drip like raindrops after continual spraying to keep it moist. The good ol' days eh!

Whilst I tidied the pile of towels on the side cabinet, I could hear Devon and Neville pacing up and down the balcony on their roller skates and skateboard (much to the dismay of the Miseries at No. 23). I started to wander towards the door and the two pranksters stood like two diagonally positioned meercats, peering their heads round the door whilst unashamedly holding their noses with one hand and covering their mouths with the other.

'Sophia,' Devon blurted out, sounding like he was under water with something lodged in his throat, 'you got any sweets?'

I swiftly walked to the door to mask their rude interruption to my professional work duties.

'I'm working, Devon. I can't just leave work at the salon and get them! You'll have to wait 'til I've finished,' I whispered.

'What d'ya call it?' Neville scoffed. 'A salon! Don't you mean a hairdressers?'

'Salon, hairdressers, it's the same thing,' I informed, unamused.

'Oh-er! She's busy at the salon, Devon,' Neville mocked as both boys proceeded to burst out laughing whilst repeatedly mocking our conversation using posh voices for effect.

'I won't give you any sweets later if you carry on,' I said trying to remain dignified and professional whilst in ear shot of the clients.

'Just tell us where they are and we'll help ourselves,' Devon suggested.

'No! You're not allowed in my room. I'll tell Mum!'

All manner of maturity was short-lived and I stormed out from No. 24's when the lady wasn't looking, hoping she wouldn't notice my brief disappearance. The boys raced behind me — excited by this new bit of drama and followed me six doors down to our front door. The kitchen window was open and I pushed my head through.

'Mum... Devon and Neville said they're gonna take my sweets! They're not allowed in my room,' I blurted out in frustration.

'Eh, eh! What is all the noise? Devon, Neville don't go in Sophia's room,' Mum said peering out the kitchen window, not really paying any mind to their escapades. The boys were cowering behind me laughing their heads off.

'Mum, they're not listening,' I complained. As the boys pulled and nudged me from behind, I turned around and warned them again that if they ventured into my room that would be the end of it: no more sharing of sweets, which firmly meant an end to their lengthy conversations about the meaning of life and putting the world to rights. Then in unison with their mouths firmly closed, Neville muffled, 'One, two...' and on the count of three they opened gobby mouths to reveal reddish tongues. With that, I barged them out the way and ran up the stairs to my bedroom. Heaving the heavy-duty books off my wooden desk, I lifted the lid and searched for any sugary remnants. Picking up the flat, crumpled white sweet bag I resignedly opened it to see only shards of red sweet droppings hiding in the corners.

'Mum... Mum,' I cried hurling myself downstairs, 'they've eaten my sweets!' I could hear Devon and Neville making baby noises and chuckling amongst themselves in their usual mocking fashion.

With that Devon and Neville were summoned inside and ordered to go to their room or they'd be hell to pay. They sulked and groaned as they stomped to their rooms, but I could hear titters of laughter through the wall that divided us. To ensure they kept out of my room, I thumped the joint wall in frustration and shouted that I hated them.

'Stop the noise up there,' Mum demanded and with that she stomped upstairs and had another stern word with boys. They moaned that mum always took my side, but she laid down the facts that they had taken from me what was not theirs and that they were not brought up to behave that way. Well, as punishment, at least they wouldn't be able to escape those four walls for the rest of the day.

I looked around my room to check if anything else had been tampered with like my period book with the big 'I' in the title which was hidden under the bed or indeed my card from an 'anonymous' Tim.

My mind passed on Lauren which brought me some consolation. Monday was round the corner and I'd be able to share my brothers' antics with a friend. But things could be a lot worse.

Satisfied that my room was still intact and hearing Mum make her way downstairs back into the kitchen, I shouted through the walls to the boys that they wouldn't be getting anything from me EVER again. Just in case they *did* decide to take revenge and root around in my room, I slipped my card with the puppy dog under my jumper and called out to Mum that I was resuming my work duties back at No.24 as I breezed out the door.

'Sorry, I just had to remind my mum about something,' I lied.

'Don't worry, I thought as much,' the lady from No. 24 replied. 'Can you make me a nice cup of tea, please? I'm gasping for a drink! And make yourself one too. You can take a break, eh!'

Pleased that the lady from No. 24 was not perturbed by my disappearing act, I willingly slinked off to the kitchen to make the refreshments. As the kettle was on the boil, I sneaked my puppy card from under my jumper. Studying the elegant writing, the whistle of the kettle broke me out of my spell and I hurriedly made the tea and gave it to the lady. Upon my return to the kitchen, I sipped my tea and let out a sigh.

Perhaps I could tell Lauren about my anonymous card since she mistakenly divulged the real reason why she was moved to our class. We'd both exchange our secrets. As I peered out of the kitchen window into the expanse of blue shy, a handwritten note outlined in bold red felt which was left on the windowsill drew my attention. It invited me to read:

"To my dodo darling. I'll be working away for the next two weeks, so don't miss me too much! Eh! I left the key next to the cabinet. See you when I get back, okay. X"

I wondered who her darling could be! Perhaps it was the male companion she shared her bedroom with the night the lady from No. 24 picked me up from the theatre? I looked again at the writing and was struck by circular dots for the 'i' which seemed familiarly unusual.

Slowly opening my card again, I read the words (which I knew off by heart of course) and noticed the similarity between a dot for the 'i' and 'j' in the words: sm*i*le, l*i*ght, en*j*oy and my name: Soph*i*a.

'You finish your tea Sophia?' asked the lady from No.24 from behind.

I clumsily spilled my cup of tea over the table surface as I tried to hide the card back under my top.

'Eh eh! Sorry, Sophia, I did-ent mean to fri-ten you! I clambered around trying to hide my card, whilst trying to mop up the spillage of tea at the same time. 'Don' worry about dat, I'll sort it out. You can attend to the ladies inside,' she joked.

I scrambled out of the kitchen with my thoughts running faster than my legs could carry me.

Chapter 10

Number 24

The next day at church, Mum said Devon and Neville had to go to confession before they could receive the host, so they'd had to wait at least a week before receiving communion! That would teach them for stealing my sweets! After the priest placed the host on my tongue, I turned and with my head held high and mouth clasped shut, proceeded to walk back to my seat.

My eyes locked with Devon's whilst Neville tried desperately to avert my gaze.

Devon's look told me that this was not over, and that I was sure to suffer in some way in the not-too-distant future. So, I decided to make the most of it by wallowing in their defeat.

Smugness oozed out of my immature pores — delighted that I'd got one over on the boys.

There was an Indian sweet-cum-grocery shop right next to the church, and I asked Mum if we could stop there before walking our customary mile and a half journey home (on the occasions when Dad couldn't collect us by car (being half-way across the world)), so I could get my weekly supplies. I could see Neville and Devon through the shop's window enviously waiting for me to emerge out from the shop — scuffing the tips of their polished, black church shoes and kicking their heels into the pavement — followed by Mum frowning at every scuff and gently clapping her hand against the back of their necks, signalling for them to stop. I double-checked how many £1 notes I had left.

'Is there anything you need, Mum?' I said as my sugary voice trickled through the crack of the shop's door.

'Oh… get me some green bananas please if you've got some change — I'll give you the money when we get back home,' Mum balled out.

I handed Mum the three bananas held in a thin plastic bag, then looked at Devon and proceeded to plop an aniseed twist in my mouth directly in front of him, which created a satisfying bulge in my cheek. Offering the boys nothing but a lopsided smile, the mile and half journey home was utter delight. Only the sound of sucking noises emanating from my mouth covered the absence of boyish chatter.

Ballet lessons were getting more intense the closer it got to our exam. Mrs Court was being even stricter than usual when she caught us with our toes not fully-pointed or legs not hyper-extended. Being an exam entrant meant we were always placed in the front row in class in the lead up to Judgement Day. Extra attention was given to the *chosen ones*, allowing others to take their 'pointe shoe off the pedal' if they weren't feeling up to performing their best that day.

That morning, whilst eating my customary rice crispies, I felt a trickle down below and rushed to the bedroom to hastily find my stash of sanitary towels before the unwelcomed flood commenced. Luckily for me, at 7:30 am, Devon and Neville would be on their second to last turnover in bed before being up for school. I did the necessaries and then placed another two pads from its packet between a hand towel and a Kleenex tissue on the bathroom floor, then pummelled the living daylights out of the offending items with the end of a yellow Jif bottle. My attempt to mould the sanitary towels into a flatter, pancake-like shape was well-executed and wholly necessary.

'What's all dat noise?' I could hear Mum screaming from the kitchen. I thought quickly on my feet.

'Erm... I'm... I'm just trying to break my pointe shoes in. I've got ballet this morning... my pointe shoes are still hurting me,' I replied with false conviction through the bathroom door — proud of the fact that this could cover as a legitimate excuse. It was customary to try to manipulate new pointe shoes by banging them against something hard like a wall or the floor, in hope of preventing blisters which would inevitably burst and weep out of impressionably youthful toes.

'Well, why don't you do it down here? You're making a racket and 'll wake everyone up!' Mum continued.

'I've nearly finished,' I said exhaustingly — using all my might to flatten the bleedin' white pads.

The thought of the girl with the train tracks (Tina) having a second round of hysterics at my expense propelled me to get the job done. I knew I should have asked Mum to get thinner towels but had forgotten. As I rushed back to my room, I desperately searched for my black girdle which would not only help to hold my stomach in at this inopportune time but help to flatten the 'towel' into a thinner shape, had it weaved itself out of place in the midst of a pirouette or grand jete!

In usual fashion, we quietly lined up in single file before entering the ballet room. I nervously looked down below to see whether I needed to go to the girl's room to make some adjustments. But it was too late, and it seemed the 'towel' had sprung back to life like a flat sponge filling with water. I thought about how I could try to restrict movement from the waist downwards. My face started to feel flushed. Ballet girls of differing heights continued to tip-toe through the double doors into the grand hall in conveyor belt-like fashion and there was no way of getting off. I felt a tap on my shoulder from behind. I looked back, dreading the thought of seeing a pair train tracks for a set of teeth gleaming in front of me, sensing my fear.

'You okay, Sophia?' Lauren whispered.

Phew, I thought. Lauren (from behind) must have seen my head turning from left to right like a roaming chicken. We entered the room and placed our belongings onto the stage.

'You look at bit peaky, you all right?' Lauren enquired again under her breath.

I gestured to her by lowering my head — eyes indicating an issue down below.

'Can you see anything?' I whispered anxiously. Thank God Lauren quickly understood. Certainly, she must have heard about my escapade before — in fact, the whole school must have heard about my unfortunate embarrassing episode. Anyhow, with that, Lauren rummaged through her bag and like a magician pulled out a thin, black chiffon skirt. I anxiously looked round to check no one was looking and quickly placed the skirt in front of my torso to see whether it would cover my incriminating evidence. The skirt adequately crossed over my front — with its length neatly reaching the tops of my bulging ballet thighs.

'Put it on, Sophs, it'll be a good disguise,' she coaxed reassuringly, nodding her head in encouragement.

In an instant, I quickly whisked the skirt on and mouthed thanks. It hadn't occurred to me that I could use the delicate ballet skirt as a way to disguise my monthly belly troubles. I looked around at a couple of other girls in class who also wore similar pretty ballerina skirts which gently framed their slimline bodies — covertly covering their privates. I remember seeing the item on the list of school kit needed (but this was optional). And anything optional remained 'not an option' for me (except for my boater of course). I wondered whether they were in the same boat as me, as one of the girls wearing the ballet skirt caught my eye and faintly smiled as she tip-toed past me before whizzing across the ballet floor at great speed whilst doing her Chaîné turns (spinning on the balls of the feet doing a series of 360 degree turns) and hurtling towards the grand piano at the end of the room, nearly landing in the poor pianist's lap! The pianist's upbeat recital piece unexpectedly ended in discord.

It was the end of our ballet lesson. Exhalation! I'd gotten away without attracting any unwanted attention. Anyway, Tina was probably more intent on focusing on perfecting her ballet movements in preparation for next Wednesday, and looked as if she couldn't see past her long, sharp, angular nose as it hung snootily in the air.

Later in the week, when things settled down below, I asked Lauren if we could get together for another tap-dancing session. I wowed her with my set of triple time steps and sequence of 'wings'. (Wings: an action which resembles a person struggling to get off the ground whilst flapping both feet in an outward then inward direction — creating two tapping sounds — whilst simultaneously flapping one's arms around in a circular motion). A bit like performing the butterfly stroke in reverse, but on land and in a pair of tap shoes. Both disciplined sequence of movements equally ungracious. In any case, my 'teacher' was proud of my week-on-week improvements and our continuing time spent together drew Lauren and I closer.

'What you doing this weekend, Sophs? Got anything planned?' asked Lauren as we walked through to the lunch hall.

'Not much really... Just working at the salon on Saturday and church on Sunday. How 'bout you?' I threw back.

'Arsenal's playing at home — got my season ticket so I'll be at the game Saturday afternoon.'

'I didn't know you liked football!' I chuckled in surprise.

'Arsenal and Barry Manilow. Whenever the two are playing — you'll be sure to find me there!' Lauren quipped before slurping on her Capri-sun. 'You should come to a game — you'd love it! It's such a great atmosphere — the grounds are just around the corner from where I live. Literally!'

'I'm not really into football! The only game of football I see is when my brother is playing. Devon plays for his school team *and* his local club — he's quite good. But I wouldn't tell him that — he'd only gloat! My dad said his schoolteachers say he's got great potential,' I confirmed exhausting myself with the lengthy explanation.

'Sounds like my kind of boy!' Lauren jested as she winked cheekily. 'You know, I mean it when I say you should come over. I mean, if not to watch football, you could stay over one weekend. We could watch a movie. Or better still, I've got lots of Barry Manilow concerts we could watch on VHS!'

We both burst out laughing, giving the last of the students in the lunch hall the opportunity to disapprovingly glimpse over and wonder what the hilarity was all about.

'Sounds like fun!' I said.

'Perhaps after our ballet exam — we could celebrate for getting through it — for all our hard work.' There was a pause. 'Hey, no pressure — it's just a thought. Like you said, ask your mum. But you're more than welcome to come over.'

'Sure, thanks… I'm not too sure Mum'd let me stay over though. Perhaps I could just spend the day,' I suggested. Lauren nodded in agreement.

After our exchange, we both sat munching on our packed lunches in comfortable silence for the rest of lunch break. I was excited that Lauren invited me to hers — it must have meant that she liked me. I wondered how likely it was though — being able to travel alone *all the way from my estate down South* to her *terraced house in the North*. Mum usually worked Saturdays, and it would be at least two hour-long bus journeys to get there (2B to Victoria and then a 38): I was certain *Highbury and Islington* was one of the places further along the number 38's bus route (having journeyed along this route after my trek to the Shaw Theatre for *Fiddler*).

The lunch hall room slowly began to empty as end of lunch neared. Feeling a warm fuzzy feeling inside, I collected my belongings and followed Lauren up the narrow winding stairs to the top of the building for a double dose of biology.

The salon was particularly busy as it was finally the weekend. Relaxed ladies with relaxed hair could finally breathe a sigh of relief now that the working week was over.

Customers sat patiently waiting to be treated to either a wash, set and blow dry, or a relaxer or steam treatment by the lady at No. 24, in eager anticipation of dancing the night away at a local party somewhere when darkness descended. I learnt early enough that black hair needed lots of attention and the lady at No. 24 gladly provided this service. But by the end of a night out, straightened afro hair would almost certainly shrink back in resistance and form curled ridges at the root of one's hair. If touched by a suitor whilst dancing, their dark masculine fingers would tease and stroke the females' hair, encouraging greater familiarity amongst the strangers. This would be closely followed by the ladies guiding sweaty palms away from their heads to protect their expensive well-coiffed tresses. In the salon, the local radio would always be on in the background in competition with the rows of wind-turbined blow driers. Some ladies perched underneath the plastic helmets — closing their eyes and attempting to sing along to tracks such as Carroll Thompson's melodic *Hopelessly in Love* or Jean Adebambo's *Paradise* — as the Lover's tunes impregnated the airwaves. Others would be sat with a towel over their wet hair having just been rinsed off, repeatedly flicking over the same fashion magazine pages in the hope it'd be their turn to be rollered-up next, with aspirations of leaving the salon looking like one of the *Black and Beauty* hair models.

The lady from No. 24 appreciated my help at the salon, as my tea-making would make clients' waiting times slightly more bearable. On the rare occasion that the lady from No. 24's two boys made an appearance, it would only be fleetingly 'in and out', carrying a load of clean dark-blue towels — and replacing old used ones with new fresh ones, and then disappearing quickly from view from whence they came.

'Would you like another cup of tea?' I would ask the ladies, particularly when I could see them checking their Timex watches and becoming increasingly irritated by the length of time it was taking to get their hair done.

The lady at No. 24 always booked in more clients than she could realistically attend to. But the pull was, her prices were reasonable, and she did a good job. However, a three-hour hair appointment was the norm.

'Yes, tanks darling. Milk and three sugahs please,' agreed a lady whilst painting her nails a rich, red ruby colour.

I whizzed around the room trying to be as competent and efficient as any thirteen-year-old with a responsible job could be and gladly pocketed 50p tips into my jean's back pocket. Tea duties kept me going back and forth to the kitchen for much of the day. It was only as time was approaching the 5pm mark that the strong aromas of hair peroxide became less intense and thankfully begun to subside.

''Ave a sit-down, Sophia, you haven't stopped all dey!' said the lady from No. 24 finally noticing as she plastered on what would be the last bits of offensive-smelling mixture onto a pretty lady's head. I faintly smiled and welcomed her suggestion by collapsing onto one of the chairs by the curved sink. 'Tired innit, Sop-hi-a! Ah — me too. I'm ready for my bed,' she groaned cheerfully. 'Where are your bruddahs todey, Sophia? Mum's at wok, isn't she?' she enquired trying to make small talk.

'They're at a football tournament. Well — Devon's playing, and Neville's gone with him,' I explained.

'Oh yes, Mum did tell me in de week. My boys said dey wanted to go but... you kno'... They have school wok to do,' she instructed. I suddenly felt sorry for her boys. They didn't seem to get any play time at all and always seemed to be stuck in their boxed bedrooms. The conversation ran dry and the lady from No. 24 turned her full attention back to her plastering skills, whilst I continued to browse through a copy of the South London Gazette that was left on a side table.

The lady and the client joked together, and I could see they were mindful about me being in ear-shot, as they'd glance over in my direction every time the conversation drifted to adult territory. Their speech at one point became inaudible and I started to flick the pages of one of the South London Gazette more vigorously to cover the talking.

'Are you hungry, Sophia? You want a sandwich and some tea or someting?'

My hesitation suggested that I was, but I declined. The lady from no. 24 went into the kitchen to grab her friend and herself a quick snack, and the pretty lady in the chair started to make more frequent blowing sounds. She desperately grabbed the nearest hairpin and used the sharp end to relieve herself from the itch on her scalp with one hand and knocking the side of her head with the back of a heavy-duty comb with the other.

'It's startin' to bu'n — we need to rinse it off Weh!' she balled out toward the kitchen in desperation.

'I'm comin', I'm coming — don't worry,' the lady from No.24 shouted back in amusement, shuffling back in her flip flop heels — making a clippy-clacky sound — and quickly putting on her even heavier-duty plastic gloves for the rinse. Just as she was making her way back to release the pretty lady from further agony and two-degree burns, the phone started to ring. 'Oh, Sophia, could you get dat please? Just get their name and number and say I'll call them back, tanks,' she added.

I rushed towards the telephone.

'Hello there,' I started hesitantly. There was a pause.

'And who is de young lady I'm speaking wiv?' coaxed a raspy voice at the end of the line.

'I'm Sophia,' I said reluctantly. 'Can I take your name and number and the lady'll give you a call back?' remembering in rote fashion the lady's instructions. Silence. 'She's... just doing someone's hair now,' I offered.

'Ah, So-ph-ia. How are you?' persisted the voice.

I shuffled towards the salon room stretching the phone wire as far as it could reach before I was pinged back; I hoped that the lady from No. 24 was free to take over the call. But she was still frantically washing off the remnants of white plaster and bits of crusted scalp down the plughole.

'Erm, I'm okay thanks,' I replied hesitantly again, not knowing who I was saying 'I'm okay' to.

He laughed like his anonymity was causing some kind of irritation for me and said not to worry and that he'd call the lady from No.24 back later. I stood looking at the phone on the wall for a few seconds wondering who it was. How did he know my name? And why was he being so familiar? Without disclosing my thoughts, I informed the lady from No. 24 of what the man said, took my well-earnt fiver with tips in tow, and made my way back home six doors down shortly after.

Chapter 11

Far From the Home I Love

Luckily, Devon and Neville were forgiven by the priest behind the black flapping curtain in the confession box before they went to the football tournament on Saturday. Both were remarkably quiet and reflective that night *and* Sunday morning. The priest must have given them something to think about. As things were back to normal, we joined in the whole church service — inclusive of sucking on the round circular rice paper half-way through the ceremony.

I decided to share some of my supplies with Devon and Neville on our journey home from church and sensed that they were at least grateful. Mum made a reverse-charge call to Dad in the Caribbean at the lady at No.24's place when we arrived home. With half term upon us, we spent most of our time either skating on our roller skates up and down the outdoor balcony, spending time at No. 24 in Mum's absence, or with our head in our books.

Our final ballet lesson at school served to tackle any gaps that needed filling (such as clarifying whether the *glissard sequence* started with a 4-bar or a 2-bar introduction). Mrs Court gave us her final words of encouragement, closely followed by a titter of claps of support from our fellow dreamer ballerinas.

When I got home from school, I placed all what I needed for my stay up North in a neat pile in the middle of my bed: ballet equipment, overnight clothes and filofax. I neatly finished darning my pointe shoes to cover the entire flat surface at the front with a cross stitch and bent the soles back and forth (which made a cracking sound on each manipulation): an action carried out to ensure pointes were properly *broken in*. My newly-ironed uniform hung nervously on the cupboard door in anticipation of the next days ahead.

The thought of having to spend two whole days not only in Tina's company but on *her* territory seemed almost too much to bear. But I tried to put it out of my mind every time the perilous thought disturbed me. Devon and Neville were unfashionably pleasant to me at dinner, and alongside mum, took an interest in my planned days up North. Mum made her famous salt-fish dinner seasoned with tomatoes, garlic and onions, and with a healthy dose of green banana salad on the side which I gobbled up in no time. Tomorrow's travel day to Bradford was soon upon us.

As we were about to leave, I put my coat on and placed my weighted rucksack on my back. I glanced at Mum — she raised her eyebrows. Sheepishly, I reached out for my boater which was propped on the white coat stand in the hallway and then plopped it on my head.

'Make sure you close the door behind you when you leave,' shouted Mum up the stairs. There was no reply. *'Did you hear me Neville?'*

'Okay, Mum,' he finally croaked, still wiping I'd imagine crusts of sleep out of his eyes.

'Bye — see you in a couple of days,' I blurted out.

Jubilant cries of *have fun Sophia* and *enjoy yourself*, bounced off the walls and down the stairs. Their voices of well wishes whirled in my head, making me feel even more sorrowful about having to leave the comfort of everything familiar and venturing out to lesser-known territories in lesser-familiar company. And with that the front door slammed shut.

Mum and I dashed across the road at High Trees as we could see a bus rounding the corner at a fast pace. Luckily, it was earlier than normal, so bumping into the South London gyals (even with Mum by my side) would thankfully be an unlikely possibility.

Euston station was over-crowded with commuters with it being rush hour. Our arrangement to meet Lauren and her mum, and Tina with her elbowing-buddy inside the station, outside the WH Smith shop at 8 am worked out as planned without any hiccups. Lauren's mum and my mum exchanged quick hellos and quicker goodbyes. As the train pulled out from the platform, we both sat by the window waving frantically at our respective mums; they both jogged along the platform as far as they could before we were out of sight.

'Ah, don't worry, you'll be back home in no time,' Tina remarked. 'Mom's meeting uz at the station and takin' uz home, sor don't worry, we'll let 'em know you've arrived safely,' Tina comforted. It was then that she did a double take. 'Where did you get that from?!' She gestured towards my boater. Forgetting I still had it on, I quickly reached for the offending item and placed it onto my lap leaving stubborn strands of afro hair to spring out of place.

'It's part of school uniform,' I answered somewhat apologetically.

'Re-ally?! I never knew that... Did *you* know that, Sarah?' Tina blurted out incredulously. 'That hat's part of *school uniform*. News to me!' still sounding amazed by this novel bit of information. Dreading a continuing onslaught, I breathed in and held my breath for protection from any further blows. 'It suits ya,' Tina approved. 'Bit posh for me though! But I like it on ya!'

'Ah... thanks,' I replied in disbelief, letting out a gulp of stored air.

''Ave ya ever be'n up North?' Tina continued, using her infamous hand gestures, and thankfully changing the subject.

'Yeah — I've been to Manchester,' Lauren injected. 'I've got some cousins up there.'

Tina then sharply turned her head to face me, signalling a contribution.

'Erm, only Blackpool,' I confessed, not going into detail.

'Ah, right. Yeah... *everyone* loves Blackpool — the fairground — the lights. You'll *luv* Bradford though. I'll introduce you to me friends. They say the best people are from up North. They're really friendly and chatty. Ain't that right, Sarah?'

'Yeah — *really* friendly,' Sarah concluded, joining in Tina's conducting by waving her stick-thin arm in agreement.

'My cousins live next door — I'll introduce you to 'em,' Tina offered. 'My aunty's got a fish and chip shop down end of road. Ehhhh... maybe we could 'ave some for tea later?' she proposed excitedly. Why would you have *fish and chips for tea?* An unlikely substitute I thought.

Sarah then warned, 'Yeah, but we've got our exam tomorrow, we don't want to eat anything *too* heavy, do we?' whilst stroking her concave belly in concern.

'Um yeah... maybe you're right Sarah... We'll just tek it easy today... and perhaps have a *pig out tomorra instead*!'

Tina's long wavy hair rocked from side to side in tandem with her laughter. Lauren and I replied by grinning and nodding in agreement. The closer we were getting closer to *Tina's territory*, 'anything Tina *said... went.'*

Even though Tina was trying her best to be nice, I couldn't help but think of the time when the *comedy duo* caused a scene in ballet at my expense. I wondered whether she ever thought about how I felt about the incident or how hurt my feelings were? Was her memory so short-lived? Or was it just not a big deal even though it felt catastrophic for me. As I'd thought, perhaps this trip was her way of making amends. So, I tried to remain optimist and let the negative thoughts drain away.

We bought some snacks off the train assistant as he wheeled his trolley full of goodies through the carriage. Lauren and I bought some tea, mini packets of custard creams and digestives, whilst Sarah and Tina afforded to dip their Twix and Kit Kats in the lukewarm, watery brown liquid, licking the dripping chocolate with the end of their sharp tongues. Slurping noises indicated they savoured every moment. I was thankful to Lauren for making small talk with Tina along the way, whilst Sarah made several trips to the toilet.

'You all right, Sarah?' Lauren asked with concern when she returned.

'Yeah, I'm okay, thanks,' Sarah responded weakly — overlapping the question.

Slumping into her seat, Sarah's concave belly formed an even greater c-shape.

'Just a bit of a funny tummy, that's all,' she continued as she soothed her introverted belly with her skinny splayed fingers. Tina darted Sarah a look. 'We should be in Bradford soon, eh Tina?' Sarah's voice just about managing to come out of her thin body.

'Yeah... yeah... not long now...' Tina threw back with suspicion.

Tina hastily collected all the empty chocolate, biscuit wrappings and teacups and pushed the plastics into the bin (which was positioned between the aisled seats), purposefully disposing of all our waste. We muttered *thanks* under our breaths. Tina dusted her hands off at the side of the table which separated the four of us, until all remnants of crumbs were well-discarded.

A varying combination of crossed arms and legs cut the conversation: four heads angled toward the train window — with eight eyes fixedly staring out at the revolving green fields for the rest of the journey.

In the distance, we could see a woman who appeared to be pulling her glasses off and on and frantically waving her arms in the chilly Northern air — beckoning us over in the process.

Tina let out an almighty shriek.

'It's me, Mom, it's me, Mom!' Tina screamed in delight, firstly jogging on the spot and then extending this action to create an array of mini-circles on the pavement. Passers-by rightfully gave her a wide berth, not wanting to spoil her fun but to carefully avoid any collisions. Then, like a whippersnapper, Tina dashed across the road towards the equally excitable stranger without looking left or right. A polite honk or two beeped out as a warning as we trailed behind her.

'Lauren, Sophia, this is me, Mom! You know Sarah of course,' Tina enthused as hugs were exchanged all around.

If Tina kept this excitement up, I'd imagine she'd internally combust — with splatters of her body hitting sides of passing cars, adding a touch of colour to the dull pavements and even duller-looking passers-by, with us unfortunately receiving the greatest impact.

'Lovely to meet you girlz,' Tina's mum said in her thick Northern accent, wiping tears of joy from her eyes. Of course, with Tina living in digs in London meant she only got to see her family in Bradford during the holidays. Maybe Tina wasn't so bad after all, as you know what they say (like mother, like daughter) — and her mum seemed pleasant enough.

With all baggage on board, we headed from Bradford station out of the city to the residential outskirts. I stared out of the car window and followed joggers along their morning runs and watched shoppers carrying their loads out of corner shops to parked cars. I could tell we were getting nearer to Tina's, as the journey became less frenetic compared to the busy-ness of the city.

As I contemplated my being in Bradford, the one thing that immediately struck me was the absence of a face like mine. I searched the streets and passing alleyways, shop doors and passengers in cars for a sighting. In school, being in the minority was something I was used to, but at least nearer to home I was surrounded by my own kind. But even in this brief time, being in a new city, miles away from home, I instinctively felt uneasy.

As we rounded the final corner, the Ford Cortina then swerved into a drive belonging to a semi-detached house. Lauren and I started to fumble with our belongings, eagerly ready to stretch our youthful limbs in recovery from the long journey. I squeezed the brim of my boater and held it tightly between my thumb and fore finger.

'We're here!' screamed Tina ecstatically at the top of her voice.

Tina's mum disappeared quickly into the house, leaving Tina to sort us out. She flung the car passenger door open and ran around to the boot and started to take out the remainder of our belongings, piling our bags in front of the front door — creating a blockade. The unease I sensed grew more intense as my ears were alerted to a stifled cacophony of barking and whimpering sounds. I twisted and turned my head in search of where the unsettling disturbance was coming from — looking over fences on either sides of the house and across the street. Sarah and Lauren were already out of the car, stretching their limbs in an attempt to awaken their weary muscles.

'Wakey, wakey, Sophia, we're here!' Tina balled in my direction as she energetically exercised her new-found hosting duties.

The sounds of dogs barking increased in intensity as the front door flung open wider, encouraged by a gust of biting wind. Scurrying wildly, the sight of two, thick set frenzied dogs — with heads shaped like funnels protruding forward patrolled Tina's hallway — paralysing me.

'Oh, don't mind them. They're just excited to see uz,' Tina quipped nonchalantly.

Beyond the barricade, Tina then proceeded to hug, kiss and playfully roll around on the floor with the bitches in the hallway — being mindful to share her love for each dog in careful succession. At this point, Lauren could see that there was no way that I was moving from the car, so she darted over to Tina and must have told her about my inability to move a limb. At the same time, I could see Lauren dodging from one side of the front door to the other, I'd imagine trying to block one of the unattended terriers from the opportunity of escaping and smelling out my fear.

With prolonged canine welcomes over, Tina finally blurted out: 'Mum... Mum. Can ya put Mitzy and Ditzy in the back garden, I think Sophia's scared of 'em! She's not coming in!'

Amongst the commotion, I could then hear Tina's mum barking orders at the dogs and scrambling around to chase the two ravenous beasts out from the hallway to the back of the house. Still, I didn't move a frozen muscle.

'Come on, Sophia, it's all right now. They're locked in the back garden. You're all right to go in now,' Lauren sympathised.

My frozen muscles started to unlock and then shake involuntarily. Lauren used the end of her sleeve to gently wipe the globules of water rolling down my cheek and comfortingly press her soft cheek against mine. Feeling the warmth of her skin helped to calm my nerves; she held me for a few moments. Plucking up courage, Lauren held my hand and calmly walked me to front door. Listening out for the stifled sound of dogs barking in the distance made it momentarily safer to enter the house full of bitches.

It was the morning of the ballet exam, and from the moment I arrived at Tina's, I'd spent most of my time locked in a bedroom with Lauren — well out of danger from the four-legged beasts. Tina got to share a bed with her elbowing-buddy Sarah — and Tina's newly-formed circles under her eyes told us her night must have been far from restful! Tina's mum informed us that our families knew we were in *safe hands*: she called them when we were asleep the previous night.

On arrival at the ballet centre (located in spacious fields in the Holbeck region), Tina's mum said she'd pick us up after we finished (at about 1pm) as she had a few errands to run. I hoisted up my newly-washed pink ballet tights above my waistline ensuring that the seams at the back were in a straight line, and securely positioned my black lycra leotard over it. The changing rooms were fairly empty with only three ballet girls who had already *been in;* changing back into their comfy tracksuit bottoms and sweaters.

'She's really nice,' one girl offered out of her diminutive frame. 'There's only two of 'em — the pianist and the examiner.'

'Re-ally, only *one* examiner,' Tina yawned, whilst looking in the mirror, applying foundation over her panda eyes. 'Well, that's good, cos she won't be able to see everythin' — she has to write things down, don't she?! Did you have to do the *pas de chat* sequence in the middle o' floor? And what pointe work did you do?' Tina asked in quick succession, like she'd known the girl all her life.

'Yeah, we did the *pas de chat* and *all* the set sequences for pointe work — but as you said, she was scribbling away 'alf the time... She's really smiley though — made you feel relaxed. Ain't it girlz?' The two not-so-talkative girls nodded their heads.

'Ah, that's good. She's not a miserable bugga then!' Tina chortled, trying to liven herself up after her restless night.

'What does she look like?' asked Lauren as she pinned her fringe off her face causing her ears to stick out.

'She's *really* posh-looking. She's got big, blonde hair — she must have used a whole tin of hair lacquer to keep it in place! *And* she's wearing *loads* o' make-up!' the girl gossiped.

With that, Tina happily slapped on more foundation, firmly concealing the circles from under her eyes and applying lashings of mascara to create a spider-eye effect. The *relieved* ballet girls collected their jackets off the hooks above the benches, gathered the rest of their belongings and wished us good luck. Tina checked her watch.

'Eh, not long now eh — only twenty minutes to go...' Tina confirmed. She turned her head right, and then left — as if practising one of the exercises from the RAD Elementary syllabus.

'Eh, where's Sarah? Anyone seen Sarah?'

'...I... think... she's in the toilets,' I admitted.

Tina used her fingers to quickly curl the ends of her spider lashes before dashing towards the toilets. But before she could get there, a frail-looking Sarah emerged out of the doorway.

'You all right, Sarah?' Tina asked, knowing that she wasn't.

'My belly,' warbled Sarah, rubbing what appeared to be a hole in her middle regions, and wincing at the same time. 'Just a bit of a dicky tummy.'

Tina put her right arm across Sarah's right shoulder, then led her to a wooden bench in front, with Sarah clearly in discomfort.

'Do you want me to tell them you're not feeling well?' Tina urged.

'No, no, I'm fine!' Sarah pleaded with a worried look on her face.

'Well, clearly you're not!' Tina curtly threw back.

'I... I... erm... I took a lax-a-tive th-is mor-ning,' Sarah eventually confessed.

'For heaven's sake Sarah!' bemoaned Tina.

And as fast as her spindly legs could carry her, Sarah sped across the floor to the girl's room again, relieving herself from any further verbal constipation.

The hypnotic sound of a classical concerto reverberated round the grand ballet hall. Evenly spaced across the sprung dance floor we stood elegantly poised — feet in 5th position and arms in demi-bras — ending the ballet exam with a customary curtsey. The examiner gave no indication as to how well we had done, but Tina seemed to capture a plethora of smiles from the pristine blonde lady with lacquered hair. As for the rest of us, we'd have to wait at least a month before Mrs Court informed us of our fate (success or doomed failure). Out of the corner of my eye, I caught sight of the tip of Tina's nose which hung snootily in the air. Her grimaced face and elongated neck with vertical ridges looked like she swallowed a couple bars of a vertical freestanding radiator. Looking further down the line, it was a surprise how Sarah managed to keep herself upright, much less get through an hour and a half without excusing herself to visit the girl's room. Having squeezed every ounce of liquid out of her thin body (just in the nick of time I hasten to add), Sarah would have surely collapsed, I thought. But thankfully she made it through to the end of the ballet exam. Lauren appeared confident enough and seemed to enjoy the whole examination experience.

In continued silence, we said our polite *thank yous* and *goodbyes* to the examiner and tip-toed out of the ballet room, clutching our pointe shoes in one hand and a *palmful of hope* in the other.

Anyhow, at least the ordeal was over, and a day closer to going back home — back to London where things would be refreshingly familiar. More pressing though, I just had to navigate mentally and physically getting through Tina's front door without losing my nerve. Enduring another night under the same roof as Mitzy and

Ditzy made me anxious — such frivolous names betrayed such savage and hostile personalities.

About an hour later, when the coast was clear, Lauren and I broke free from the bedroom we shared, which (with a stroke of luck) was positioned at the front of Tina's house. Tina and Sarah were busy chatting outside, discussing how well they thought they might or might not have done in the ballet exam.

'Oh, well I'm glad that's over girlz. We can relax now and have some fun, eh!' said Tina, chewing on a Hubba Bubba as Lauren and I bolted through the front door. 'The chip shop's on't corner. It won't take uz five minutes.'

We started to walk along the pavement towards Tina's aunty's take away.

'I'm gonna have cod and chips and a pickled onion...' Lauren enticed excitedly.

'Mine's a steak and kidney pie!' Tina scoffed back.

'What you gonna have, Sophia?' Lauren asked.

'Erm, probably a Cornish pastie and chips... and a gherkin,' I added.

'Err, yuk... not those green nobbly things,' joked Tina, 'they're disgustin'!'

'They're really tasty — you should try 'em!' I threw back, my voice bravely bolting out of my body from nowhere.

Lauren and Tina looked at each other in surprise. Lauren then flashed me a look of admiration whilst Hubba Bubba girl *(sans-expression)* abruptly chose to burst her pink bubble in dissatisfaction. She then used her tongue to dislodge the gum from her braces before chewing again. Before anyone dared to ask, Sarah said she was looking forward to eating a saveloy and chips.

'Well, you definitely need *something* in your belly ya silly sausage!' Tina quipped, 'you must be bleedin' starvin'!'

We couldn't help but see the funny side and all joined in laughing, releasing much pent-up tension.

'And don't worry, we won't say anything,' Tina conspired.

Lauren and I ashamedly nodded in agreement. We were still on Tina's turf and what Tina '*said…*' I was just pleased the spotlight was off me for once, even though Sarah's eating issues *did* seem a huge cause for concern.

We had barely trodden a few paces before reaching our destination. Tina got a mixture of hugs and thumps on the back from her extended family, who were overjoyed upon seeing her once familiar face. Tina's warm introductions made us feel *like family* as we ordered our chips with differing portions of sides (cod fish, pasty, pie and saveloy etc).

Like a carrier pigeon, Tina filled the northern folk in with the glamours of posh school mixed in with grubby London life down South. Her opinions of the North/South divide (favouring the North of course) were passionately and vehemently in agreement with the locals: a long-running grievance with the South seemed firmly rooted in northern soil. Tina then brought her relatives up to date with details about our ballet exam, whilst being careful to leave out Sarah's mishaps along the way. Her audience hung onto her every word, and the Northerners enjoyed listening intently to Tina's rallying.

Delving into our open packets of chips (greased with fat and drippings of vinegar), we scoffed our bingeing treats along the way back to Tina's. Even though it was bitterly cold, we enjoyed the fresh air. Then, it felt as if the air had dropped another five degrees with muffled voices coming from behind.

It was not until the voices came nearer that the scathing, aggressive tones — interjected with the odd four-letter expletive thrown into the mix — alarmingly alerted our attention. More unnervingly, it wasn't until Tina urgently shoved her grease-ridden hand into the small of my back, forcing me to move along at a quicker pace, that I realised that it was *my* 'unfamiliar' figure which was the apparent cause for hostility.

Chapter 12

Musical Youths

"Everyone of us is a Fiddler on the Roof — trying to play out a tune without breaking our neck!"

Lauren lowered her pretty voice by about one and a half octaves and applied a limited range of vocal inflections to imitate the famous words spoken by *Tevye* from *Fiddler*. Gravitas and sincerity filled the air as she addressed her audience made up of: a spinning washing machine; a Zanussi dryer; and a room full of freshly-washed clothes in a bathroom the size of our living room on our South London estate!

Tevye continued, *"As the Good Book says, send us the cure we've got the sickness already!"*

Lauren recited the well-known script with equal pathos. She set her feet unfemininely wide apart — firmly rooted in her manly stance. Her application of Stanislavski's technique urged me to gallantly join in and recite one of my favourite lines from the musical with equal measure. In character, I spontaneously whisked a newly-dried white sheet off a nearby clothes horse, causing it to fall over. But I continued in earnest. The sheet covered my head like a *tichel* and crossed over my dwarfed body. My equally caricatured voice morphed to resemble the character of Tevye's daughter Mottel, *"Even a poor tailor is entitled to some happiness,"* 'I' mourned, looking deeply into 'Tevye's' eyes.

Tevye solemnly sang back, *"And look at my daughter's eyes... so hopeful."*

'He' searched deep into my soul, looking for answers, pathetically searching for 'hope' into the vacant distant corner of Lauren's spacious bathroom. Our version of *Tradition,* singing every line (word for word), included us stomping away in an attempt to raise Lauren's North London terraced Victorian roof. Devon and Neville would have been proud I thought!

Lauren and I fondly reminisced our time spent in the school production of *Fiddler on the Roof.* Again, we would instantly break into song and perform exerts from the musical for the duration of Mrs Harrison's *second* washing cycle, ending with a rendition of *Matchmaker* by Hodel, Tzeital and Chava.

We ended up collapsing into a piled heap on the bathroom floor — two bodies entirely covered by Egyptian cotton and smelling sweet from an abundance of fragrant fabric softener.

The door flew open.

'What on earth are you two doing?' Lauren's mum asked incredulously.

We scrambled round on the floor using our arms and legs to release our bodies from further entrapment.

Lauren's head was the first head to greet Mrs Harrison and bear the consequences of our childish frolics.

'Sor- so-rry m-u-m! ... So-phi-a and I were... were.. ju-st... we were just ch-eckin' the...'

Lauren couldn't even finish her sentence before ending up in fits of giggles. By this time, I had given up fighting my way out from under the cover. I desperately tried hard to stay as still as a corpse wrapped in cotton like an Egyptian mummy, hoping Mrs Harrison wouldn't notice I was there.

'I can see what you're doing, love! Making a mess of my clean sheets, that's what!'

There was a pause. 'You all right there, Sophia?' Lauren's mum asked.

'Yes, thanks,' a muffled voice cried out, making its way through the fabric.

'Oh, I don't know. Just pop it back in the wash, Lauren, when you're done,' Mrs Harrison concluded as she shut the door behind her.

Once her footsteps disappeared, remnants of stifled laughter freely flowed out again, then Lauren and I obediently observed her mother's request.

Life on the estate was becoming quieter as Winter was drawing in. People moved around in more staccato-like fashion in pursuit of their homes after a hard day's work. An abundance of information was gifted to us through books and three television channels: BBC One, BBC Two and ITV! Minimal channels were sufficient for the youth, and less over-whelming in the world that existed prior to media explosion. What more could we want? Life seemed simple. Life *was* simple: that was our gift. Regrettably, simplicity is no longer a luxury preserved for the youth, or indeed adults.

Devon and Neville enjoyed nights at the local youth club after school, and I'd sometimes join in with Devon trampolining. Devon was a proper little athlete and took pride showing off his skills at whatever sport he turned his hand to. I remember hanging out on the ground floor café area of Tulsen School and watch the teenage boys play pool and slurp on hush puppies and crisps — exchanging jokes and laughing about the things young people laugh about — with their assortment of blue and red tongues. I preferred the company of boys in preference to the South London gyals any day!

Chapter 13

Of Dust 'til Dawn

'Move along de bus please,' demanded the bus conductor as we made our way onto the lower deck, finding a place to stand. 'And noh standing upstairs please!'

The bell attached to the rope which rang out in the bus driver's carriage was pulled only once, beckoning him to turn off the engine and for everything to grind to a halt. Tuts and sighs could be heard out of the mouths of passengers who sat comfortably in their seats, as they willed the offending standing passengers down the stairs and *off* the bus. It was a common daily occurrence. And our journey resumed quickly enough once the offenders complied.

As I moved along the lower deck, standing near the front of the bus, I caught sight of the familiar outline of a man with a brown balding head, dressed in a beige trench coat with his arms placed either side onto his briefcase. He stared straight ahead. The seat next to him was unoccupied and I was to be the nearest person to oblige. I nervously gestured to the person behind me, to see whether they would like to sit down, but the moustached gentleman warmly declined. Not wanting to be scolded by someone for not allowing more passengers to board, I tentatively sat down next to the balding man, careful that my newly pressed uniform didn't come into contact with any part of his oversized body. I tugged the end of my kilted skirt to cover a newly formed gap, ensuring privacy from his peering eyes.

The man's bulky figure could barely contain itself in *his* half of the two-seater nearest the window, making our separation of bodies difficult. Within moments, the gap between the balding man and myself grew smaller and smaller as he appeared to spread himself further — his solid legs widening to form a more obtuse V-shape, and his arms finding room to suggestively fill the gap. My body remained rigid as I could hear the saliva-induced warmth of his smile and his deep exhalation of breath stalely linger in the air. It was as if he knew that his smile was causing some kind of irritation for me. I remained poker-faced not wanting to invite any unnecessary conversation.

As we approached my stop, I urgently bolstered out from my seat, mindful not to make any bodily contact with the overly familiar man or catch his gaze. The bare sight of him made my skin crawl, like a plethora of tics trapped underneath my skin's surface, desperately trying to find a way out.

I managed to shake off the uncomfortable thoughts running through my mind on my walk from the bus stop to school.

It being a typical Wednesday, selected pupils had to sing prepared solos to the whole class in *Song and Movement*. In customary fashion, we would each give the pianist our sheet music, followed by an indication of the song's tempo to the pianist: a choice of fast, middle tempo or slow (for a ballad). Or according to Mr Murphy it would be a choice of: *allegro, mid-tempo*, or *adagio* in his Italian-come-Sheffield accent. Most pupils tried to vary their songs, but one girl insisted on singing the same song every week. In her *'Zip-a-Dee-Doo-Dah'* song, she'd even match her actions with the lyrics by pointing to the imaginary, *'blue bird on my shoulder,'* and irritatingly give the air an over-zealous fist pump every time she sang the title line, *'Zip-a-Dee-Doo-Dah'*. I could see the teacher's eyes glaze over as the girl started her much-loved rendition of the song and politely clap when the final chord thankfully resolved.

That week, there was a certain amount of excitement and buzz in the air as we heard there was going to be a list of names going up on the notice board for candidates to audition for a new big European film. The Heads of Department were *doing the rounds,* on the look-out for talent. So, everyone was on their best form in class, with some pupils over-extending their personal chats to teachers. Selected pupils were invited to go the school's agency at lunchtime, and everyone flocked around the noticeboard to see if they were *the chosen ones*. As luck would have it, Lauren was on the list — it really lifted her spirits. She was still getting some stick from some girls from her previous class (although her troubles were nothing like before) so the opportunity to appear in a film was a great distraction. Lauren and I had lunch together and we arranged to spend the coming Friday at hers (if mum allowed). I said that I could help her with learning her lines.

The week had *'Zip-a-Dee-Doo'd* by, and luckily, we got to finish early on the Friday at lunchtime as the staff had their termly afternoon of planned meetings. Lauren and I sat on her Barry Manilow-covered single duvet with script in hand, reading through the scene she had to learn for her film casting the following week. I had never come across a casting script before and was excited to read in the other characters — adjusting my voice to suit the other adult roles in the scene. We had the house to ourselves until Mrs Harrison arrived home at around 4 p.m. She was excited about the prospect of meeting a famous film director as Mrs Harrison said she would be Lauren's chaperone if Lauren was to get the job!

Mrs Harrison kept popping her head through Lauren's bedroom door every five minutes, asking if we wanted cups of tea, or any biscuits, sandwiches, or anything. She repeatedly asked Lauren how she was getting on, and she would simply say, *'the same as the last time you asked, Mum!'* On the fifth occasion, Lauren cut to the chase and told her mum that she *interrupted her flow* every time the door creaked open. Mrs Harrison politely took the hint and left us to it.

By the time we finished Lauren was word perfect, so we spent the rest of the time catching up with stuff that happened over the week at school. Spandau Ballet's *True* came on the radio and we sang alongside Hadley's voice whilst miming using microphones. On my departure, Lauren's mum said she was looking forward to seeing me again soon and that our time together was *time well spent*.

By the time I got back to the estate at around seven o'clock after a near two-hour journey, Mum greeted me at the door, handing me my overnight bag from my room, as I would be staying at the lady at No. 24's overnight! (Mum got a last-minute call to do a sleep-over at the residential home, and Devon and Neville had been picked up earlier by our uncle who lived in east London).

On the doorstep six doors down, Mum gave me a quick hug goodnight before darting off down the balcony and out of the estate. I recognised some of the ladies who had their coiffed hair sealed with sheen spray before bouncing out of 'the salon' another four inches taller. My nostrils twitched as remnants of peroxide merged with an assortment of cooking from the kitchen which stifled the air.

'Would you like something to eat, Sophia?' the lady from No. 24 offered warmly.

'Erm, can I have a cup of tea, please?' I asked.

'You no' hungry? Eh, eh, you mos 'ave someting to eat Sophia.'

'Erm, well maybe some toast as well, thanks,' I decided.

The lady threw her head back and chuckled as she placed two anaemic-looking slices of bread on the grill at the top of the cooker.

'Go inside and rest you' feet, Sophia, I'll bring it in fo' you.'

I placed my school bag beside the table in the living-room-come-salon and rested my tired feet. The familiarity of No. 24 soon made me relax and my nostrils adjusted to the amalgamation of smells, and it was beginning to feel more and more like a second home.

After a quick bite, I offered to help the lady from No. 24 tidy up and with two sets of hands the place was tidy in no time.

We sat and enjoyed a stream of Friday night tv from Blankety Blank to the Generation Game, with the lady from No. 24 interjecting jovial comments along the way. Then, the phone rang.

The tone of the ring pierced the air and my eyes darted towards the grey plastic intruder on the wall. The lady turned towards me, but just as she was about to give instructions, she stopped herself in her tracks and hurriedly dashed towards the front passageway, making clicky-clacky sounds with her feet as she went.

The conversation began in her usual manner. But as the conversation lingered her exchanges became inaudible — not more than a whisper. I tried to focus on the questions from the TV quiz show, but my attention kept returning to the conversation further on down the corridor. When the exchange came to an end and the lady from No. 24 delicately placed the receiver down – she sauntered back to the living room — her hips swaying from side to side.

'You mos' be tired, Sop-hi-a. Let's take your things upstairs and get you settled for bed — it's getting' late,' the lady persuaded as if tiredness had suddenly descended upon the both of us.

Friday was usually our family's staying-up late night, ending with the TV watching us instead of the other way around. She closed the downstairs curtains and promptly switched off all the hair-raising appliances. I collected my belongings and followed the lady to *my room* (adjacent to her boys' room at the front of the house), glancing at the *intruder on the wall* as we passed by on our way upstairs.

The boys' room next door was closed as usual. The lady opened the door to the adjacent bedroom and gestured me in.

'Night, So-phi-aa,' she said with a warm smile, closing the door behind her.

'Night.'

I placed my uniform in a neat pile on a wooden chair in the corner of the room and positioned my boater carefully on top of the boys' chest of drawers, then pulled out my pyjamas from my overnight bag and got changed for bed.

An orange light from an outdoor lamp post sneaked its way through a gap in the curtain onto the chest of drawers underneath the window. The light drew me in, and before I decided to take a sneak-peak out the window to see if the familiar black car was there, I noticed different objects in view.

I admired the boys' collection of beautifully carved tiny wooden animals and felt the smoothness of the surface of what looked like a leopard and ran my fingers over its smooth humped back. Their marble set was positioned on a wooden frame (mancala) board game, which lay to the right of the drawers. I ran my fingers along another wooden spiral-shaped object until I felt a sharp edge on the end of my finger. I picked up the offending item with its rough edges and tipped it on its side to have a closer look at where I caught my finger. As it tilted sideways, bits of dust and what appeared like pot-pourri fell out of the spiral-shaped item and onto my boater and the tabletop. I hurriedly used the palm of my hand and scooped the dried flowers back into the boys' object, dusting my hands off to clear any remnants and quickly snuck into bed.

Not a sound could be heard from the boys next door, and I wondered whether they were actually there, as not a stirring sound evidenced their presence. My mind lingered on the lady's telephone conversation earlier, followed by our hasty retreat upstairs. I tossed and turned for a while before finally falling asleep.

In the small hours of Saturday morning, I was awoken by the slow creak of a car's tyres scraping along the gravelly tarmac outside before it came to a halt, followed by a car door slamming shut. Footsteps creaked on the stairs before reaching the top of the landing — ending with the quiet clink of the lady's door shut behind them. A blend of soft and raspy tones intertwined, merging into one to form a mechanically sounding *ebb and flow*: the sounds of coiled springs through intermittent breathy gasps for air. I put my fingers securely in my ears.

The light streamed through the second storey window causing my eyes to blink before welcoming in the new day. I noticed the bedroom door was slightly ajar. Collecting my school uniform from the chair, I placed my clothes into my overnight bag and got changed into my joggers and sweat top. I reached for my boater and tiny specs of dust trickled and danced to the ground in the stream of sunlight. Hastily, I dusted off any remnants before Mum could catch sight of it and inspected the tabletop to remove any evidence of further spillage, whilst searching for the prickly wooden item, but noticing it was no longer there.

'Is Sophia up?' I could hear Devon calling out from downstairs.

Inside the kitchen, the lady from No. 24 was finishing off eating her breakfast. As I entered her two boys dashed past me — returning to their rooms upstairs, barely looking my way and mumbling good mornings under their stale breath.

'Did you sleep well, So-ph-i-a?' gleamed the lady.

'Yes, thanks,' I said politely remembering the multiple times I had been woken up during the night.

'I hope I didn't wake yo', I had to collect someting from the boys' room when I got up this mo'ning. You looked fas' asleep.'

I smiled indicating all was well. I figured the bedroom door left ajar was the explanation for the missing object and then sped off six doors down the balcony towards home.

Chapter 14

Heart Through a Letterbox

Schools out for Summer!
At last, we could let our hair down, or in my case *let my afro hair out* now that school was over for the academic year. My parents proudly attended the End of Year ceremony at Covino's. Both Lauren and my mum met for the second time (in person), even though they had managed to speak on the phone a couple of times in between my visits to Highbury. Mrs Harrison's white summer dress was held together by a thin belt which tried its best to hold in her podgy waist. The mothers seemed to like each other's company as I caught sight of lots of head nodding in agreement and exchanging of smiles. Poignantly, the joyous occasion symbolised a welcomed celebration of newly introduced reforms to the 1980s education system. And helped to shake the South London streets out of its government-controlled misery.

A favoured part of the End of Year show was a Street Dance performance to Janet Jackson's *Rhythm Nation*. As the count down to the song began, blood pumped venomously through my veins. My wired body lashed out the clipped choreographic movements in notorious Jackson-esque military fashion as our dance troupe moved as one. 'Us' girls looked cool in our all-black tight-fitting lycra outfits with uniformed baseball caps and black trainers to boot.

Synchronised movements were perfected after drilled afternoon rehearsals undertaken throughout the summer term — instructed by our highly-desired dance teacher: Mr Baldwin!

Lauren (alongside most of the female pupils I hasten to add) said she had the *hots for him* and was clearly disappointed when she wasn't chosen as one of the sixteen Jackson dancers! I think she was secretly jealous of me being selected, so I made sure I didn't talk about our sweat-ridden dance rehearsals too much. Or if I did, I played it down!

After the ceremony, we collected our accolades, certificates and well-wishes and ventured into the damp-smelling pub next door to the old Academy. The decision to have the ceremony back at the old building in South London was met with disapproval by some of the more hoity-toity parents, who would have much preferred to clink champagne glasses in a Lounge Bar somewhere up West End. Lauren and I then spent most of the afternoon drinking orangeade, eating cheesy Wotsits and playing pool, whilst our parents (dads included) sat on beer-stained, imitation velvet-covered chairs in the corner of the pub, talking about summer holiday plans and hopes for the future.

Devon was wearing dark-blue Lois jeans, a pristine Lacoste polo-shirt and Kenny Dalglish (Liverpool player) trainers. Neville was similarly attired but wore a cool, red and black, *'The Fonz'* t-shirt (notably to show who was boss!). Undoubtedly, my brothers had no choice but to be on their best behaviour in public with the parents around. More amusingly though, it was not long before Devon and Lauren were flirting with each other. Lauren continually flicked her brown, wavy hair, taking every opportunity to sashay past Devon in her polished school uniform, whilst Devon stuck out his chest, desperately trying to lower his voice every time he spoke. He must have found it hard maintaining his act, as he kept clearing his throat and taking lots of sips of lemonade in-between pool shots. They especially hit is off after Devon told Lauren about his favourite player David Rocastle who played at Arsenal — what with Lauren being a season ticket holder! Lauren even suggested Devon could perhaps see a home game (with the two of us!) at some point, since the grounds were only walking distance from her home. I couldn't think of anything worse. When the evening was over, Devon looked mightily disappointed as we said our goodbyes: Lauren and her parents headed fashionably up North London, whilst we remained firmly rooted down South.

'Lovely to meet you, Devon,' flirted Lauren.

'You too, Lauren,' Devon replied in his usual higher-pitched voice. 'I mean…yeah, see ya around,' he bellowed attempting to lower it again.

Fortunately, we were blessed with sunny weather for the most of August 1989, which enabled us kids to play out most days on the estate. Devon and Neville up-graded their roller blading and skateboarding skills from the confinement of our balcony to the tarmac of the grand prix track that circled the houses on the estate — much to the relief of the miseries at no 23. (I tagged slowly behind, keeping out of danger from passing cars and stuck to the pavements). Luckily for the miseries, they wouldn't have to keep disinfecting their patch outside their front door with a hard broom as often. I was certain that the old lady who lived there didn't have any teeth, as her pursed lips were always clamped firmly shut whenever she walked past our front door. It was a surprise that she never complained when we had our parties on the estate: she must have heard the pulsating calypso music and secretly danced to the free entertainment when her husband wasn't looking!

The 'Kray Twins' were still up to no good terrorising us neighbours with their incessant noise and constant banging on our front door and then running away. My parents didn't seem to be too bothered by the five-year-old critters, but I'd often wait in the passageway in anticipation of a knock on the door and swiftly bolt out to chase them away. I would see two sets of podgy legs escaping around the corner of the communal walkway and the two mites laughing like hyenas as they waddled through their open front door to the *safety* of their home. Complaining to the Krays' mother never made any difference — they'd only be at it again after a ten-minute reprieve to catch their five-year-old breaths!

Over the month of August, I was allowed to sleep over at Lauren's house a couple of times.

She'd whip her new vinyls out and turn up the volume loud, drowning out our timid voices as we'd sing along to 80s pop music without a care in the world. My bed for the night was a sleeping bag on the floor of her bedroom — the closest to camping as I'd ever get. Lauren told me all about her camping adventures in the UK — I couldn't imagine anything worse than sleeping in water-drenched tents; washing in communal showers with a bunch of strangers; and taking long walks in the British countryside! We'd talk until the small hours of the morning, mainly about girly things, but not without an injection of Arsenal football club, Barry Manilow and most pressingly: Mr Baldwin!

'Do you know if he's got a girlfriend?' Lauren whispered curiously.

'I'm not sure... I think so...Well, he must be at least in his 30s!' I whispered back, pulling the metal zip of the sleeping bag under my chin.

'Yeah. You're right. He's definitely *old*, so he must have a girlfriend,' Lauren affirmed from her bed above. 'I know he's shaven off his hair, but you *can definitely* see a bald patch. But I'm not too bothered about that.' Lauren thought for a moment. 'He must be about… say fifteen… sixteen years older than me? I guess round about the same age gap between Mum and Dad,' Lauren proudly affirmed. She let out a weary sigh and then continued, 'What do you think I should do?'

'What do you mean?' I replied not knowing where the conversation was heading.

'How can I get in touch with him?'

'What for?'

'To let him know how I feel,' said Lauren plainly. 'Do you think I should write him a letter or something? I think he knows deep down how I feel, but someone's got to get the ball rolling!' Lauren quipped. I hesitated for a moment.

'Er… yeah…you could do,' I said, trying to be encouraging, 'but if you write a letter, where would you send it? It's the school holidays remember!' I party-pooped.

'Well, I could send it to Covino's. I'm sure they'd send mail on to his *home address*? What do ya think?' Lauren asked excitedly.

'Erm… yeah, I'm *sure* they would,' I ping-ponged back, trying not to burst her bubble.

'If I put *'private and confidential'* on the envelope, I'm sure they'd just send it on, wouldn't they? They wouldn't know it was from me!'

'No, they wouldn't know it was from you,' I encouraged. I could hear Lauren's exciting new plan whirling in her head.

'Would you help me write a letter, Sophia?' Lauren suggested just like an excited schoolgirl (which she clearly *was!*).

'Yeah... course — let's do it in the morning,' I replied in hushed night-time tones (aware that Mr and Mrs Harrison's bedroom was only next door).

'Thanks...Night, Sophia,' Lauren sang under her breath. I harmonised, 'Night.' I pictured Lauren and Mr Baldwin looking into each other's eyes with him romantically caressing her soft rosy cheeks. I smiled to myself before mischievously continuing: 'Sweet dreams Mrs Baldwin!' I giggled — unable to resist! Lauren let out an almighty laugh unsuitable for the night-time and pulled the duvet over her head to deaden her laughter.

'You cow!' she muffled under the sheets, trying to stifle her laughter.

I was awoken by the sound of a front door slamming shut. I wiped the crusts of sleep from my eyes as the sun peeked through a gap reflecting on Lauren's Paula Abdul pillowcase. Shadows of angular, stick-thin tree branches danced on her bedroom wall whilst trills and chirps of a morning chorus gaily brought in the new day.

'Are you up?' Lauren croaked.

'Yeah. *You?*'

'Course, silly!' Lauren then chirped, as she readily checked the time on her alarm clock.

The long hand pointed to eleven and the small hand neared seven. 'Mum and Dad won't be back 'til later. We've got the house to ourselves!'

Dear Mr Baldwin (or should I say Chris?! Hee hee!),

Hi there! It's Lauren Harrison here from Form 6!
I hope you're enjoying the glorious weather and your free time in the Summer holidays!
*I just wanted to say how much I loved your Janet Jackson choreography for the end of term show at Covinos. I **REALLY** wanted to speak to you on the last day of term, but you were busy speaking to lots of parents and I didn't want to be rude and interrupt! I **SO** wanted to be a part of the dance troupe for the Janet Jackson number — it was fab! Everyone said it was the highlight of the show and I totally agree!!!!!!!!*
Sophia Healey is staying over at mine at the moment and she told me all about the funny things that happened in rehearsals. (Wish I was there to witness it — sooooo jealous!!!!).
Anyhow, Sophia and I have been making up some of our own dance routines to Miss You Much. Maybe we can show you when we get back in September??? Maybe next year, if I practise hard enough, I can get into the dance troupe for the next production! What do you think?! I'm much better at ballet and tap, but Sophia and I have been practising lots of street dance at home — I'm always keen to perfect my street dancing skills!

*Anyhow, I hope you enjoy the rest of your holidays. And I **really** look forward to seeing you next term. Feel free to drop me a line in the meantime if you want! Bye for now Chris,*

> *Massive hugs and kisses,*
> *Miss you lots and lots,*
> *Lauren xxx*

*Ps. Really **really** looking forward to hearing from you!*

I suggested to Lauren to write her address on the back of the letter instead of the envelope just in case any prying eyes would give way to her anonymity. She thanked me for my ingenious idea and clutched the letter close to her chest — being careful not to crease it.

'Do you think it's all right, Sophia?' Lauren pleaded for approval.

'Yeah... course. He'll be well-chuffed having a young admirer like you!'

'You don't think it's a bit cringe,' she said, gently stroking her hair, as if Mr Baldwin was present in the room.

'No... no! It's lovely — I'm sure he'll write back. He seems like a lovely man.'

'Yeah, he's got *gorgeous* eyes — I could just gaze at him *all day*!' Lauren drooled before we both burst out into fits of laughter.

Lauren stained her letter with Body Shop's strawberry-scented perfume, then air-kissed it before folding her love note neatly into the tiniest of white envelopes. Her alluring pink tongue navigated its way from one end of the sticky strip to the other, ensuring her saliva consumed the sticky substance as much as Mr Baldwin consumed her love-stricken mind.

'Shall I put a kiss on the back? To seal it? My mum's got a ruby red lipstick I could use,' Lauren enthused.

'No, you don't want to give it away! You don't want anyone knowing that it's a letter from an admirer. They might open it and find out that **Lauren Harrison** sent **Mr Baldwin** a *love* letter!' I toyed.

'NO!! That would be *tragic*… soooooo embarrassing.' Lauren began fanning herself vigorously with the tiny envelope which was too miniscule to relieve her from her juvenile hot flushes. 'Gosh, yeah! Not only that, if he has got a girlfriend (which I'm *sure* he has) she would be right jealous if she sees red lip marks on a letter sent to her man! If *she* gets the post before *he* does, she'd probably open it, read it and put it in the bin before he even sees it! Yeah, I'll make it look as formal as possible.' Lauren's talk was full of nonchalance: the prospect of Mr Baldwin having a girlfriend didn't seem to bother her or *her* pursuit of *him*. The time was nearing eleven — not long before the next postal collection was due on her road. 'I've got an idea!' she blurted.

Within seconds, Lauren's feet noisily clambered up the stairs (to the second landing of the Victorian house).

This was closely followed by a succession of taps emanating from an old Maritsa 30 typewriter. Lauren ploddingly tapped out MR BALDWIN and the school's address in singular succession onto the tiny envelope. Her novel attempt to formalise the envelope (using typed letters instead of handwritten ones) was somehow betrayed by the stench of its strawberry-perfumed scent!

The postal van rounded the corner. Looking like a deer in headlights, Lauren pushed *her heart* into the red post box at the end of her road just in time for the day's second collection. As we heard the feeble sound of the envelope hitting the interior of the post box, Lauren jumped up and down as she knew it was the point of no return! As her accomplice, complicit in her frivolity and audaciousness, I was certain that whatever was to be Lauren's fate, I would be there as a friend to fan the flames of a newly-found romance or to help soothe any heartache! Mr Baldwin would soon know he had a fourteen-year-old admirer in his midst and nothing and no one was going to stand between them.

Chapter 15

Plain/Spice

It was a third week into the holidays and Mum and Dad were preparing for our summer party — celebrating Devon's success at qualifying for the under 16s local boys' Football Team. I helped Mum all week making a banner noting Devon's name and football club, icing cakes with red and white splodges all over it and then adding tiny silver balls in the middle of each splodge. There was also cut cheese, pickled onions and hot dog sausages to be squeezed onto cocktail sticks and stuck onto half-cut grapefruits covered in silver foil to be made.

Mum's cake speciality always went down well after servings of curried goat and rice. Mum's alcoholic concoction always sent party goers into a spin after only a few sips, so it was always wise for the adults to line their stomach with some food first in preparation of the deadly rum punch. I helped to cut up the fruits: apples, oranges and limes to add to the potent mixture which reeked of an array of Mamajuana, Bacardi and spices (to add some zest).

Lightweights were afraid to even sip the rum punch and said just the whiff alone was enough to send them over the edge.

I thought about whether I should invite Lauren around for the party. I desperately wanted her to come to mine and get to know my family. I was certain she'd love the music, good humour and dancing in a house packed full of friendly faces. She would surely enjoy a party atmosphere like never before and be surrounded by things that belonged to me, in *my* world.

Lauren's spacious North London home dwarfed ours in comparison. But what we lacked in terms of materialistic wealth we made up for in richness of spirit, benevolence and togetherness.

Devon's face lit up at the prospect of Lauren coming over. I'm sure he thought Lauren might like him even more especially since the party was a celebration of *his* footballing achievements. Devon's desire for Lauren to come fuelled me to ask Mum if she could be invited. Mum didn't sound too sure about the idea and came up with an array of excuses: *it's more of a night-time affair, I don't think Mr and Mrs Harrison would be too keen for some reason. I don't think they'd be able to collect her from the estate so late at night. And what about finding a suitable sleeping place for Lauren with all the family around?* Aunt Cassy always sprawled out on my bed after parties were over. I informed Mum that I always slept on the floor of Lauren's bedroom when I stayed at hers, so I'm sure Lauren wouldn't mind me returning the favour! Anyhow, the fact remained: sleep overs or visits between Lauren and I were never reciprocated. So, I guess the idea was a non-starter.

With the sun blazing down on the estate and the party just warming up, Calypso beats could be heard blaring out from the living-room speakers where Dad was DJ-ing. On hand to help was Neville who selected a number of vinyls to be played. Desperate to change the musical flow somewhat from a Caribbean flavour to further up Stateside, Neville handed dad De La Soul's *Me, Myself and I* before taking to the floor to bus' some dance moves: the pulsating intro started. Helping Mum in the kitchen was Aunt Cassy who was cackling about Mum's *flat* and not *round* bakes (fried dumplings). She hastily cut up onions for the curried goat dish (to be served later). Whilst Mum tossed the flat, circular-based pieces of dough in the pan, they sizzled until reaching a golden-brown colour. It was De La Soul who managed to relieve Aunt Cassy and her crying eyes away from the kitchen to the living room.

Bursting through the multi-coloured plastic strips which dangled vertically from the kitchen doorway, Aunt Cassy elbowed her way through to join Neville on the dancefloor. Jostling her elbows up and down whilst moving her hips robotically from side to side in time to the music, she looked more like she was on Round Two with Mike Tyson. I completed the finishing touches to Devon's football banner and cello-taped it high up on the living-room wall.

Slowly, the front room began to fill up with more friendly faces — aunts kissing cousins — kissing uncles twice removed. Devon then came running frantically into the front room, weaving himself in and around the mass of people, skilfully manoeuvring himself like a player on a football pitch ready to score a winning goal. He ducked back and forth between bodies and managed to dodge an odd elbow or two and saved himself from being foot trampled by dancing feet to the sounds of Soul II Soul's *Back to Life*. My ballet skills came into good use as I stood barefoot on my tip toes on the wooden armchair rest, securing the end of the banner to the wall. As I turned around, I caught sight of Devon moving like a pinball wizard towards me and I carefully made my way down onto the 'dance' floor. His eyes widened in devilish delight.

'Sophia, Sophia, come here!' Devon blurted out in excitement above the music.

'What it is?'

'Quick, quick…Come with me! Quick!' he exclaimed, pulling me towards the front door as I bumped into an assortment of bulging bopping bodies along the way.

'Hold on a minute, you're hurting me! What's the rush?' I agonised, as he dragged me along at a quickening pace.

'You're never gonna believe this!' Devon cried out — his voice getting higher and higher the closer we got to the desired destination.

Devon and I finally arrived at the passageway near the front door. He put his hand over my mouth before I could say anything; I danced around on the spot, desperate to be released from my gagging order.

Directly in front of me, I could see the back of a petite, well-postured body fashioned in a polka-dot dress, standing with feet in first position encased in brown, strappy sandals.

The mis-placed girl was surrounded by a sea of black and brown faces looking incredulously at her. Her curly hair cascaded down her back; her diminutive voice contradicting her surroundings. A conversation between the girl and mum was in mid-flow… but she hardly took a breath…

'No, it didn't take *that* long to get here, Mrs Healey. Dad said it was much quicker than he thought it would be! We could hear the music as we turned into the estate and figured the party would be in this direction which led us to here!' she joked, trying her best to raise her voice above the music. The sea of intrigued onlookers laughed animatedly in response to her *joke*.

'That's good, that's good,' Mum continued. 'I'm so glad you could make it. Sophia's gonna be really pleased to see you!' she said grinning in my direction over the girl's shoulder, and then back at her again.

By this point I was fit to burst. As I wriggled out of Devon's grip, the girl sensed a commotion from behind. She did a 180-degree turn ending in a theatrical scream.

'Sophia!'

'Lauren! I... I... can't believe you're here! You didn't tell me you were coming!'

'Mum said it'd be nice to surprise you!'

Aunt Cassy cackled her way over and joined in.

'Is this your friend Sophia?' Aunt Cassy asked using her poshest voice. I nodded in disbelief. 'Oh, lovely to meet you... what's your name?' she nosed.

'Lauren,' said Lauren.

'Oh, nice to meet you, Lauren. That's a pretty name.'

'Thanks,' Lauren answered politely.

'I'm aunty Cassy,' said aunty Cassy. 'Lovely to meet you and welcome to the Healey family.'

Mum raised her eyes to the ceiling. 'Yes, welcome, Lauren. Just relax and enjoy yourself. Sophia will show you around.'

Lauren looked excited by all the attention she was getting and had probably never been in the company of so many non-white people before! As Mum danced her way back to the kitchen to resume her hosting duties she concluded, 'Put Lauren's things in your room, Sophia. I hope it's tidy!'

You could tell Mum already had a few rum punches as she appeared quite relaxed about Lauren visiting and staying over for *the first time — ever*! By this point the party revellers made their way to various parts of the house with 'the show being over'. Some family members went to the kitchen to grab patties and rum punch; some ventured to listen to the sounds of the calypso and reggae beats in the living room, whilst others decided to rest their weary dancing limbs on the stairs. I pulled Lauren's over-night rucksack out of her hand and whisked her up the stairs to my bedroom with Devon tagging closely behind.

'You all right, Lauren?' Devon asked once we got to my room.

'Hi!' flirted Lauren. 'This is a great party!'

'Thanks,' Devon quipped, taking all the credit. 'I'm glad you could come,' he continued, lowering his voice.

'Me too! Mum and Dad got invited to a dinner party, so they said they'd take the opportunity for once and go!' Lauren confessed.

'Oh… right,' I answered.

'So, you're staying over?!' asked Devon eagerly. Lauren nodded.

'That's brilliant! I'm so glad you could come,' I continued. Lauren's rosy cheeks reddened as I hugged her tightly again.

'Me too,' Lauren squealed.

Devon looked at the two of us and appeared unusually awkward. He proceeded to ask Lauren if she'd like something to drink and quickly hot-footed downstairs to help quench her thirst.

Lauren told me about how her parents spoke to Mum on the front doorstep before they quickly dashed off into town to attend their friend's Silver Wedding anniversary dinner party somewhere in Holborn. As Mr and Mrs Harrison had to dash, they didn't get the chance to speak to Dad, who was too busy entertaining the partying crowd (and much of the estate for that matter). But they said to say hello.

'Your dad's got some cool music!' Lauren commented, as the thumping reggae beats reverberated off the bedroom walls. 'I've not heard this one before,' she continued whilst robotically doing a two-step to a slightly off-beat rhythm. I joined in dancing and introduced a few head bopping movements and sultry facial expressions to match which Lauren attempted to emulate.

'Oh, that's how you do it,' she jested whilst copying my body movements.

'Ahem, ahem! Sorry to disturb you girls!' Both Lauren and I turned our heads sharply towards Devon at the door. 'I got you a cherryade, Lauren,' Devon gushed.

'Ah, thanks Devon,' she gushed in return. 'Just what I needed!' I busied myself putting Lauren's overnight bag out of the way, underneath my wooden school desk.

'Hey, why don't you come downstairs, and we can bus' some moves on the dance floor!'

'Sounds good to me!' Lauren threw me a look. Sensing my hesitation, she continued, 'Erm, Soph and I will come down in a bit, won't we, Soph?"

'Yeah... course. We can get something to eat too, you must be hungry,' I reckoned.

'Yeah, nothing too spicy though, I don't think I've got the stomach for it,' Lauren warned warmly.

Devon and I knowingly looked at each other and smiled.

'Don't worry, we've got lots to choose from. We've even got sausage rolls and crisps. So, you won't go hungry!' I joked.

'Oh no... I'll try some of your Caribbean food — it'd be nice to try something new. The food smells *lovely*,' Lauren injected, trying desperately not to offend.

Lauren slipped off her sandals and made herself comfortable on the bed. I watched as she took in her surroundings. She probably couldn't conceive having such a tiny bedroom. Nevertheless, Lauren appeared relaxed and quite at home which made me feel good.

We would burst out into fits of laughter more frequently as the night went on; despite our tender years you only had to breathe in the aroma of the rum punch to feel intoxicated.

The evening breeze breezed through the window which helped to cool us down, and also served to lower Lauren's temperature after she downed a plate of curried goat and rice.

Devon coaxed us several times downstairs onto the dance floor. Lauren and I even did the whole choreographic routine to *Rhythm Nation* too (courtesy of Mr Baldwin!). Our audience (made up mainly of family members) whooped Lauren and I on, whilst fascinatedly clapping in time to the music. Devon and Neville attempted to copy a few of the repetitive moves directly opposite us in mocked humour, which naturally amused Aunt Cassy who was crying with laughter... again! Hopefully, it was *their* moves and not *ours* which was the cause for hysteria. I don't know how I was so brazen to 'perform' in front of our footballing home crowd, but I guess being in the company of Lauren gave me the impetus to forget my shyness. When the record finished, Lauren and I darted upstairs to a round of applause, zig-zagging through the crowd as we made our way up the stairs to my bedroom… our sanctuary.

'Wow Lauren! You've got some moves on ya!' complimented Devon after he tail-gated us to my bedroom.

'You're not too bad yourself!' jested Lauren, trying to catch her breath. 'I can't take all the credit though — Soph taught me well!'

Her mouth hung open as she plonked herself in a heap on the bed. Devon leant against my bedroom doorway gazing admiringly at Lauren (as if I wasn't there). He was definitely smitten. I found it hilarious though as I had witnessed an unexpected side to Devon which was quite touching for an annoying pubescent teenage brother!

'Did you have something to eat, Lauren?' Devon asked, trying to fill a gap in conversation.

'Yes, thanks. I had that lovely, curried meat dish — it was delicious. And some sausage rolls and crisps!' We all burst out laughing.

'Yeah, curried goat's a favourite of mine too,' Devon agreed. He stood stiffly with his hands on his hips, and one foot crossed over the other, like one of the wooden-looking modelling men out of a Littlewoods catalogue. Then, he purposely uncrossed his legs mid-conversation, as if taking an alternative stiffened position for another photo shot, with Lauren as 'the camera'.

'Where's Devon?' a voice called out from downstairs over the blaring music.

'I think he's in Sophia's room,' a cousin third-removed called out from the queue for the toilet.

'Tell him to come down please, we're cutting the cake,' Aunt Cassy balled from the kitchen. It was her perfectly-formed football cake which was the spectacle of the evening.

She promoted her cake to the main table for the celebratory toast and cake-cutting, much to the amusement of mum.

A head poked around the corner, 'Did you get that, Devon?'

'Yeah!' laughed Devon.

'Let's get some cake — we can come back up after,' Devon suggested.

As we entered the heaving living-room again full of sweaty dancing bodies, we made our way through to the middle of the floor, dodging *jutting arms* and *stomping legs* that moved in defiance to Bobby Brown's *My Prerogative*. It was a clever move by dad, as the track was a sure way of getting Devon downstairs. Neville and Devon (alongside a couple of cousins around the same age) mimicked some Bobby Brown dance moves — inclusive of the shoulder isolations (minus the shoulder pads). This was followed by repeatedly crossing one foot over the other and thrusting their pelvises vehemently forward in time to the strong beat. I looked over and could see Lauren with her curly locks dangling down her back, joyfully doing her own thing and shaking around like a rag doll in random time to the music. When the song ended, everyone held their poses for a couple of seconds in mocked seriousness and then burst out laughing. I could see Mum standing by the table with a cake knife in one hand, beckoning Devon to join her at the table. Aunt Cassy ducked out the way and let out an *'Eh eh! Mind my face'* with a disapproving side-look, followed by an exaggerated cackle which always lasted a tad longer than necessary. Devon awkwardly shuffled from one foot to the other. The room buzzed with chatter as the music came to an abrupt backsliding halt.

The evening sky was slowly beginning to descend upon us.

'Someone turn the light on, please,' Mum shouted above the din. You could see a roomful of eyes squinting and adjusting their eyes to the bright light, and people making adjustments to their clothing which hung awkwardly over their bodies after a succession of over-zealous dance moves. Mum put on her best telephone-speaking voice before she put her lips to the microphone:

'Well, first of all, I'd like to thank you all for coming today,' Mum gushed. Whoops and cheers could be heard all around in congratulatory fashion. 'It has been a long time since we've come together. So, I'm delighted that we could hold this party... for Devon... to celebrate his success in gettin' into the local youth under 16s football team!' The cheers got louder (followed by a Mexican wave but in voice form) with sounds of *BO-BO-BO's* to show support for Devon's achievements. Mum continued, 'I'm sure Devon will continue to do well and progress with his football. And one day... you never know he could make it to the First Di... what is it? The First Div?' Mum's words tailed off.

'The First Division for God's sake woman!' shouted a cousin forth removed in his Dominican-cum Cockney twang, ending in laughter reminiscent of Sid James from the Carry On films.

'You know well what I mean!' Mum joked. She continued her public onslaught of the *Sid James* character in patois, "Sa ki wive'w? Eh eh. Ou to hadi!" The room erupted in laughter. The young people laughed too even though they hadn't a clue what Mum said! I think it meant something along the lines of being too rude!

Dad and Neville said a few words and Aunt Cassy cut the first slice of the cake with Devon.

After the laughter died down, in usual fashion, there was a line of speakers ready to share their well wishes — ending with a call for the LIPs to come to the floor to speak.

Throughout the speeches, Devon's eyes darted back and forth towards Lauren to catch a glimpse of her reaction. Her continual smile reassured him, but you could see he was looking forward to the speeches ending and getting out of the spotlight. But before he could be freed, an elderly man who I didn't recognise creaked out of his chair and came forward to speak. He wore a stylish trilby hat and white suit which had an orangey-yellow stain on its lapel (probably shared by someone in the midst of an energetic dance move). He took the microphone and commanded silence by just standing there, waiting for the chatter to stop.

Then, 'Ahem. Good evenin' everyone,' the old man projected in an upbeat tone.

'Good evening,' slurred the crowd in return.

The old man continued at a slow, deliberate pace.

'Some of you may not know me... but I would just like to say... how much... I have enjoyed watching you all... this evening — especially seeing the youngsters having such a good time tonight... dancing... smiling... having fun... Yes, it's so good to see... yes...'

You could feel the crowd thinking along the lines of: 'I know you're an old man, but I hope this isn't going to take too long. Please get to the point — we wanna paaaaa—rrrrr—ttttty!'

Aunt Cassy decided to cut the football cake into triangular slices and then wrapped them in *football-covered serviettes* whilst the old man prattled on.

'Now, I've known Mr and Mrs Healey since... 19..69...' The old man looked over to dad for confirmation: dad speedily nodded his head in agreement willing the old man to politely get on with it. 'Yes... 1969...' The crowd let out a uniformed groan, which the old man was blissfully ignored. 'Mr Healey remembers...

yes!' said the old man pointing his finger to the heavens. 'And I... I consider them to be like... *family...*'

Party revellers stood with vexed faces, desperately willing the old man to cut to the chase and put them out of their misery. The elderly man in the sharp suit continued with a lengthy account of life growing up in the Caribbean: his journey to England and the difficulties he faced along the way. He concluded his speech though by saying there was more for black youth in Britain to pursue in life other than a career in football or entertainment for that matter, causing mum's lips to jut forward and make a sucking noise with her teeth.

Sparked off by a *heckler*, an impromptu round of applause helped round off the old man's speech. He was kindly led back to his seat by Aunt Cassy, who failed to conceal her cackles along the two-metre journey to his chair. Needless to say, the old man's sprint *home* gained another raucous round of applause; he sat upright in his chair grinning from ear to ear as proud as mum's intoxicating rum punch.

'A toast to Devon,' blasted a voice.

'To Devon,' the crowd cheered.

Mum gave Devon a massive hug and continued her calls of *well done, keep it up* and *I'm proud of you* which made Devon recoil even more, shrinking in embarrassment, especially with Lauren in sight. Devon relented by hugging Mum back quickly before speeding back upstairs, calling for Lauren and me to join him as he dashed out the living room. I hastily collected some football cake for the three of us before anyone had a chance to ask me for a song to entertain the crowd. Lights were set to *off* again and the party resumed.

I weaved my way through bodies, being careful not to spill any crumbs of cake en-route. As I zig-zagged my way up the stairs, a firm hand snaked its way through the banister and clutched onto my right ankle — stopping me in my tracks.

'Cassy... Cassy,' the drunken voice called out over the stairwell, with one eye fixed on my face and the other one just left off my chest. 'You gonna give us a song tonight?' he teased above the din.

For some reason this family member always referred to me as Cassy, even though Cassy was the name of my aunt and was about 30 years older than me. I was her spitting image apparently, minus the cackles. I tried to wiggle my foot free from his firm grip whilst making my excuses: explaining that I was attending to my *guest* upstairs.

Thankfully I had managed to escape his grip after a relative with plaits half-way down her back playfully slapped his arm, balling for him to *leave me alone,* helping to release me from his drunken charm.

'Ah... maybe later then. Cassy!' he continued in a stupor, craning his neck as I crept further up the stairs. 'I look forward to it!' he smarmed. 'Ou ka gade bel jodi-a,' I could hear him mutter under his rum-fuelled breath. I didn't know what it meant, but knew it was most likely something lecherous. The lady with the plaits gave the man an even harder wallop.

'Don't mind him,' she said whilst shaking her head disdainfully.

I found Devon and Lauren sitting side by side on the bed, chatting about the footballing skills of various Arsenal and Liverpool players. They happily munched on their cakes, whilst I sat picking out offending currants from my slice. Devon told Lauren about his new football team and the pristine kit which Mum and Dad recently bought him. In bold excitement, he nipped to his room next door and within seconds posed in the doorway of my bedroom in his kit — with hands on hips. Lauren's eyes were transfixed on Devon's caramel-coloured legs as he paraded along the 3-metre length of my bedroom. After the second stride, Devon spun on his heels and strutted towards the door in sultry teenaged fashion. Lauren sized him up and down some more and commented on his toned, muscular legs which made Devon's head (and other parts I'm sure) swell even more!

'Great kit Devon — very swank,' Lauren complimented.

'Thanks,' revelled Devon, lapping up the attention. 'You must come to a game when the season starts.' He started to do what looked like warm-up exercises, showing off his fancy foot work skills.

'Yeah, course, I'd love to!' Lauren turned to me. 'I'm sure Soph'll let me know when you're playing, won't you, Soph?'

'Yeah... course,' I agreed — feeling a bit like three's a crowd.

Devon continued with his fancy footwork (minus the football). 'Here, Lauren!'

Devon gestured passing the 'football' to Lauren and she jumped up from the bed to join in the action. She then picked up 'the (imaginary) football' and started throwing it overhead to Devon. Back and forth it went as they playfully mucked around. Lauren quickly searched my room and clasped her eyes on a fitting substitute. Nabbing my school boater which lay on the shelf above my wooden desk they continued their throwing game.

'Hey. Careful with my hat!' I pleaded, trying to catch the boater mid-air between throws. Mum wouldn't have been too pleased either if had she seen my expensive piece of school uniform being used for a game of catch!

'You're not quick enough, Soph!' laughed Devon as he held the boater above his head, twisting and turning away from me. I attempted to snatch it back. 'Catch Lauren,' Devon teased. Lauren was on her ballet toes, transferring weight from one pointe to the other, avoiding my flailing arms. I jumped up on the bed in another attempt to re-claim my precious possession from a higher position.

'Give it back please! Mum'll tell us off if she sees us,' I warned, trying to dissuade them both from continuing the game.

Devon delighted in *teaming up* with Lauren against me. Bobbing up and down on the mattress, I swung my hand aggressively towards Lauren, but she ducked down, still managing to clench my boater. She then darted under Devon's outstretched arms, and like a gazelle, bounded towards the bedroom door and sped along the top-floor landing, down the stairs to the darkened ground-floor level of the (maisonette) house. Music was still pumping out from the living room where most guests could be seen dancing to the mesmerising reggae beats.

'Wait, Lauren! I'm coming!' laughed Devon as he chased after her, with me lagging (a close third) behind.

A man dressed in Farah trousers and a blue short-sleeved shirt with his belly sticking out stood over a lady with relaxed curls cascading down her cheeks. The intimate couple were engaged in whispered conversations and weren't interrupted by the succession of teenaged feet clambering down the stairs. Lauren made her escape through the front door which was slightly ajar. She fleetingly rounded the corner onto the communal balcony — the sight of her white polka dot summer dress billowing in the wind. Two more party-revellers who huddled outside clutched onto their plastic cups full of alcoholic beverages and continued to blow smoked ringlets into the midnight air.

Devon sped along the communal concrete landing, down the stairs and then u-turned down the slope towards the playground. As seconds rapidly passed by, I could faintly hear Lauren's titters diminishing in the distance... until they disappeared. At this point Devon made his way in another direction to the right past the gardens beneath the maisonette, until he *too* was out of sight. In the blackness, I hurried straight ahead and darted along one path then onto another near the playground, calling out Lauren's name as I went. The only source of light came from a flickering streetlamp on the stretch of the racing circuit which enclosed the houses on our estate. Hesitantly, I ran towards the light hoping to see Lauren ducked somewhere behind a playground wall in her mischievous attempt to frighten me.

As I paced further from home, I could feel my breath quickening. With Lauren out of sight, and now Devon too, I became anxious in the dark, open surroundings and hastily decided to retreat. All of a sudden, I felt my body falling forwards and my hands darting out in front of me, helping to break my fall. I lay there motionless for a second. Lying against the concrete surface, unexpectedly I felt my right calf brush against something soft on the ground, so I tentatively reached down to grab it. I felt the familiarity of the trimmed edge of the object between my thumb and forefinger and impulsively clasped the object towards my chest. For a moment I had forgotten where I was. Soon remembering, I frantically clutched onto the playground wall to help me get to my feet, but as I looked up, I caught sight of a small figure… standing, staring out of a bedroom window straight ahead into the distance. It looked like one of the *Kray* boys. It was certainly the house — three doors along from ours. As I steadied myself a hand grabbed me from behind.

'…Lauren!' I turned around shaken by the presence of someone emerging from the darkness.

'It's me. Sophia,' I tremored…

Chapter 16

Our Little Secret

Long after Lauren's disappearance, the nightly visits continued. Lauren's figure would appear as if in soft focus and I would marvel at the warmth I felt of her being with me momentarily. But something more had been disturbing me for a while, and I didn't know what to do.

On that school night I sat up in bed in anticipation of another visit. I tried hard to focus, to adjust my eyes to the darkness. But nothing was there. Then I waited and waited, and then plucked up the courage to finally speak back. I whispered Lauren's name in return. A faint responsive voice came back. It was light, jovial and untroubled.

'Soph... *finally*! I've been waiting. What took you so long?!' Lauren quipped.

I paused for a moment, shaking my head in disbelief and quickly shot back under the covers.

'Hey Soph, did you get to speak to Mr Baldwin? Tell him I'm still waiting for a reply?' Lauren teased.

My head slowly peered out from beneath the covers as I looked furtively towards the bedroom door, then all around me. I carefully eased myself to a seated position with my knees to my chest, resting my chin on my bony kneecaps — covering myself with the duvet as if for protection. I took a deep breath.

'Lauren…' I coaxed. 'I… I didn't get the chance to… I… I…'

'I know,' Lauren predicted. 'I didn't think you would! You think they'll think you're *crazy*, don't you?! I understand!'

I jumped in quickly, 'No, it's not that…'

'Don't worry, Soph, you don't have to explain… In fact, perhaps we should keep it our little secret. That way, no one can try and pull us apart — at least not for the *second* time,' Lauren figured. I nodded hastily in agreement whilst trying to listen out beyond the door and walls, concerned that Devon and Neville might hear us through the thin divider.

'…I… I couldn't say anything because… well… Mr Baldwin left.'

'Really!' encouraged the voice.

'Yeah. He found another job — Head of a Dance Department at another school,' I informed, pleased that I had a legitimate excuse.

'Ah, too bad! Those Covino girls can't get their mitts on him anymore. Just as well 'ey! If I can't have him…!' Lauren mused, ending in a giggling fit.

I fell silent for a moment, trying to take it all in. Then Lauren continued, 'Hey Soph. Don't let those girls get to you. That's why they hang out together… they haven't got the bottle to face you alone. Don't worry, I'll always be here for you,' she soothed.

'Lauren...' I whispered. There was no response.

That's when it started.

Our little secret, although a comforter at the beginning was the start of the spiral of descent. Lauren's parting words echoed in my head: she'll always *be here for me.* I couldn't help but see the irony. That was typical Lauren though. My head fell back onto the pillow; my knees tucked into my chest as the night faded into day.

At school, when the towering Academy walls would climb higher and consume me, I'd think about Lauren, finding comfort in the knowledge that I could now talk to her when darkness fell. Finally, I had Lauren by my side again to share my thoughts with. I looked forward to our nightly chats and it helped to ease my internal struggles.

It was the middle of Spring 1990. The school had organised a trip to the theatre in Stratford- upon Avon and a workshop/talk was organised for the following day for the Covino pupils as amazingly a student from the Academy had landed the lead part in a theatrical production of *Carrie*. Mrs Court our ballet teacher was one of the staff members accompanying us on the trip. The seat next to me was empty and she gracefully took the seat beside me and we talked practically for the duration of the three-hour coach ride to Warwickshire. We spoke about school but also interestingly enough about Mrs Court's early career as a ballerina — training at White Lodge — and all that it entailed. It was fascinating to hear her life story and I was so intrigued by her openness about her life beyond the Academy.

More astonishingly, Mrs Court said I should think about taking the RAD ballet examination at Intermediate level. I was shocked that she thought I would ever be a contender, as I didn't think I was nearly good enough to enter. Not only that, but my weight also hadn't plateaued as yet; I still had puppy fat as my cousin twice removed always had the habit of reminding me. Whenever I looked in the mirror, I only saw the bulges — and it made me self-conscious.

There were mirrors practically *everywhere* in Covinos. So much so that I'm sure everyone's over-imagined over-sized reflecting image was firmly implanted in their memory. There was no respite from being self-critical about one's weight or in some stick-thin girls' cases — lack of it. The only place that didn't have mirrors was the academic school rooms at the top of the building. At least you weren't reminded of your physical imperfections up there.

I couldn't help but think Mrs Court only suggested that I take the forthcoming ballet exam entrance out of pity; it would be something to help take my mind off things after what happened to Lauren. Although things went seemingly well previously at Tina's stayover in Bradford, Mrs Court knew that Tina and I still weren't the best of buddies, and I was still bearing the effects of her malevolent influences on the other girls at school.

But as the weeks progressed, I was beginning to become more of an island. I guess Mrs Court was trying to be protective and tried her best to keep the *sharks from swimming nearer shore* and taking pleasure in viciously attacking its prey at any opportune moment.

The journey from our school in London to the Warwickshire countryside was a lengthy one, and with Tina and her fan club putting on a performance at the rear of the coach for most of the duration; I was grateful for Mrs Court's company. It appeared she made a conscious effort not to bring Lauren into our conversation... and neither did I.

The evening performance of *Carrie* ended at about 11 pm, and our year group (of about sixty girly theatricals) chattered with excitement along the cobbled streets of the market town where the Swan Theatre was situated, back to our dormitories nearby.

A voice piped up from a group from behind, 'Did you enjoy the show, Soph?' the familiar Northern voice rang out.

I turned to see Tina with her clan grinning from ear to ear, joining in with the hubbub and post-show excitement. I forced a smile and waved to her out of politeness to show some acknowledgement.

'Gosh, you're just trying to make conversation,' I could hear one girl say.

'No wonder she hasn't got any friends,' said another.

'Yeah, she can't even be bothered to be polite. You would think she'd try harder after what happened to Lauren,' scorned another.

'It's midget girl I feel sorry for, she's got to share a room with her for the night. You never know what might happen!'

Then the crescendo of cackles reached its climax before Mrs Court warned, 'Keep the noise down, girls. Remember we're in a public place.'

I took a deep breath and tried to block out chatter. I continued walking along with my paired partner from Song and Movement class. Thankfully, it didn't look as if she was listening to the commentary and seemed oblivious to what was going on around.

When we arrived at our dormitories, I took the bottom bunk bed for the night and *midget girl* (as she was so lovingly named) claimed the bunk above. The boxed room contained mainly of a bunk bed, a small wooden table and a window over-looking a vast green open space beyond the confines of the pint-sized dormitory room. With lights out, I lay down facing the ceiling, studying the metal grids that supported the mattress above, my eyes darting from one rectangular wire to another — thoughts running through my head like the intertwined connections between each wiry segment.

Earlier that day, Mrs Court informed me about the classic original film (which came out in 1976) with the lead actress Sissy Spacek and the furore and critical acclaim it received at the time. *Carrie* was one of the films I heard Mum talk about too, but my brothers and I weren't allowed to watch it. I guess Mum figured it would be good for me to go on the school trip, perhaps being out of the school might help to forge new friendships. But the theatrical production stirred up pitiful feelings inside. Carrie was humiliated by the harrowing, bloodied incident that she encountered and although my experience was not as gruesome, Carrie reminded me of *me*. *I* felt like the lone girl in the story, a girl tormented and bullied by her classmates. Like her, I felt shamed by my peers for being an *outsider*, not looking the same, not being the same, not feeling the same. I was shamed in the same way for *the change that occurred in me*, when I was shamed about my menstruation in ballet class. And I kept thinking about the time when I was ridiculed in ballet class for my own *bumpy road to puberty*. And now I felt that people resented me even more because of what happened to Lauren on the estate. It was my fault and it seemed I would never be forgiven.

Tossing and turning, I couldn't seem to drift off to sleep even though the country air should have worked its magic and sent me into dreamland. The bloodied dramatic climax of *Carrie* kept whirling round in my head.

I tried to sleep, but I couldn't put the disturbing scene out of my mind. My agonising recollection kept playing over and over in my head, causing me to turn restlessly from one side to the other, trying to shake the thoughts off, willing a visit from Lauren to relieve me from my torment.

Then, finally, a voice teasingly called out my name.

'Lauren...' I blurted softly, aware of 'midget girl' in the room in earshot.

'Is that you, Soph?' a voice called out. 'Are you awake still?'

There before me was a silhouette of a head hung upside down from the top bunk with plaits swinging like ropes on either side. Pretending to be asleep, I muttered something under my breath — unconscious of my *sleep talk*. Peeking through squinted eyes, I could see the plaited girl mumbling a string of incoherent words in return before disappearing from view again. I listened out intently for her breathing — a sure indication of her return to sleep, ensuring it was safe to make to contact with Lauren again, but I stopped myself in my tracks.

With thoughts of the Covino girls perilously scrambling through my mind and their conversation on the way back to the dormitory together, with the dramatic scene from the musical I began to work myself up into a state. I pictured the white opulent staircase dominating the entire stage that night, and my eyes transfixed on the bucket of pig's blood cascading down the porcelain staircase from the *heavenly* top to the *hellish* bottom of the staircase. I imagined Tina, Sarah and her clan standing all around me, laughing, their bodies animatedly rocking *to and fro*, from *left to right* — with me in the centre of the furore.

Anxiously, I clasped my face with both hands, trying to squeeze the image of the *fitting* girls out of my mind, as gasps and gawps could be heard out of the mouths of audience members reverberating around the theatre.

I then thought about the next day's events. Certainly, the bloodied scene was going to be the big talking point the next day! All the Covino girls in the theatre workshop would willingly *play their part* in the dramatic re-enactment of the scene with me (I visualised) at the centre. *The insiders* would revel in my doomed fate, and I as the outsider would have no protector from further ridicule. The climactic part of *Carrie's* story would merely be a repeat of my own shameful escapade only for *more* people to witness. The more I thought about it, the more I felt the urge to talk to Lauren. She'd help me calm my thoughts. I needed her to curtail the negativity and temper my anguished mind from blazing full speed ahead.

I pushed the covers to one side and hastily clambered out from the bottom bunk, put my slippers and dressing gown on and crept towards the door, closing it quietly behind me so as not to disturb sleeping girl.

The walkway was near pitch-black. No voices could be heard as girly night-time chats had finally subsided. As I tip-toed along the narrow corridor, my hand searched for the rounded door knob at the end of the walkway. Slowly, I creaked open the door and entered the girls' communal toilets. Even though I was slightly perturbed by the dark night, I decided to leave the lights switched-off, so I would be alerted if anyone was to enter the girls' room.

Pushing the aluminium door of the cubicle open, I snuck inside and closed the door behind me, locking myself in.

As a draft of air seeped through a closed window, I could feel the swift breeze brush against my face. Using the palms of my hands I rubbed the sides of my folded arms, in an attempt to warm myself up, feeling comfort in the soft touch of my furry dressing gown. Then in the silent darkness I called out Lauren's name and waited… then…

'Funny old place this is eh, Soph!' Lauren mused.

'Lauren, I'm so glad you heard me. I couldn't sleep. I just wanted to talk,' I anguished.

'What's bothering you, Soph? Not those girls again?'

'Well, no… nothing's happened really… not yet… I'm just worried about tomorrow.'

'Why's that, Soph?' Lauren sympathised.

'Well, the girls were teasing me again and we've got a workshop tomorrow,' I whispered. 'I just know all eyes are gonna be on me… I'm sure the girls are going to be thinking about me and my incident in ballet… 'Cause that's what happened to Carrie. They all made fun of her… like the girls did to me…' I said before breaking down in tears.

'Hey Soph, you're getting yourself all worked up. Hey, listen, I'm not being funny, but think about it. They're gonna have all the important people there in the workshop. Those girls'll be on their best behaviour. They'll want to impress the director more than anything else and not scupper their chances of getting into the production,' Lauren amused. 'You know they're already looking for the lead for the next production on Broadway!' she added before laughing.

I thought about it. Perhaps Lauren was right. Perhaps I was just over-thinking things and letting my thoughts run away with me, making my own stories up before they even happened.

'Well... yeah... when you put it like that... why *would* they be more interested in me?'

'Hey, Soph. You're doing fine...' Lauren encouraged. 'Now you make sure *you* impress the directors too... you're a talented girl, Soph. Don't let others stand in your way... you deserve a break as much as anyone else.'

The toilet door cubicle rattled against the lock, signalling an end to Lauren's brief appearance. I reflected on Lauren's words and made my way back to the dormitory, feeling a sense of ease and temporary release from my troubles. After de-robing, I settled back into bed and pulled the blanket over my face, drifting off to rattling sounds of the girl above as she slept.

The next day thankfully was more as Lauren predicted. In fact, our workshop conversation about the girls in the story ganging up on Carrie appeared to make the Covino clan more sympathetic and soften somewhat towards me; even to the point where Tina said goodbye to me on the Wednesday evening when our coach got back to school.

Even so, by the time I got back home to South London, all my built-up feelings of anxiety had worn me out and sent me into a deep sleep as soon as my head hit the pillow.

At school the next day, Mr Hodge's dulcet tones reverberated around the lower floor of the Academy. He combed his huge hand through his greasy slick-backed hair as he over-emphasised the words to the '*Betty bit a bit of butter...*' tongue twister, whilst simultaneously spewing out bits of saliva in the process.

Our weekly dose of elocution was aptly renamed *Execution* by some pupils: Mr Hodge would often single out a pupil to repeat verses aloud if they couldn't replicate the Queen's English.

Being publicly slaughtered was something we all dreaded (and a common theme amongst teachers in the school), and Mr Hodge had a good ear for weeding out the chaff.

The small room which accommodated about twenty pupils sitting poised in their chairs echoed a precocious chorused imitation of Mr Hodge's pronunciation and inflection of each word from the well-known verse. Three chairs down to my left, I could still hear Tina's grating voice spouting out, with her flattened vowel sounds refusing to take a back seat to Mr Hodge's preferential RP, making her loyal audience of fans giggle. As we repeated the verse over and over, I could see Mr Hodge squinting his eyes and grimacing at the sound of her betraying Northern dialect. Luckily for Tina, she was saved by the buzzer, marking the end of the lesson. Otherwise, I'm sure Mr Hodge would have summoned her to recite an executory solo performance. Anyone would have thought Tina would at least have tried to make her voice from up North blend in with the southerners, or perhaps she secretly wanted the attention and raised her voice louder than anyone else on purpose! Anyhow, Tina didn't pay me any mind that day as she was still revelling in the great impression she made with the directors at the theatre.

School was almost bearable for the last couple of few weeks of term before the Easter holidays and speaking with Lauren at night was a real comforter. Also, with Mum escorting me to and from school on most days, I also felt protected in the event that I bumped into the south London gyals on route. So, that was one less thing to worry about. When I did see the girl gang, they'd flash me a wry smile (disappointed that I wasn't alone) and simply walk on by muttering their disapproval of me under their breaths. Anyhow, it was nearing the Easter holidays and at least I would have a couple of weeks reprieve from the churlish chatterers at the Academy also.

It had been a number of weeks since I had received the Body of Christ (the host) at church leading up to Easter. Mum must have had an inkling as to why. She knew it was difficult for me to talk about Lauren's disappearance to anyone much less talking to a figureless man behind a black, draped curtain at church. Perhaps Mum was fearful I might have told the priest a different story — another version of events to the one I told her, the police and the social services. Whatever she thought, Mum never forced me to go to Confession.

It was the Saturday before Easter. Devon and Neville played out on their roller skates and skateboard along the communal balcony, whilst Dad was in the garage below tinkering around on his Ford Escort. Mum and I said our goodbyes and made our way out of the estate up the road to church.

She sat on a pew in the empty church with her palms pressed firmly together and the weight of her body on her knees. I left her side and entered the small room at the front of the church as she mouthed a dozen *Hail Marys* and rolled the tiny rosaries of her necklace between her thumb and forefinger. With knees pressed together, I sat primly on the wooden seat, watching the black, draped curtain flapping every time the priest spoke.

'And what happened after that?' barked the Northern Irish voice, which was always set not too many decibels short of the level of a lawnmower. Whether he was in mass addressing the congregation or speaking to an individual in a tiny confession box the priest's voice was set at the same ear-piercing level!

The next day on Easter Sunday, Father Delaney stood impressively in his white tunic behind the lectern — his wide body bulging out from either side as he stood there stony-faced. His grandiose voice echoed around the holy space, with just his lips barely managing to prize itself apart whilst he bellowed his outpourings. The congregation was packed full of families, with parents holding tightly onto their cherished tiny off-springs.

The priest's brash voice filled every crevice of the Catholic church. 'And let's give a thought to our dearly beloveds who are suffering at dis special time. Easter is a time for family — a time to reflect on the sacrifice Jesus made for us, who died on the cross. It's a time to remember the resurrection of Jesus Christ, a man who lived and died for us all. It's a time for forgiveness for our sins, a resurrection of the dead and the life of the world to come. Let's remember those who are no longer with us… Let's tink and pray for dem and dere families…' He bowed his head and the congregation followed in timely succession.

Mass was nearly ending. The boys and I always looked forward to the half-way point where we could relax, knowing that the church service was nearly over — with thoughts of a big fry-up and the scoffing of lots of chocolate Easter eggs to look forward to. My thoughts then turned to Lauren. I kept my head bowed and said a prayer for Mr and Mrs Harrison.

    Father Delaney then changed tact and shuffled awkwardly behind the wooden lectern before continuing in a less formal tone. 'I don't know if you have seen in de papers the continued reporting and speculation about the young girl, Lauren, who went missing in our local area?'

Remaining straight-faced, the priest shot Mum a quick side-look and then addressed the congregation again. 'Let's remember de young girl whose family and friends are still grieving, as she is still missing. Let's remember the many *other* families who have lost loved ones and who have family members who are missing. We continue to pray for Lauren's safe return,' Father Delaney concluded as he lowered his eyes and head.

Mum put her arm around me and pulled me closer, squashing my face against her arm as a roomful of eyes penetrated us. Devon shot me a look and lightly pressed his palm on top of my hand.

The chiming of the bells at 12 o'clock signalled the end of mass. Father Delaney stood at the front of the church wishing members of the congregation a good Easter before families trundled home with a lighter more optimistic spring in their step. Mum simply locked eyes with the priest and mouthed, 'thank you' on our way out.

Dad picked us up from church and whisked us safely to our home on the estate. Television programmers repeated the usual lengthy offering of *The Ten Commandments* which kept Dad entertained for most of the afternoon. Mum spent most of her time in the kitchen rustling up lunch and then dinner. And as I had given up chocolate for Lent, it was now time for the boys and I to secretly scoff our faces full of Easter eggs upstairs in our rooms between lunch and dinner time, against Mum's command of course!

For the months and years that followed I learnt to hide my struggles well. Not only had I lost my one true friend, but as time went on and I grew older, I felt immense guilt and responsibility for what has happened. Had I really put Lauren in harm's way? Should I have disclosed the activities at No. 24 to Lauren? Did that have anything to do with Lauren's disappearance? And furthermore, nothing could console Lauren's parents. These thoughts and the guilt that I felt plagued my mind for years to come.

Chapter 17

Make Believe

It had been a long time since Lauren and I had a nightly chat… years even…

After graduating from Covinos some ten years on, I had managed to find a number of dance jobs travelling in the UK and abroad. Devon had been selected to play for a semi-pro club up North in Leeds. Dad had re-settled back in Dominica with Neville following swiftly behind to work with him on a car business he got going, leaving Mum and I to weather the storm back on the estate. Only newcomers would appear quite talkative when they first arrived on the estate, but it was not long before the polite conversations were reduced to strained *hellos and goodbyes.* The lady at No. 24 moved out not long after the oppressive forces (the police) continued its presence on the estate. She never gave Mum a real goodbye, much less an inkling as to where she was going to. Although we had sought to move out, buyers for the maisonette were hard to come by and the recession had left Mum with a situation of negative equity, so after things had calmed down, we decided to stay put.

Life after Covinos wasn't the glamorous existence that we hopeful students were led to believe it would be. Checking in and out of crammy hotels and being allocated dressing rooms the size of a broom cupboard (with only a saucer full of half-decaying fruit to welcome you) were some of the disappointments. Chasing payments for jobs three months after you clinked glasses of wine with theatre producers (who only sang your praises about the wonderful performance you had given on the opening night) were other setbacks.

Attending countless auditions only to be told months later when the production was in full flight that they were *going in another direction* added to the slow wearing down on one's psyche. These experiences weren't the life us wannabes at Covinos were prepared for, and undoubtedly the culmination of these factors added to the stress of it all.

However, what the business *did* afford us was the escape from the humdrum of normal everyday living: an escape from the nine-to-five, an escape from the prospect of monotonous pavements *to* and *from* the same place of work — an escape from a life of permanence. Chorus girls and boys would be afforded the chance to execute razor-sharp choreographed routines whilst sweating buckets — welcoming the release of their contagious endorphins onto their audiences and the stratosphere. Our sugar-coated lives when the right jobs came along placed you in a state of daily euphoria.

Our *'make believe'* world helped to create an illusory life anyone would crave. And more personally my world in my fragile liquid ball helped to ease the past painful events.

Showbiz life, however crummy it might have been, helped to curtail the stark reminders of what happened on the estate nearly a decade ago.

Mercilessly, Lauren's disappearance was becoming a distant memory. The emptiness I felt slowly began to dissipate as the years rolled by; I parked the painful feelings of loss submerged in the depths of my mind.

But even so, sometimes things must have appeared quite differently on the outside. Mum often said I should speak to someone (a professional) about what happened. Perhaps it was on those days when she caught me in my bedroom staring at a spot on the wall, motionless, that she knew the torrid memories still plagued my youthful mind. Any 'therapy' I had was only short-lived. I didn't like the idea of people prying into my life, drudging up the past and tormenting me further by re-surfacing old wounds. I wanted to forget. As time went on, I learnt to live with moments of anxiety and negative thoughts that filtered in and out of mind.

And like a great actor, I learnt to hide it well from the world and others too. I learnt to cope with combatting cyclical feelings of low self-worth, self-esteem and self-pity, just as I had learnt to live in the knowledge that Lauren was never coming back…

It was May 1998. I struck up a friendship with a girl named Charlie, who was around the same age as me: 23. We had gotten to know each other on a dance gig we did abroad in Ossen, Germany. It was another high-flying dancing job I had managed to clinch in a dingy nightclub in the middle of nowhere! Our glamorous 5-day gig involved promoting a well-known aftershave by treating the club revellers to a choreographic routine whilst advertising the pungent intoxicating astringent! Being allowed to enter the nightclub free of charge and getting our own sample of the goods were some of the perks of the job! Not only that, we had the freedom to hang out in the smoke-filled venue every night after our three-minute performance, so long as we wore the t-shirt emblazoned with *Cool Mountain* on its front, whilst sipping on our free cocktails and nibbles from the bar. Failing that, we were left to our own devices and headed back to the hotel nearby when it was time to silence the noise.

Young clubbers hung out in all corners of the venue. Muscular legs were draped carelessly over sofa armchairs positioned in *chill out* zones; flexible arms and legs moved effortlessly in time to the soulful music; and alcohol flowed freely and guiltlessly down elongated youthful necks. Charlie and I got to know each other a bit more one evening over the slow intoxication after a series of rum shots.

'I love this track! Let's dance!' Charlie encouraged, whilst pulling me off the wooden stool at the bar.

Charlie smouldered her way through the buzzing crowd onto the dancefloor, an invisible circle began to form around her and others were in line for a bruising from her strutting limbs as she showed off her professional dance moves.

"My love won't hurt you... Don't Walk Away boy..." Charlie sang out at the top of her lungs.

We improvised a string of dance moves which may have looked as if we were on stage giving a choreographed performance to a paying crowd. Hit after hit kept us on the dancefloor until I needed to go the bar for a refill. I downed a glass of cool water and sat back on the stool at the bar. Charlie was still going, and it didn't seem as if she was going to get off her platform anytime soon.

As I sat perched on the stool at the bar, I scanned the room watching club revellers enjoy their evening. Moments later, an older man wearing a jean jacket came and sat on the stool next to me. At first, I remained in the same position as the man placed his beer bottle down defiantly on the bar. He sat there quite still, looking straight ahead, whilst all movement continued busily around us. It felt as if the man was about to engage in small talk, then for no reason I suddenly felt my guard rising. I swiftly turned my whole body towards the bar with my legs clenched firmly together underneath. My skin began to tingle, like an open wound that was about to be doused in sulphur. As my heart began to beat faster and accelerate, the man thrusted his bottle towards the girl serving at the bar but more at an angle in my direction. Seconds later, I instinctively stumbled off the chair, feeling the urge to get away, but not wanting the man to sense my uneasiness. With my breath still quickening in pace I could feel my chest woefully trying to slow my breathing down and fight my anxieties. Once I had managed to move a few feet further away, I stealthily turned to look back at the man at the bar; he sat there unwittingly knocking back another bottle of German beer.

'Heh Soph! What's up? Someone troubling you?' Charlie asked plainly as she saw me gazing perplexed in his direction.

'Ah… no, I… I was just about to try and find you,' I replied lost in thought.

'Hey, we can go back to the hotel if you want?' Charlie offered. 'We don't have to stay here.'

'No, let's stay a bit longer,' I answered unconvincingly, not wanting to spoil Charlie's enjoyment.

We found a spot at the other end of the bar and stayed at the venue for a little while longer. But behind my façade, Charlie read something different; the sense of unease was noticeably etched on my face. I kept turning my head to check whether the same man was there, and finally relaxed when there was an empty place where he was seated.

Charlie told me I needed to *let myself go* and that I needed to *get out more* if I ever wanted to meet someone. It was as if being with a significant other would be the answer to my insecurities. To make matters worse, she nearly found herself *under* the bar when I told her about my history with boys to date (which was virtually non-existent). In a sisterly fashion she insisted that I needed to *find someone special who would treat me how I deserved to be treated.*

She joked that she didn't want me to end up living alone — spending most of my days behind a sewing wheel with three cats circling round my ankles — brushing against my calves in need of their evening feed! Finding 'my match' was to be Charlie's mission.

Once back home from Europe, Charlie said she needed a place to stay for a couple of weeks before sorting out a flat she was going to rent out in North London. Mum was kind enough to oblige and put Charlie up in Devon and Neville's old room for a few weeks, which turned into a few more weeks after that. It did cross my mind that Charlie's friendly ways may have been harmlessly rooted in her own practical needs, but I appreciated her friendship.

One Friday night, Charlie and I drove in her Mini from the streets of South London to the bright lights of the West End to find somewhere we could meet a potential date. We parked across the way from Green Park tube station before seeing a long line of night-clubbers waiting in an orderly fashion outside a nightclub, so figured it was one of the better ones to try out. Most girls wore mini-skirts without jackets and stilettos, and the guys wore proper shoes (square-toed black ones) with open-necked shirts whilst trying their best to steady themselves on their feet as they queued upon entry into the club.

Charlie and I were next in line. With bags and coats checked into the cloakroom in exchange for a 50p, Charlie shot off like a pinball onto the dance floor and created a space where she could cut some shapes to Salt n' Pepper's *Let's Talk About Sex* (a track by the prominent American 1990s hip-hop girl group). As I was not quite as ready to make a statement on the dance floor, I tailed sheepishly behind her and nestled myself amongst a group of teenage clubbers and moved self-consciously in time to the hip-hop beats, but making sure Charlie was still in sight.

Every so often Charlie would pop over and dance with me for a bit. Sometimes she would bring over a rum and coke in one hand whilst fist pumping the air to the music with the other.

'Seen anyone you fancy, Soph?!' I shook my head. 'Don't worry, it's our first night out. Plus, they say it's more likely to happen when you're not looking anyway!' she advised before taking off again.

Charlie had a side line in selling cooking pans when she wasn't performing. She had no qualms about boldly approaching strangers in the club in order to recruit members and party hosts for her pan-fried business! This time, Charlie found herself chatting to a model couple near the bar.

I decided to stay on the dance floor — it felt more comfortable being amongst a crowd. After a few drinks, the room full of strangers began to appear not so daunting as the night drew on. It was then that I caught sight of a tall pleasant-looking figure in the crowd, who made it known that he had his eye on me. Whilst dancing, I'd glance at him every so often and meet his persistent gaze.

To my delight, the young guy maintained *his pursuit* for most of the evening.

I could see my *pursuer* wasn't one for dancing as he stood like a bean pole on the other side of the darkened room, whilst I intoxicatingly moved to the rhythmic soulful music. The more I'd catch a glimpse of him peering at me, the more I started to exaggerate my body movements and sensually contort my body. Our eyes were fixated as if *we the only ones in the room*.

'That's another three!' Charlie gloated, before she was off again.

At about 1:40 am, after an evening of flirty non-verbal posturing, I could see my voyeur watching as Charlie and I headed to the cloakroom to collect our belongings. Having had our fill of music (and recruitment), we strutted out of the nightclub, our heels making clicking sounds as we made our way to the car. Just as we collapsed onto our seats, a guy wearing an open-necked dark maroon shirt sauntered up to the car window. Charlie cracked it open, leaving just a two-inch gap for the inquisitive guy to speak through.

'Hi,' he smarmed.

'Hi,' flirted Charlie after she wound down her window on the driver's side a few inches more. Charlie looked in the rear-view mirror and pushed her lips together, ensuring her ruby-red lipstick was still adequately spread over her sizeable lips.

'Don't worry, they're still there!' he quipped, as he brushed the palm of his hand over his *Fresh Prince of Bell*

Air high-top. Charlie flashed her eyes at the young man and teasingly chuckled to herself, amused by his attempt at a chat up line.

'Did you just follow us from the club?' Charlie brazenly confronted.

'Well, I couldn't let two ladies just leave without saying goodbye!' the young man charmed.

'I didn't see you in there,' Charlie threw back flirtingly. 'Did *you*?' Charlie turned to ask me. I shook my head, not wanting to confess to our evening's game of ping pong.

'You didn't look hard enough,' the young man returned. Charlie made a sound which suggested it hit her spot, and then recovered from her weakened composure. 'So, why are you ladies leaving so early? Where are you off to?' he enquired, whilst throwing some side-eye (attention) my way. The brazen man then looked over to his friend and raised his hand as if to say, *I've got this!* After a few more rounds of chatting, the young man put his hand into his shirt pocket and produced a business card. 'Have you got a pen... sorry, what's your name?' he asked.

'Charlie,' flirted Charlie. 'And this is Sophia,' Charlie continued, smiling in my direction.

'Lovely names...' he continued whilst gently taking the biro from Charlie's feminine grasp. 'It would be lovely to see you ladies again. Perhaps we could hook up another time?'

Charlie turned her head acutely in my direction and pulled a face, then turned her head sharply towards the gentleman after she adjusted herself. After the young man scribbled on the back of the card, he proceeded to squeeze his long athletic arm through the small gap in the window, clumsily leaning over Charlie in the driver's seat. His outstretched limb reached the passenger seat where he placed his credentials between my thumb and forefinger. I froze in embarrassment by his manly gesture.

'Well, lovely talking with you Charlie... and So-ph-ia,' he flirted, whilst giving me a long lingering look before striding off into the night. In a frenzy, Charlie briskly wound the car window down, letting in a surge of chilly air, then ungraciously stuck her head out of the window.

'Yeah... thanks... lovely talking to you *too*!' she bellowed, ensuring her sarcasm reached the back of his head before bouncing off his faded afro. I could see the young man continuing to stride forwards without a pause for breath, and coolly raise his right hand in acknowledgement.

With her nose still firmly out of joint, Charlie speedily wound the car window back up to the top and let out a disapproving gasp. The business card was still awkwardly positioned between my thumb and forefinger.

'The cheek of it!' Charlie pouted, her eyes rolling to the skies. 'Tell me you're not going to call him!' she urged, showing no signs of hiding her bruised ego.

'I don't know!' I pretended, trying to make out it wasn't a big deal.

Charlie's bite continued, 'I guess he thinks he's *fowine (fine)* just 'cause he looks the way he does. I know *loads* of models much better looking than he is! I even met this couple in the club tonight. *And* I got their numbers, *and* they're gonna come to one of my pan parties!'

I remained composed, knowing that Charlie just needed to let off some steam. She then grasped her handbag awkwardly from behind the driver's seat and rummaged through it before pulling out her *Cool Mountain* and squirting it in a frenzy around her neck. A stream full of light from the streetlamp allowed Charlie to admire her profile in the rear-view mirror before sulkily asking, '*Well?!* What does he do then?'

I lifted the business card towards the streaming light and read out his credentials:

Mr Dean Sutton
Manpower Services Commission
Managing Consultant — Recruitment
0171 872 3671

'Hmmm? He works in Central London then. I wonder what kind of Recruitment he manages?' I could hear Charlie's mind working overtime. 'I guess you'll have to phone him to find out,' she resigned, changing tact.

I presumed that was her way of signalling her approval for me to call him. In spite of her bruised ego, perhaps she thought Mr Sutton might be a good contact for her pan business! In any case, I was just glad that Charlie had settled down from her mini temper tantrum.

'What did he write on the back?' she asked curiously.

'*Call me,*' I chuckled. 'And he's added a mobile number.'

'A hopeless romantic then?! A man of many words!' Charlie smugly chuckled to herself. 'I'm taking it you like him, then?

'I... I don't know? I don't *know* him!' I said, feeling a bit flustered by the continued firing of questions.

''*Course,* I know you don't *know* him! I mean, do you *fancy* him?' Charlie relented, whilst half-laughing in exasperation.

'Well... yeah he's kinda cute,' I replied coolly, not wanting to upset her further.

'See. Well, I told you it always happens when you're not looking! Stick with me girl and you'll be loved up in no time!' Charlie paused for moment. 'If not, you could always chuck him my way!' she threw in. 'Just kidding, Soph. I hope it works out for you,' Charlie finally concluded.

Charlie then revved up the engine and sped off from our spot like Nigel Mansell behind the wheel. I tried not to focus on the speed of her driving and instead concentrated on the London landmarks along the way. Our journey home was filled with the music from early morning pirate radio station which filled the awkward silence. But underneath I was secretly excited by the night's turn of events. I clasped onto my future in my hand and looked forward to calling *Mr Sutton* in the next few days.

Dean was to be my first boyfriend. When I first asked him why he picked me out of anyone else in the club that night, he said it was a combination of my dance moves and my sprayed-on tie-dye trousers that did it for him! As I grew to know Dean, what did it for me was his undivided attention like nothing I had ever experienced. Not that my limited number of dates to date had anything to go by, but I was flattered that Dean wanted to be with me morning, noon and night. It was the sort of undivided attention that would be any young girl's dream (until you were old enough to know better!). Co-incidentally, we only lived about ten minutes driving distance from each other (with him living in nearby Streatham and me still in Tulse Hill). We were practically joined at my tie-dye hips! Initially, I told Dean that I wanted to take things slow, but as we know when love comes knocking on the door, taking things slow doesn't quite flow!

After the first few weeks of us officially dating, Dean whole-heartedly declared his love for me and said he never wanted to let me out of his sight! Of course, I was totally over-whelmed and completely besotted with him. Although, the smooth talker with a high-flying job as a Managing Consultant for a big insurance company was still living at home, he had his own stylish car, great dress sense and money in the bank — often lavishing me with the usual gifts of flowers, chocolate and perfume, mixed in with trips to the local cinema and the odd dining out at a Chinese restaurant! Romantic cosy nights in were precluded by a trip to the local Blockbusters and getting our hands on the latest VHS American film releases like *Falling Down, Indecent Proposal* and *The Pelican Brief*!

At first, Mum erred on the side of caution and said that I shouldn't get ahead of myself, and that she didn't want to see me get hurt. Why she wasn't more trusting in the beginning I didn't understand. I just wanted her to be happy for me and welcome Dean into my life with open arms. After a few weeks Dean started to help out Mum a bit more, like driving her to get our weekly groceries at the local supermarket and picking Mum up from work when she was on a late shift. As Dad was no longer around, Mum found Dean to be quite helpful and soon relied on him and grew to like him probably as much as *I* did.

'Let me know if you need anything, Mrs Healey?' Dean would say, flashing his porcelain teeth encased in his killer-watt smile before he departed our home on the estate after his nightly visits.

As Dean and I were growing closer, thoughts of Lauren kept consuming me. Dean and I were in a whirlwind romance at full speed ahead, and although Charlie had essentially *opened the floodgates* by giving me the opportunity to meet someone, Charlie was too busy in her own loved-up-ness in bushy North London to take any interest in my new romance, especially after how it started.

I often wondered what Lauren would have thought about Dean — whether she would have given me the seal of approval. Brimming with sentimentality, the more I thought about it, the more I felt the urge to 'contact' her; it had been a while since we last 'connected'.

Over the years, I had been continually comforted by Lauren's voice in my head. Well actually, it was something that I grew accustomed to; it was so second nature and commonplace that I never used to give *her guidance* a second's thought. On many occasions she would tell me what I needed to do if I was unsure about something, or if I was in a difficult situation, she would offer me advice. Only now I needed her more than ever, I wanted someone to speak to, to confide in.

Was Dean *the one?* Should I put my trust in him? I was scared that I may have been too quick to let down my guard, to have shared my heartfelt feelings with him, only to be let down. I didn't want to risk getting too close and being hurt... to lose someone dear again. I just needed Lauren's voice, her guidance... her approval. But where her voice was prominent before, it now fell silent.

More poignantly, I was beginning to feel fearful that Lauren had only been a figment of my juvenile imagination (that our nightly chats following Lauren's disappearance were simply imagined). I also wondered whether the rumours were true: that Lauren had run off with Mr Baldwin to distant lands and started a new life together! Over the years, there were some alleged sightings of her, but traces never amounted to anything.

When Dean left home nearing midnight one evening, I waved to him from my bedroom window and got myself ready for bed. His tender kiss lingered on my lips long after he'd left my arms. I pulled the duvet cover over me and played back our kiss over and over in my head. It would only be a matter of minutes before Dean would call me on my mobile (which I kept protected underneath my duvet cover) before he wished me a final goodnight. I then rested my mobile next to me on the pillow.

Soon enough, I fell asleep but was strangely awoken, not with dreams of Dean but visions of Lauren swirling around in my head. I could see her smiling face with us in different places that we had frequented together (like a camera shot flashing in quick succession).

As I lay under the duvet, I tossed from side to side and couldn't get back to sleep. I looked at my phone: it was 03:24. It would've been too late to call Dean to soothe me back to sleep. I tossed and turned some more.

'Lauren… I hope you can forgive me,' I confessed, 'I'm so sorry it's been so long.'

I remained still for a few moments in hope of hearing her returning voice. But nothing came; Lauren remained unreceptive to my call. And who could blame her?

It was about six months in and I was in complete lockdown with Dean. If he wasn't at my house on the estate, I'd be at *his*. But since Lauren's disappearance, I still never ventured out alone at night. *Theirs* was a terraced house on a tree-lined Roman Road with respectable working-class neighbours. His mother, Janice, was a feisty, small woman who adored her son. In spite of holding down a full-time job at the local hospital, she always made sure Dean had a well-cooked meal ready for him as soon as he stepped through the front door from work. She whipped around the kitchen like a Michelin chef, ensuring his belly was full of his customary daily meat with special fried rice. Dean was a creature of habit. Every other day, his washing would be perfectly folded in the clothes basket at the foot of the steps, ready to be taken to his room. Dean always joked that I had a hard act to follow, and sometimes I'd feel the wrath of his mum if I dared oppose something he'd say. I took it on the chin and tried to not upset the applecart and learnt to savour my opposing thoughts for when Dean and I had some privacy.

In contrast, Dean's dad was a bit of an enigma. He worked on the buses, so I never really got to see him, as he'd often stumble in after a late shift. I'd just hear an inaudible grunt as his father came home late at night and strolled past the mottled glass panel of the living room door at the front of the house (where Dean and I would be watching MTV videos or action-packed films). Dean would reluctantly return the same disdainful grunting noise back. So, no love lost there. I didn't ask why Dean had so much contempt for his father. Whatever had gone on between them I didn't want to know, that was *their* business. I didn't want to get into any family politics. In any case, I didn't want anything or anyone (more importantly) to spoil the honeymoon of our relationship.

Mum was doing more late shifts at the residential home, so on those nights Dean would stay over at mine and we'd have the place to ourselves. However, whenever I stayed over at Dean's, I would sleep on the couch in the front room. I was never invited into his bedroom; I wondered what it looked like inside. Knowing Dean, he probably had a desk set out with all his work and business stuff at one end and accolades and certificates from his high-flying time as a university student at Leeds University on the other. I admired Dean's world — a world far away from my own — away from the insecurities of life in so-called 'show business'. I was beginning to imagine that life might have not been so dismal in the world of the 9 to 5. Dean was able to buy what he wanted and wine and dine me at the drop of a hat, as well as have savings in the bank. These were luxuries I was yet to be afforded.

Even though Dean and I were about seven years apart it felt like there was no age gap between us. We shared the same sense of humour and outlook on life. He knew I was full of ambition and wanted to conquer the world with my ambitions of life on the stage. And even though as time was passing by and nothing significant was happening in my career (no roles of significance materialised) my dreams were still alive, and Dean encouraged me to keep on striving for what I wanted in life! Refreshingly, the combination of our business and creative worlds appeared to be a fitting match.

After months of cosy nights staying in, Dean said that we should go out somewhere up West to have a bit of change of scenery. I recommended a singers' hang out called *The Eye* — a bar venue in Leicester Square that Charlie had told me all about. She said A&R men used to frequent there when on the look-out for new talent, so it was the place to be if wannabes wanted to get signed by a recording company. Failing that, it was just a great place to hang out, apparently! Of course, I wouldn't have the audacity to *take the mike* as it were, but I thought it sounded like a lively venue to try out. Plus, I wanted Dean to embrace a bit of my world and be amongst artistic and creative people.

Before the evening of entertainment started, we hung out by the bar: I sipped on my southern comfort and coke whilst Dean slurped on his lemonade-on-ice. Dean was dressed in his usual business attire: suit and tie, whilst I glammed myself up in a tight-fitting long skirt with two slits up the front that was bordered with amber stones along its length. My clingy top emphasised my ample top-half which allowed Dean's eyes to comfortably drown themselves in.

Strangely, it felt a bit awkward as it was the first time Dean and I had gone '*out-out*' together since we first met in the nightclub over six months before. We stood at the bar like two strangers on a blind date, not quite knowing what to say or do. I notably felt quite self-conscious in the middle of the buzzing crowd, and Dean in his *executive-suited and booted outfit* stood out like a sore thumb! Many of the people around us were quite animated and extrovertly gave each other hugs and kisses every two seconds, saying *lovvie and darling* at the end of every single sentence.

As I was about to make polite conversation by asking, '*Do you know where the toilets are?*' (even though Dean's guess would have been as good as mine) I could feel someone's fingers tickling my neck from behind, which made me surprisingly titter. Swiftly, I turned around to see a beaming familiar, yet un-placeable face before me.

'Hey, Sophia, darling, you look very glam. I hardly recognised you! How are you doing?' exclaimed the smiling, young guy — wearing a fashionable hat with multi-coloured beads around his elongated neck.

'Hi… I'm good thanks…' I replied with equal measure as if we were best buddies.

'I haven't seen you here before. What you been up to, lovvie?' he charmed.

'Ah not much… Just doing auditions really… It's the first time I've been here actually! My friend Charlie said I should check it out.'

'Charlie? You don't mean Charlie Wootten? Charlie! Oh my god, she's fierce darling, I didn't know you were good friends! She said she might be coming down tonight.'

'Oh really?'

At this point, I was trying desperately to remember where I knew the excitable pup from so that I could introduce him to Dean. I looked in Dean's direction, aware that he might have been feeling a little left out, then suddenly remembered.

'Yes!' I gestured, pleased that my memory was finally restoring. 'I met Charlie on a dance job in Germany — she's great! Have you seen anyone else since *the...* Hammersmith... gig?' I asked in hope.

'No... no darling... well... Nick's my flat mate, so we see each other all the time of course, but other than that, 'no'! I haven't bumped into *anyone*! Oh, it's so great you came. I'm gonna go on the mike tonight, are you?'

I couldn't have thought of anything worse than singing in front of the crowd, much less in front of Dean (a reminder of the past I'd rather forget). Based on my performance so far, I could barely string a sentence together in Dean's company much less sing in his presence.

'Hey, sorry Dean. I haven't introduced you. This is Marcel,' I said, gently pulling on his arm, desperate to bring him into the conversation, 'Marcel... Dean.'

'Oh my god, I didn't know you were together? Pleased to meet you... *Dean?* Like the suit!' Marcel perked up some more, as if that was at all possible!

'Hi, you 'right,' Dean replied with a normal level of enthusiasm, which could have been interpreted as plain rudeness. He took Marcel's outpoured hand and used a businessman-like handshake to greet him, then slowly turned back towards the bar and took another slurp on his lemonade.

'He's cute,' Marcel whispered in my ear, giggling like a little schoolgirl. 'A man of few words. I *like*. I guess more of an action guy, eh!' Marcel winked suggestively. I coyly reddened at his comment, but I was more concerned about Dean. Not wanting to leave him out of the conversation any longer, I raised my eyebrows, indicating that I should get back to him. Marcel gave me another wink in agreement and made a poised demi-point turn to exit.

'Sure, see you later, darling,' Marcel warmed as he gave me another hug. 'Lovely to meet you, Dean!' Marcel's voice raised over the few heads between us, as Dean had become increasingly separated in the room from us as it started to fill. Dean lifted his hand towards Marcel in acknowledgement.

'Catch up with you later, Marcel,' I said hurriedly.

That evening was the most I had ever spoken to the guy in the fashionable hat with the multi-coloured beads around his neck. I wished Marcel had been as friendly when we worked on the dance job in Hammersmith those few months back. It wasn't a surprise that he knew Charlie too. Everyone in the dance world knew Charlie! I wondered if she was going to turn up that night, as I hadn't spoken to her in weeks — well, we hadn't really spoken since Dean and I had got together. I squeezed through the crowd to reach Dean again, accidentally stepping on a few toes along the way and mouthing *sorry* as I passed by.

'Sorry about that… Marcel kept talking!' I apologised whilst comfortingly rubbing Dean's back.

Dean remained facing the bar and looked deeply into his glass. He swirled the last bits of flattened lemonade around like it was a shot of white rum, before knocking it back and slamming the tumbler onto the wooden bar (a bit *too* firmly for my liking). I instantly lifted my arm off Dean's back as he backed off, noticing that he wasn't quite the same.

With the atmosphere in the bar still buoyant and jovial, I nervously looked around me to see if anyone noticed Dean's rebuttal. I tried to keep the mood between us upbeat by continuing to make light of Marcel's interruption to our 'quiet' evening.

'Hey, in case you didn't know, Marcel's not into girls. He's probably more interested in *you* than *me*!' I quipped, hoping Dean would loosen up.

Still, the temperature descended a couple degrees lower. Dean adjusted his tie, making sure it was perfectly centred before he turned to face me head on, and then started speaking (I imagined like he does with his work clients).

'Do you know you spoke more to that guy in those few minutes than you've done with me all evening?' Dean breathed into my ear.

I stood in shock, not quite sure if Dean was being serious or not. I shuffled awkwardly from one foot to the other, waiting for the joke. Dean then raised his eyebrows as if to say, "*So what's your response?*"

Was I to be unnerved or flattered by Dean's obvious craving for my undivided attention? I put it down to male pride and then assuredly encased my hand in his, interlocking our fingers.

Dean looked me deeply in the eyes and drew me closer, then kissed me passionately on the lips before slowly brushing his cheek against mine.

'Don't ever do that to me again,' he whispered with intent.

I put his churlish reaction down to his bruised ego, which only re-enforced what I already knew. *Dean truly loved me, and he didn't want anyone or anything to come between us.*

Totally forgetting my surroundings, I lovingly kissed Dean some more.

'Do you want to go home? We can always come back next week?!'

'Hey, I don't want to spoil the evening for you. You'll miss the main event,' Dean toyed, now lightening his tone (and in turn, the atmosphere).

'Depends, what's the main event!' I batted back. I teasingly pulled Dean towards me and we exited the venue, grabbing our coats along the way. (It felt like being in the films when a lover leads the other upstairs to the bedroom following a bit of downstairs' foreplay!)

When we got back to the car Dean made it known he was pleased we left early.

The week went by quickly enough and Dean and I decided to remain cosied up at home the following Friday night. He said he had a tough week in the office and just wanted a bit of *chill out* time rather than be in the company of *lovvie darlings*. I completely understood as I wasn't in the mood for a bumping into Marcel again either.

On the Saturday morning, Dean said he had a bit of work to catch up with, so he'd be making business calls from home. With time on my hands, I decided to attend a dance class at Appleton Studios in London. Like all dancers, I needed to make sure I was maintaining some semblance of dance condition in case of any potential calls to audition! As I approached the studios on Wardour Street, W1, Dean called me on my mobile to make sure that I had got there all right. He even said that he would pick me up in town after I finished dance class if I wanted. I said he needn't worry as it was easy enough to jump on the train and get a bus back from Brixton station to home, what with all the Saturday road traffic. Plus, darkness wouldn't have descended as yet.

On my way home, when I got out of Brixton station, I joined the crowds of people waiting eagerly for a bus to reach further south of the river. As I stood in front of Woolworths' shop front, I was aware of a man with a Nike baseball cap who kept dashing past and then stopping and then coming back and positioning himself beside me as he busied himself on his mobile phone. The more it happened the more I became anxious and kept looking around me. The dashing man seemed to be looking towards the opposite side of the road at a guy in his 20s (dressed in a khaki jacket, jeans and white plimsolls) who kept looking back over in our direction. The man then darted into a red telephone box. All of a sudden, like a mass exodus, swarms of people gravitated towards an already packed 2B bus which ferociously approached the bus stop.

As I moved hastily towards the bus with a surge of people, the man grew closer, now invading my personal space. So much so that our bodies collided. He must have read the look of fear in my eyes as we moved in tandem when he reluctantly apologised for bumping into me. I looked defiantly at him and pulled my bag closer to my chest. Most of my bus ride was spent looking to see whether the man on the top of the bus was getting off before me or not. I breathed a sigh of relief when he got off a couple of stops before and made sure I speedily made my way through the estate home.

Our home on the estate hadn't changed much over the years. Although Mum had treated me to a few new pieces of furniture for the room which I had outgrown, much of the interior had stayed the same. We weren't too bothered about *Keeping up with the Joneses.* The newest item we had purchased (many years ago) was our television (with Ceefax and tele-text) and novelty remote control! I remember spending many a night scrolling through the pages of news information and stories just so that I could flick through the on-screen pages. Dean and I spent most of the evening at ours locked in each other's arm in our joggers and slumped in front of the TV. Mum was at work on the overnight shift.

'So how was your dance class, Soph?' Dean asked, stroking my forehead as we lay on the sofa in the living room.

'Yeah, it was really good. Walle's such a great teacher. All the girls *love* him!' I joked.

'What about you?'

'Me?'

'Yeah, do *you* love him *too*?'

'Course I don't, don't be silly,' I giggled, playfully hitting Dean on his arm. 'I just love his choreography. We did a routine to *That's the Way Love Goes* today,' I enthused.

'*Really*. I *love* Janet.'

'Do you really? I mean, do you *really* love Janet?' I mocked in return.

'Ha-ha, very funny!' Dean succumbed. 'Well, show me the routine then, I wanna see your moves,' he teased.

'I can't remember how it goes now!' I faked, whilst wrestling with him on the sofa.

He tried to tickle me all over and then pushed me off the seat towards the middle of the living room, enticing me to dance for him.

'I'll sing Janet's tune to help you out… I'll start with the verse… ahem. *"Da-dah-da- dah-da-da-da.. Da-dah-da-dah- -da-dah-da, Da-dah-da-dah-da-da-dah dah."* Dean hummed painfully out of tune, whilst accompanying the melody with a drummed beat. *"That's the way love goes…!"*

"Oo!" I injected.

"That's the way love goes..." Dean blurted out in full voice. 'See, I can sing! You don't have to go to special school to learn how to sing. It's *eau natural.*'

It was a rare moment to see Dean break loose from his more conservative ways, and I welcomed his more laid-back-ness and attitude.

'I never said you *couldn't* sing!' I threw back.

I lay on the living-room floor (legs akimbo) as if limbering up in preparation for a dance class, continuing without coming up for air.

'Actually, we did a routine to Jackson's Rhythm Nation when we were at Covinos. It was *so* cool. There was this dance teacher called Mr Baldwin and he choreographed a number for our end of term production. *Everybody* wanted to be part of his dance troupe. My friend Lauren — she was my best friend at school — she was sooo jealous that I was chosen to do the routine, 'cause she had the hots for him. So much so that she wrote him a love letter in the summer holidays and posted it to him! Well, *I* helped her write the letter and we sent it off and... and...' Then, I caught myself.

'Yeah... *and...*?'

'And... and *what*?' I panicked.

'What did your teacher do? Did he write your friend back? You know teachers are not allowed to do that. They can lose their jobs if they have a relationship with their students! It's against the law!'

I immediately clambered up. Crossing my legs, I slowly bent forward and lowered my head to the floor, then stretched them out in front of me.

'Come on, you can tell me,' Dean teased.

'No… no he never wrote her back…' I replied, staring straight ahead.

'Hey, never mind, Soph, I'm sure she got over her teenage crush!' he quipped.

Months had passed without as much as a phone call for work, but I wasn't too bothered by the *season of drought* I was experiencing as I had other things to dominate my mind (namely Dean!). On the grapevine though, there was a new film that was being cast and the US producers were on the look-out for a cast of young dancers from the UK. Everyone in the dancing fraternity was trying to get an audition. I managed to get the casting details from a classmate when I attended my weekly dance classes in town, but the closing date had come and gone, and it was too late to follow it through. I heard they didn't even select many UK dancers anyway, so I didn't feel so bad about missing a so-called opportunity.

It was coming up to my birthday and previously Dean had proposed that I leave my birthday weekend free. With Mum working the whole weekend, Dean must have confided with her about his arrangements, as she left me a birthday gift and card on the downstairs table together with a note saying: *Have a wonderful time and I'll see you on Monday!*

Although not one for surprises I was excited by the prospect. I made sure the house was spruced clean and spent most of Saturday morning relaxing in a long hot bubble bath; painting my nails a rich Autumnal colour; straightening my already relaxed hair and taking my time over dressing-up in anticipation of a weekend adventure. I tried on a number of outfits before I was finally satisfied and squeezed into a pair of tight-fitting Levis; some red-heeled sandals; and a cropped top to complement.

'Happy birthday, Soph! Nice jeans,' Dean complimented. 'Turn around so I can see you properly.'

Self-consciously, I spun around at speed, knowing that it was my *derriere* which was what he really wanted to gawp at! Dean pecked me on the lips (being careful not to smudge my well-moisturised lips) before placing my belongings into the car boot. With my inflexible denims disallowing a bend in my body from my torso to my ankles, I cautiously side-stepped into the passenger's seat and was delighted that my jeans fittingly held my excesses of fat firmly into place.

I fastened my seat belt and checked it over a number of times before we took off. Dean coolly got into the driver's seat and sped off out of the estate, leaving a trail of rubber behind.

As we drove up Norwood Road, we passed our local church — St Luke's. As we got caught at the traffic lights, I gazed through the double-doored entrance to the main church and was transported back in time... I could picture our three small afro heads (mine with a ballet bun lobbed on the top) sitting next to mum with her head of roller-relaxed hair. I re-imagined Devon and Neville pulling some kind of prank and laughing at an inopportune time during church service. Then, I remembered Mum clipping the boys around the ears when Father Delany wasn't looking, as the comedy duo couldn't contain themselves when the church choir continued to 'sing' *Hosanna in the Highest* dreadfully out of tune from beginning to end! Father Delany wasn't too pleased either when he witnessed the boys misbehaving and I could see him giving them a cut eye which only served to encourage their mischievous antics even more. Neville and Devon's shoulders were body-popping in sync to the hymns, whilst hysterical tears naughtily streamed down their sinful faces. That incident earned the boys a hasty trip to Confession the following week! Reminiscing the moment of youth brought a smile to my face but filled me with sadness at the same time. How I missed those days… the time before…

As the lights turned amber, I could feel the acceleration of Dean's pulse before he even put his foot down. The car jolted forward which arrested my transportation back in time, forcing me to apply some imaginary brakes. Dean glanced down at my feet and shook his head in jest, noting my habitual anxiousness when travelling in the car.

Five minutes later, we arrived at our destination. I scanned the streets wondering where we were staying for my birthday weekend. Dean manoeuvred his car with boastful ease into a space off the main road, just outside where a Volkswagen car showroom was situated on the corner of Streatham High Street.

'You ready then?' Dean asked.

'Are we here?' I asked quizzically, unsure where we were headed to. 'I've no idea where we're going!'

'That's why it's a surprise!' Dean mocked.

Chapter 18

The Weekend

Trying to keep up with Dean's gainly strides, my high heels scrapped noisily against the pavement. Feeling the warmth of Dean's hand, I grabbed onto his arm with my other hand as he led me across the busy high street, trying mostly to steady myself and ease the throbbing pain from my crippling toes.

'Can I take a name please, sir?'

'It's Mr Bailey. I'm booked in for 2:15 p.m.,' Dean offered assuredly, 'I faxed you the documents last week.' The salesman ran his grubby mechanical oil-stained finger down the white form, stopping about half-way down.

'Oh yeah, right. It's for the missus, ain't it? So-ph-ia Healey?' he checked, whilst giving me the once over, stopping short of a chuckle at my red-heeled sandals. 'It's the VW Golf Cabriolet ain't it? *Larv-ely* motor. It's just come out — *really* popular with the ladies. We've got quite a few on order already, so you'll want to get in there quick if you wanna purchase,' he continued going full-steamed ahead with his sales patter. 'You're a managing consultant at Lexington's ain't ya?'

Dean tittered with a sense of pride. 'Great firm. Last time I read they turned over about £250 mill... You guys must' a been buzzing.'

Dean nodded again, adding a heartier laugh to boot. 'Yeah, yeah they're not doing too badly,' Dean said modestly. 'Gotta keep it rolling.'

'Yeah, too right, sir, gotta keep it rolling!'

The man with the grubby fingers imitated the same dog head-nodding action, whilst trying to keep the upbeat momentum going and then pointing to a gleaming red, soft-topped VW through the car showroom window.

'Just look at her, she's a real beaut,' the man relented, shaking his head.

'Yeah, I thought she'd give it a test drive first. You know what it's like, you gotta put the feelers out first. Don't buy til you try it, they say.'

I stood there lamely, not knowing which *she* they were referring to. They both burst out laughing.

'You got a right one here, missus. I'd hang on to him if I were you!' the man gestured.

'Yeah, well, gotta keep the missus happy, innit,' Dean joined in, maintaining his eye contact.

Feeling like a spare part, I sheepishly turned to look at Dean for comfort whilst they continued to throw around some more boyish banter.

'Too right,' he bounced back as they shared another testosterone-filled laugh.

Still unsure of what I was about to encounter, the salesman led us to a glimmering motor on the forecourt and plonked the car keys in my hand. Dean casually strolled over to the passenger side before the man started again:

'Now, right. Just a few things before you whisk her away! Car horn's here, windscreen wipers there (not that you'll be needing them!) looks pretty clear to me,' he said gazing up at the sky. 'Top speed — 110 mph just in case you get the urge,' he joked, cocking his head through the car door, so Dean could also witness his professionally amateur comedic skills. 'Oh yeah, and if you wanna pull the top off, you can just wind it down using the lever on your right. The rest is pretty much *as per. All right?'* his voice inflected. 'And don't worry Mr Sutton, they've got air bags on the passenger side too!' the man got in before traipsing off to see another potential customer waiting outside his office.

My manufactured smile informed him that I was rearing to go, but I was just happy to rest my derriere on the driver's seat and get some relief from my aching feet.

Only then it dawned on me: I hadn't driven since painstakingly passing my test (on my fourth attempt) years ago, and now I was about to drive about the streets of South London in my new pair of designer heels! Not wanting to make out like I was incapable of such a feat, I securely clinked my seat belt into the fastener, checking it over several times until I was duly satisfied. I let out some air like deflated tyres after a lengthy drive and wiped the steering wheel from the droplets of moisture which surfaced as a result of my sweaty palms. Next, I proceeded to turn over the engine over. Before take-off, I noticed Dean securing himself into the passenger seat too: buckling up and repetitively checking that his seat belt was securely fastened.

'It's yours, babe, if you like it?' he offered, slapping his thighs indicating that he was rearing to go.

'Really?' I said in amazement.

I didn't know whether it was more appropriate to say thanks *before* setting off in my heels to test drive the new car (potentially ramming it into a wall at 110 mph as a result of my heels getting caught under the driving mat); *or* to wait until when we got back after we had suffered an onslaught of abuse from other drivers on the road, simply because I was going at a snail's pace and holding up the traffic!

If this wasn't Dean's way of showing me he was in for the long haul, it certainly was an indicator that he took our relationship seriously and he wanted to show me his best intentions.

I tentatively reversed out of the tight spot — amazed that I at least got the car moving at first attempt whilst trying not to put too much pressure on my 3-inch heels. Finally, we exited the forecourt together with a dozen or so eyeballs trailing us (including the grinning grubby-fingered man with the sales patter).

'See ya in about 20 minutes then. Enjoy!' he barked.

We were now about 30 miles out of London and Dean was back in the driving seat of his car, where he belonged.

I had finally recovered from my test-driving ordeal navigating the back streets of South London! The VW was handed back intact to the oily-fingered man in the showroom only minus my confidence in ever getting back onto the roads again. Dean *did* warn me that I had to drive like a madwoman in order to maintain my position on the roads, otherwise I'd be run off of it (which was what more or less happened). In conclusion, Dean told the comedic salesman that he'd give him a call the following week about a possible purchase once we had a chance to mull it over!

The winding roads trailing off the A40 soon led us to an impressive manor set amongst 440 acres of Oxfordshire countryside. A field full of sheep welcomed us before we found a parking space in front of the Grade II listed building. After we checked in at Reception, a portly porter led us up a grand spiral staircase and along a hessian walkway to our suite at the end of the corridor, which overlooked a restaurant terrace on the ground floor at the rear of the stately building.

Dean thanked the porter and dutifully slapped him a fiver and a wink. I pulled back the net curtains covering the impressive sash windows and looked out onto the fields taking in the magnificent surroundings.

'So? Do ya like?' Dean asked.

He was busily unpacking his belongings and putting them into the mahogany wardrobe with matching-drawers which were positioned on either side of the spacious room.

'Wow, yeah it's so peaceful here — great to get out of London once in a while I guess. What made you choose this place?' I asked.

Dean continued whilst unpacking, taking his toiletries out from his washbag in the en-suite bathroom. 'A colleague from work suggested it. Well, we held a conference meeting here last year — we invited some international business guests over. Don't worry, I've got a few more surprises in store for you later!' he said as he came back into the bedroom. 'We won't be locked up in our suite for the whole weekend! Not that that would be such a bad thing!' Dean remarked as he strode towards me. Placing both of his palms around the back of my neck, he pulled me towards him and tenderly kissed me.

'I love it here. Thanks Dean,' I kissed back.

'What, you *really* wouldn't mind if we just stayed in our room all weekend?' he suggested with a glint in his eye.

I laughed *no*. Then, it suddenly dawned on me. I couldn't use the excuse of feeling funny doing it at home now. No family — it was just us and the luxury of an executive suite in the Oxfordshire countryside all to ourselves! Six months into a relationship I guess is a long time for some to wait for intimacy.

And now, thinking about it, I don't know what Dean's expectations of me were.

'Hey, look. Don't worry. I'd never force you to do anything you don't want to do. I've always said that. We should only do it when the time is right... okay?' Dean comforted.

'Sure... thanks. That means a lot,' I said, feeling like a failure.

The sensual aroma of essential oils and therapeutic treatments filled the Beauty Rooms. A massage appointment was booked courtesy of Mr Sutton for 5:30pm in the basement of the grand building. A lovely petite Japanese lady's soothing hands eased out knots and stresses in my pent-up body. She gently tapped me on the shoulder to awaken me at the end of the session, wished me a *Happy birthday*, and gifted me an assortment of miniature essential oils.

I made my way back to our room to find Dean sprawled out on the King size bed, watching the tail end of an afternoon football game.

'Enjoy your massage, Soph?'

'Yeah, thanks for the treat. It was just what I needed,' I said before blissfully collapsing on the oversized mattress next to him.

'Who did you have?'

I looked at Dean quizzically.

'Oh, the masseuse? She was a Japanese lady — beautiful thick hair in a bun.'

'Oh right. Yeah, sounds like Mayu. I *did* ask for her when I booked, but they weren't sure if she'd be working today. I must go and say hello before she clocks off.'

It was the first time I felt my hairs stand up on end from pangs of jealousy. The fact that Dean knew her by her first name meant that they must have been friends, or at least acquaintances. Perhaps he too had been a recipient of her feminine touch. I enviously enquired further.

'Yes, Mayu, that's it. She was really nice. She gave me these massage oils as a treat. You know her then?' I probed.

'Yeah, through work. You know our company likes to keep its workforce in optimum shape. We get vouchers for a free massage once in a while. Perks of the job, eh,' Dean gushed.

'Ah right. That's good,' I lied.

Dean changed the subject. 'The night is young... I'm sure you must be wondering what's happening this evening. You hungry?' Dean asked.

'I guess I could eat something.'

'Well, that's what's next on the agenda, believe it or not! I've just got to sort something out at Reception first.' Dean rummaged through his bag for his wallet and keys and made his way over to the suite door. 'We've got over an hour, so you can relax now and get ready a bit later. I'll be back shortly, okay.'

I locked the suite door behind him and pulled out a copy of Cosmopolitan from my bag.

Flicking through the photos, I sized the stick-thin female models up and down, mentally comparing each and every aspect of their hair and body with my own. Having brought a choice of two dressy outfits, I tried on both to see which dress was more flattering, around the hips.

Dean had been gone longer than anticipated, so I decided to start getting myself glammed up for the evening. As the night was drawing in, I admired the view from our room. From the window overlooking the woodland I noticed a couple of guys talking outside, under the terrace. Before I was about to draw the curtains, one of the men looked up at me and waved. It was Dean. I smiled and waved back before closing the curtains.

Within moments, I could hear the door handle depressing two or three times.

'Is that you, Dean?' I asked from the inside.

'Yeah, Soph, open up.'

I greeted Dean in my black fish net tights and sparkling mid-length asymmetric dress.

'Wow, you look great, Soph!'

'Thanks,' I blushed, closing the door gently behind him. 'I'm nearly ready. Just gotta do my nails!'

'Okay, I'll take a shower then. I won't be long,' said Dean.

Painting my toe nails a scarlet red, I suddenly remembered the other guy from downstairs on the terrace.

'Who was the guy you were talking to down there?'

'Oh… Max. He's been here donkeys,' Dean projected from under the shower. 'He's the guy who sorted our trip out for this weekend. I'll introduce you to him later.'

Just as we were about to head out the door, Dean gave me the once over. He fleetingly scanned the room and picked up my silk scarf which was draped across the bed, then arranged it decoratively around my neck.

'There. That's better, Soph... You don't want eyes wandering where they're not supposed to be. Only if they're mine, of course!'

The dimmed room was full of buzz and chatter as the maître d' showed us to a table on the far side of the hotel restaurant. Dean said 'hi' to a table with seven seats which had two empty spaces. I noticed a balloon with 'Happy Birthday' on it. Then a lady with black shoulder length hair turned around and greeted me.

'Hi Sophia. I hope you enjoyed your massage?'

'Oh, hi. Yes... I... it was great. Thanks so much,' I beamed back.

I immediately recognised it to be Mayu the masseuse from my earlier Beauty treatment. She was out of her white cotton slacks and tunic, and glammed-up with immaculately applied make-up which accentuated her beautiful dark eyes.

I noticed an empty table for two beside the party table, then looked back at the five well-dressed guests. Dean stood chatting to a man with an open-necked shirt and slicked backed hair. Another guest at the table got half-way out of his chair, reached his hand out to me from across the table and introduced himself.

'Hi Sophia, I'm Tom. Very pleased to meet you and *Happy birthday*,' he greeted, "take a seat." His open palm indicated the seat with the birthday balloon' on it, tied to the slatted back of the chair, beckoning me to sit down.

'Hi, thanks so much,' I smiled back, realising that this group of strangers were our dinner guests for the evening. I kept glancing back at Dean, who stood talking in hushed tones to another man. I began to feel a bit uneasy about having to carry on a conversation with the group of strangers and willed Dean to cut his conversation short.

'And this is my fiancé Neve,' Tom offered.

'Pleased to meet you Sophia,' Neve started, politely toasting her glass of champagne in my direction. 'I guess you'll be wanting some…'

And before she could finish her sentence Dean loudly interjected, 'Ahem. Sorry everyone. You know Max and I — always got some important business to attend to!' Finally taking charge, Dean then took my hand, 'Everyone, this is Sophia.'

I shyly waved to all the guests at the table as if meeting again for the first time, then Dean sat down beside me. With our flutes filled to the brim, seven crystal glasses clinked ceremoniously in the middle of the table — and we simultaneously knocked back mouthfuls of bubbles. A lady, who sat directly opposite me introduced herself as Lisa. She shared a smile and gushingly complimented me on my dress. Apparently, she worked at Dean's Management Company but was good friends with Max and was his 'date' for the evening.

'Well, it's lovely to finally meet you, Sophia,' said the confident lady. 'Dean has been planning this for weeks, hasn't he, Max?' she informed, flicking her auburn hair.

The gentleman beside her brushed his hand against her head to smooth her red flaming tresses.

'Yes, darling. Well, everyone knows Dean,' he addressed. 'He calls me up and says, "I've got a wonderful lady I would like you to meet". She's a dancer, on the stage. And you know me,' he joked, 'Dean, what was it I said?'

'Ah Max. You've just met Soph, at least give her the chance to settle in! I do apologise, Soph. Please excuse Max, he's like this all the time,' Dean half-joked, enjoying the verbal titillation.

'Come on, Dean, it was only a bit of banter. You can imagine what I said, can't you?'

Max continued holding court. The other nonchalant guests, who were only too familiar with his dominance, joined in the laughter at the dinner table.

'Yes Max, you said something about *laps*. And you didn't mean the running type either,' Dean blatantly divulged, without disguising his complicity. 'I'm sorry Soph, please excuse Max, he means no harm!'

I tried to laugh it off and took another sip of my champagne.

'To be honest,' Max continued, 'I didn't know you were dating *anyone* — you know Dean can be a dark horse,' he continued jesting.

Lisa tapped Max on the arm, indicating him to stop and then took over.

'Have you had the chance to see the sights yet, walk around the grounds?' Lisa piped up.

'Erm, not yet. I suppose we'll get a chance tomorrow?' I inflected, looking for Dean for 'guidance'.

'Yes babe, don't worry. I'll show you around then. Or perhaps Max can give us a guided tour?!' Dean bantered back.

'Hey, why don't we go on an exploration this evening — after dinner?' Lisa suggested.

'Yeah, we could take some drinks out. Seems like a mild evening. Let's explore the Oxfordshire countryside and show Soph around,' Neve proposed.

It seemed they were all set on the idea. As much as they were eager to show me around and were welcoming, part of me just wanted to snuggle up and spend the rest of the evening alone with Dean. The conversation continued flowing over our first, then second-course meal.

'So, where do you live Sophia?'

'In South London…'

Apart from the sounds of knives and forks scrapping the plates and the general hubbub in the restaurant, a silence continued. Then I elaborated, "Tulse Hill."

'Ah yes, I know it well. Used to have a client who worked in the kitchens who came from there. Endless housing estates.'

'Yes, I've lived there practically all my life,' I replied in defiance.

'Good for you!' commended Max. 'Good for you.'

He laughed heartily. I could see the flame-haired lady wriggle in her seat, probably giving Max a kick under the table at the same time.

'It must be a welcomed change then, coming here,' Neve offered, thinking her comment would offer some support.

Then, Dean took over. 'Soph has just come back from Germany actually, from doing a dance gig.'

'Where was that then?' Max's ears pricked up.

'Erm, in Ossen,' I expanded.

'Oh wow, that must be glamourous, getting to travel the world with work,' Tom innocently joined in.

'So, what was the venue? They've got the most beautifully-designed theatres in Germany. The Germans are well-renowned for their architecture,' another voice added.

All heads turned towards me, waiting for my answer.

'We performed in this… night… club,' I revealed.

Max nearly spat out his half-chewed lamb chop in laughter. 'I do apologise Soph. Please forgive me,' Max relented. He could hardly get his words out for laughing. 'But I wasn't far wrong, was I Dean?!'

Dean shook his head from side-to-side half-smiling.

'Lap… yeah Max, I know that's what you're thinking!' Dean laughed.

I failed miserably at swiftly trying to defend myself.

'Well, we rehearsed for about a week in Appleton Studios in London with a well-known choreographer — he's choreographed a load of West End shows.'

'Oh right,' Tom responded raising his eyebrows in admiration. 'I've heard of those *studios*. Quite famous in London,' he encouraged.

A number of heads nodded in affirmation.

'Yeah. We had about three rounds of auditions, before they selected us for the job.'

'Wow, great. That sounds great,' Neve assisted.

'Yeah. Very glamorous. Getting to travel the world,' her fiancé said in support.

'Yeah, and also Soph's waiting to hear about a lead role she's just auditioned for,' Dean offered.

'Oh really, what's that for then? A show in the West End?' Neve asked with interest.

'Oh, well I can't really say much at the moment,' I explained.

'I understand. Got to keep it hush-hush, eh.' Neve enthused in conspiratorial tones.

'Well, let us know how you get on. We'll be the first ones to book — front row seats!'

I felt comforted by Neve's comments, and we continued to chat a bit more freely for the duration of the meal. Then, I looked across and noticed Mayu at the dinner table. She hadn't said a word; I had forgotten she was there.

'Hey Mayu,' Max started. 'You gonna come for a night walk too? You're more than welcome to join us.'

'I'll see. I might have an early client tomorrow morning. Someone provisionally booked in for a treatment, but I won't know for sure until a bit later,' Mayu affirmed.

Silence descended again, and Neve and Lisa shared a look.

A number of hours had passed, and our meal was rounded off with a delicious chocolate gateau (my favourite) which Dean had aptly selected. I blew out the candles on the cake and made a wish. The ladies said they had never known Dean to go to such lengths for previous girls he had dated, so he must be smitten or going soft in his 'old' age!

It was nearing a quarter to eleven, and Dean decided to gift me with a delicate emerald bracelet at the dinner table. He clasped the new jewelled accessory onto my wrist as the ladies admiringly looked on. I was warmed by his charm, care and attention and felt secure in the fact that Dean wasn't afraid to publicly show me affection.

I had already consumed several glasses of bubbles and rum cocktails by this time, and the awkwardness and anxiety that I previously felt began to subside. Even though Max's initial opinion of me wasn't the greatest, it appeared he warmed to me slightly. He began to pay me little compliments and made sure I was included in the conversation whenever I fell silent.

'If you'll excuse me everyone, I'll have to love you and leave you I'm afraid — I need to get some sleep-in-beauty!' Mayu spoke, flashing her seductive eyes.

'No little amount of sleep will ever stop you from looking gorgeous Mayu,' Max creepily slurred as he slid his hand down the side of her arm. 'I thought you might've wanted to join us for our mid-night walk.'

Mayu tittered politely, then continued to tuck her chair under the table, 'Perhaps we can catch up tomorrow. I'll have the afternoon free.'

'Ah. Never mind, yes, perhaps we can all catch up tomorrow,' Max concluded, slamming his hand on the table. The rest of the group agreed and said their goodnight wishes to Mayu.

She paused for a few moments behind her chair.

'Oh, and thanks Mayu again for my birthday treat. That was very kind of you,' I said interrupting the silence.

Dean meanwhile had his arm across my back and gently stroked the middle of my neck with the tips of his fingers; his head was in profile, beside me. But Mayu lingered some more, before grimacing, then finally left the table. Max checked his watch. Max and Dean followed Mayu's trail out of the restaurant.

'Well, if everyone is still up for it, let's reconvene by the terrace at about say... eleven thirty?' Max piped up again.

Dean and I were the final couple to arrive at the terrace. Both Neve and Tom looked cosy in their duffle coats linking arms as they stood next to an impressive concrete lion statue. Max and Lisa too in deep conversation stood huddled on the other side at the top of the concrete staircase. I tentatively looked out in the darkness, barely able to see the vast acres of grounds that belonged to the Manor. This time though I was wise enough to change into suitable shoes (converse trainers) for the occasion!

Clutching onto Dean's arm, a sense of unease overcame me as I perused the dark open space.

'You cold, Soph? I can run up to the room and get you a sweater if you want,' Dean proposed.

'No, I'm fine. I'll soon warm up once we start walking. How far are we going?'

'Hey, you're not scared are you, Soph? Don't worry, there aren't any mad axe murderers out in the woods! At least not since last time I was here!' Dean joked.

'Ha, ha — very funny,' I teased back, trying to steady myself on my feet. The trees were dancing more frantically in the wind.

'Well tell a lie, there may be axe murderers, they're just not *mad*!'

I shook my head at Dean's attempt at humour and convinced myself that I was in safe hands.

Intoxicatingly comforted with Dean by my side, the alcohol was still having its effect and making me less apprehensive about going out into unfamiliar territories.

Max rallied up the troops and we set off. The further we got out the more I kept mentally calculating the distance back to the Manor, looking backwards and sideways — and now becoming nerved by any rustles in the darkness.

Max told us about the history of the grounds along the way, about the previous wealthy landowners and tales about their lives and the mischiefs they got up to. Then Max uprooted a story about a decrepit hermit who lived in the woods, who possessed a rifle, and would use it without hesitation to protect his land if anyone dared to trespass!

'Let's get as far as Pointer's End, then we can make our way back!' Max guided as he stumbled over tree roots, his voice fading into the steely night as he led the way ahead.

I could tell Neve and Lisa were growing tiresome. Although they kept pace with their partners their conversations were diminishing. It was my birthday, and I didn't want to be the one to quit our 'adventure', but it seemed there was no *Pointer's End* in sight. The nocturnal sounds around began to swell, and the winds were growing in pace. I felt a drip on my forehead, followed by another one, until the patter of rain became more rapid and heavier.

We quickened our pace, following Max through the dense woodland.

'Under here everyone, let's shelter here,' Max called out over the sound of the torrential rain saturating the earth. The six of us settled beneath a huge tree, holding onto our respective partners — trying to shelter from the rain pelting us from all angles.

'Whose idea was this?!' Tom joked, shaking his head at Neve.

'*I* never suggested it, I only agreed with Lisa,' Neve defended whilst affectionately slapping Tom's arm.

'Thanks, Neve, don't mind me, I'll take the rap for the crazy idea then,' Lisa interjected, clinging onto Max some more. 'Anyhow, come to think of it, I recall it was Max's hair-brained idea to go out into the woods!'

'So, it's *my* fault now?' Max jested. 'I simply wanted to give Sophia a grand tour of the grounds. Give her a bit of a feel of the place. Beats going out in the streets of South London at night, wouldn't you agree, Soph?'

Another downpour of train pounded the earth around us, and everyone laughed in unison. It appeared that the effect of alcohol was rapidly wearing off; Max was on original form, returning to his bouts of sarcasm. I just smiled and shrugged the comment off, feeling more preoccupied with the suffocation of darkness that surrounded me. Everyone agreed to stick together and wait under the shelter of the tree until the rain subsided before heading back to the Manor.

The conversation continued… I clung tightly onto Dean's arm but couldn't help but fixate on the open space around us. Tom, Neve, Lisa and Max's faces were barely visible in the night.

I'd sharply turn my head from one direction to the next when alerted to midnight sounds, yet faintly heard the group's sobering voices as they skipped from one topic to the next. I watched their mouths going ten to the dozen and felt completely removed from the conversation.

'Sophia? What are you doing here?!'

I was quick to respond, 'Max organised this trip. It's for my birthday,' I explained.

'But you can't just go off with anyone. You haven't known him five seconds.'

'It's okay, he's been looking after me, I've been trying to…'

Joltingly, I felt my left arm being shaken until I fixated on Lisa on the opposite side of the tree just staring at me. Dean kept repeating my name.

'Yes, I *have* been looking after you, Soph, haven't I!' Max started. 'I'm glad you appreciated it!' I could see Max and Lisa sharing a joke. Even in the cold and rain I could feel my body temperature rising and my heartbeat gradually quickening.

'Why did you bring us here, Max?' I started with a vehemence I'd never felt in me before. Everyone turned to face me drowning in a spiral of descent.

'Hey Soph, it's all right, the rain's laying off, we can go back,' Dean intervened.

'I thought you just said I've been looking after you? Make up your mind!' Max joked. I think your lady has had a bit too much to drink Dean,' Max pointed out, staggering on his feet. 'Let's make our way back before World War Three erupts!'

'He's not right for you. Don't trust him, Soph. Listen to me, don't trust him. I only want the best for you,' the voice continued.

'I called out for you, but you never came. What was I to do?' I continued — unaware of anyone around me.

'Ask me what, Soph? I'm right here,' said Dean.

'What is she rambling on about?' Max got in. 'I don't know if this is some kind of joke or just a B-rated actress having a funny turn!' Max flittingly remarked to Dean. 'I'm sorry about your job in Lapland Sophia, it didn't sound the greatest and I'm not a West End producer I'm afraid, so I can't offer you your next job on the West End stage!' Max quipped, hoping his audience would join in laughter at his tragic comedy piece.

I could feel the inside of my palm red raw, and throbbing from the strike I inflicted Max with across his left cheek. The cowering man stood there dumbfounded and silenced for the first time that night — shocked into submission. Lisa quickly pulled his hand away from his cheek to inspect the damage.

'*You f***ing B******. Why did you do that?' Max roared.

I could see the rage in Max's eyes, his head shaking partly from the blow but most probably more from the fact that he had to restrain himself; he wouldn't dare retaliate and lay a finger on a woman, as much as he probably wanted to!

'Come on Max,' Tom exploded, 'you asked for it. You haven't stopped all night. Just lay off the poor girl for God's sake!'

'Stay out of it, Tom,' Neve interrupted as she tried to pull Tom away from the commotion.

Dean meanwhile was wrestling between Tom and Max, trying to prevent another physical altercation. Lisa managed to prise Max away and lead him off into the darkness. Tom apologised to me on Max's behalf and agreed that Max deserved all what he got before setting off with Neve by his side. Dean held my trembling body in his arms — a tsunami of water flooding down my reddened face. It wasn't the end to my birthday that I had hoped for!

Early hours television filled the empty gaps of conversation for pretty much the rest of the night before we fell sleep.

Uncertain of the fallout, Dean left the room around 7:30am the next morning, saying that he needed to speak with Max. Just a few minutes after he left, the phone rang, but the caller put the phone down upon hearing my voice. With the morning sun streaming through the window, the brightness of the day appeared to block out any misgivings of the night before. I tried not to dwell on it too much. I was keen to start the new day afresh. With Tom's voice echoing in my head saying, *'Max deserving all what he got'*, I was hopeful everyone would see it that way too (even Lisa).

When Dean returned, he said the others were just finishing off breakfast, so we could probably just have something to eat in our room. I was relieved we were spared the awkward conversation around the breakfast table. Plus, it was a treat to get *Room Service* consisting of a full English breakfast, and a champagne and orange juice to take the edge off!

On the side of my tray was a small teddy bear with the sign, *'I love you'* written across its chest. I had never heard such words uttered from Dean's lips, so felt warmed by the soppy sentiment. Dean's attempts to make my birthday as special as possible gave me hope that the 'glitch' between Max and I last night wasn't going to spoil things between us.

At around 3:15 pm, Dean decided to take me for a drive in the Oxfordshire countryside, so we could *admire the idyllic surroundings*. I routinely checked to see if my seat belt was securely fastened numerous times before sitting back in the passenger seat. After about ten minutes, Dean slowed down, stopping at an inlay of a country lane — with only a few lone cattle in the distant fields to come between us!

Still feeling uncertain about Dean's thoughts on the drama that unfolded the night before, I stared out of the passenger window, my perturbed reflection staring back at me in the car wing mirror. Surely, I should have been the one to have felt aggrieved by Max's antics. With Dean going to the trouble of arranging a special weekend for me though, I couldn't help but feel I acted ungratefully and worried that Dean was about to give me my marching orders.

'I know it must have been difficult for you last night,' Dean started. 'I guess I didn't really think about how you'd feel celebrating your birthday with people you didn't know.'

'Oh, I didn't mind,' I got in there quickly. 'It was sweet of you wanting me to meet your friends and arranging the dinner. I had a really good time... I... I hope you've forgiven me for what happened last night... I didn't mean to cause any trouble between you and Max...' I perked, apologising like a disobedient schoolgirl stepping out of line.

'I mean I couldn't really invite any of your friends... because I don't really know of any.'

As much as Dean was being honest, it cut deeply. It was a fact. I didn't have any *real* friends he could call on to share my celebrations with. I felt embarrassed, inadequate... unlikable even.

I internally damned myself for my social inadequacies and my absence of friends amongst an ever-increasing list of shortcomings. Desperate to make it up to Dean, I thought about how I could make amends with Max before the weekend was over. I could write him a note or buy him a gift from the shop in the Manor as a way of saying I was sorry? Or perhaps that was too sentimental? Knowing Max, he'd probably laugh at the gesture. He didn't seem the type to appreciate or surrender to any displays of kindness I would imagine. I could feel a tightness in my throat and swallowed hard to try and relieve myself from the aches. What must Dean really think of me? I was beginning to think why he would even be attracted to me.

'Hey Soph, it wasn't your fault,' Dean interrupted, 'Last night... Max knows he went too far. You don't have to apologise, we're cool. He doesn't mean any harm you know.' I couldn't believe Dean was being so forgiving, but still braced myself for what was about to come next. 'I was thinking...' Dean continued.

'Yeah?' my voice waivered.

'About this evening...'

'Uh hum...'

'How about we do a sep-ar-...'

Dean didn't even have to finish the word. I could feel my gut agonisingly pulling me forwards, sideways...

'..-ate girls' and boys' night? How's that sound?' he inflected. 'You can get to know the girls a bit better.'

'What do you mean?' I nerved, wanting Dean to clarify.

'Max, Tom and I can catch up over a drink whilst you Lisa and Neve have dinner together.'

Relieved at Dean's clarification, I nodded readily in agreement. 'Yeah... yeah, I'd like that,' I spurted out, burying my chin into my chest, not wanting Dean to see my water-welled eyes.

'Great. We can always meet up afterwards, after dinner,' Dean persuaded as he comfortingly touched my hand.

I felt a sense of relief, elated that our trip to the peacefulness of the countryside wasn't the 'perfect intended place' to mark the end of our relationship! I was getting a second chance. I would even have sacrificed another torturous dinner with Max that night if it meant that Dean and I would remain together. How pathetic.

Dean started up the engine again and we weaved along the meandering country lanes towards the Manor. I thought about meeting up with the girls later, and what things I could talk about to try and be a bit more sociable and interesting. But suddenly, like a shot, I was bolted upright. As I gazed at the dense woodland through the car window, parts of the conversation from last night filtered back to me: the conversation prior to me striking out at Max.

Lauren! It was Lauren's voice that called out to me in the woods: her stark warnings made clear. As fragments of the conversation unnervingly swirled around in my head, I was reminded that my *uncontrollable wandering hands* were not the only thing of concern.

Fortunately for me however, like the preliminary rounds before a boxer's fatal knock-out blow, visions of me talking to the wind last night were hopefully buried and forgotten. Dean hadn't mentioned a thing.

The meeting room in the eastern part of the Manor was reserved solely for our ladies' evening. Lisa said Max was able to gladly accommodate *our* wishes.

'How did you spend your day, Sophia?' Neve perked.

'We went for a drive in the countryside earlier. It's beautiful around here,' I perked back.

'Ah that's nice. How romantic. Did you have a fumble in the forest?' Lisa got in, laughing. I shook my head in embarrassment. 'Dean's been planning your birthday weekend for weeks. Hasn't he, Neve?' she regimented, deliberately turning to face her — almost as if their conversation had been rehearsed.

I couldn't help but feel it was said to make me feel guilty about what happened in the woods.

My paranoia again getting the better of me. I tried to fight the negative trails of thought and poured another glass of wine while offering to top up the other ladies' glasses.

The two 3-seater Chesterfield leather sofas facing each other were separated by a glass table. Lisa and Mayu sat on one side with Neve and I on the other. Double doors led out to a patio, with the woods yet again serving as a stunning backdrop, even though the night was descending and was soon to obstruct our view.

Somehow, I couldn't help but stare at Mayu — her dark eyes drew me in. Dean didn't mention she was coming. She intrigued me. But I was dispelled from my gaze by Lisa's beguiling voice.

'This is very civilised. A bit of a break from all the testosterone, eh!'

'Yeah, it was a good idea to have a girlie evening,' said Neve.

'Yeah, we can talk about the men!' Lisa quipped. 'Who needs them anyway?'

Lisa looked at me.

'I'm only joking, Sophia. Dean's one of the good ones.' Neve and Lisa shared a look.

'*And* Tom — he's such a gentleman. I'm really pleased for you, Neve. When's the big day again?'

'Next Summer. We haven't finalised the guest list yet. You know weddings can be a nightmare. I'm gonna leave that for someone else to do!'

'Well, if you need a make-up artist, I'm all yours, Neve,' Mayu politely interjected, trying to get in on the conversation.

'Oh, gosh that's a good idea. I never thought of that,' returned Neve. 'I forgot you did hair and make-up as well as all the masseuse stuff. I'll speak to Tom about it.'

'And what about you, Mayu? Who's lighting up *your* life? I heard rumblings of you seeing the manager here, is that right?' Lisa boldly asked, whilst darting her suspecting eyes towards Neve in the process.

Mayu chuckled sweetly and flashed her penetrating eyes before playfully flicking her ponytail.

'Oh, we're just friends,' Mayu replied, tittering. Her knees firmly locked together.

'That's what they all say!' Mother Hen diced back. 'You just be careful girl. Don't let anyone take advantage of you. You're still young.'

'Thanks Lisa, it's okay. But I'm not only interested in *one* man!'

The room erupted.

'*Pray tell, Mayu!* You *are* a dark horse!' Lisa threw back nearly falling off her seat.

'I'm just teasing.'

'Oh, no. No backtracking now! You've started so you'll finish! Who's the lucky man?! I like her style!' Lisa appraised, whilst seeking Neve and I's approval.

Mayu tittered some more. 'I can't say for the moment. It's early days. Who knows what will happen?' Mayu smirked — now trying to play it down.

'All right girl — watch this space, eh!' Lisa concluded. 'Well, I don't about you girls but that came as a surprise! Your love life sounds more exciting than mine. Perhaps I'll take a leaf out of your book.'

Mayu lapped up the attention she was getting from *Mother Hen* some more — her growth in confidence increasing by the second.

'How about you, Lisa? What's going on with Max?' Mayu shot back.

'Oh, he's just my ***k buddy. We're not serious,' Lisa said curtly, ending any further room for interrogation. She slurped on her wine and stared blankly towards the window, thought for a moment, and then said, 'I'd give him a 7.5! Needs to be more attentive. And you, Neve?'

'Well, I'm not going to score my fiancé, but he's pretty much up there! I wouldn't be getting married otherwise.'

'No, course you wouldn't. Just report back after a few years of marriage then!'

'Cynicism will get you nowhere, Lisa. You know you're not gonna find the right one if you stay with Max.'

'I know, it's just a temporary thing 'til I get my knight, don't you worry!'

'You'll be looking for a long while if a knight's what you're hoping for!' Neve stated.

'I know, I know. I've heard it all before. Well, I'm really a commitment-phobe at heart. And as Bobby Brown says — it's my prerogative,' Lisa clawed back, doing the shoulder body-popping actions to suit. Lisa turned to face Mayu. 'Don't worry, at nineteen you're exempt from this one!'

'Agreed,' said Neve. 'Plus, she's got too many men to score anyway!'

The wine continued to flow freely; the ladies' lips loosened more as I became tenser by the second.

'Now, we wouldn't leave you out, Sophia,' Lisa jested. 'I don't know about you guys, but I'm *really* curious to know what Dean's like in the bedroom,' Lisa stated blatantly.

I caught sight of Mayu's face as she cleared her throat. I didn't know if it was female intuition, but something troubled me. I tried hard to not let my imagination run wild. Yet, worse still, how was I going to get out of divulging the intimate details of my love life? I wasn't about to admit my sex-less relationship with Dean!

'Come on, you can share, Sophia. It'll be our secret. What did you *really* get up to in the woods yesterday?!' they toyed. 'You're a dancer, you could teach us a few moves!'

Neve and Lisa playfully poked around some more, forming even more grotesque and contorted shapes across the leather bonded sofa, one out-doing the other with their alcohol-fuelled gesturing. When they realised I wasn't partaking, Lisa sprung to her feet and dashed across the room.

'I know what will help. Let's set the mood!'

All went black and all I could see were silhouettes moving around the room, dis-orientating me further. Lisa's impersonation of a voice an octave lower repeating sexually suggestive phrases was used to *get me going*. Her persistence at playing the ill-advised game sent my heart quickening and my chest started to ache further from the dull pain. To cover my anxiousness, I immediately started rambling about when Dean and I first met in the nightclub, trying to latch onto something to 'entertain' *the audience* and distract from the discomfort I was feeling. But my mouth and brain seemed to disconnect. Foreign words fumbled feebly out from my mouth and in jumbled order.

Hazy images whizzed across the room like speeding cars flashing past in the night across a television screen. Blurred visions of a figure advanced towards me, and a raspy voice softly called out my name, then built into a crescendo with more urgency and aggression. The small, boxed room closed in on me, suffocating me further.

Goosebumps raced across my skin and became more prominent like tiny red pimples ready to burst...

The next thing, I found myself lying on the floor, my eyes fixed straight ahead, writhing in pain. My knees bent towards the ceiling with my own hands forcefully covering my mouth. A muffled youthful voice found its way through the gaps of my fingers, instructing me to count each two-penny coin for each stroke of his finger, "Four... six... eight..."

As my body was pulled and shaken every which way, I remember looking up and seeing Lisa waving her hand frantically over my face, desperately trying to 'waken' me. Neve and Mayu stood on each side towering over, their hands covering *their* mouths in dismay. Paralysed, I lay there motionless. Only blinking. With each successive blink, I slowly pieced together the moments that got me there.

Chapter 19

A Decade of Decay

A couple of weeks had passed since our escapade to the Oxfordshire countryside. Dean had been busy with work, so we hadn't seen each other as much as usual. I was still feeling insecure but tried to blot out the negatives of that weekend away. Mum was almost permanently at work with her shifts — we needed some money to keep our heads below the parapet.

Mum tried in vain to sell the house for what it was worth, but still with no offers in sight, we had to endure tangible memories of what we had lost: *our family, our hopes and dreams for the future... Lauren.*

Dean promised that we would spend a night out together once things calmed down at his work. I kept myself busy by attending dance classes over the coming weeks and fortunately bagged a dance job for a corporate event at a hotel venue in the city. Although, our nightly chats kept me believing that Dean and I still had something special between us, I sensed something wasn't right. *Yes, intuition*! I also struggled with incessant chatter in my head. Voices kept dissuading me from continuing the relationship. Lauren's voice was no longer a voice of calmness and encouragement; instead, she kept telling me Dean was no good. Other voices would even have conversations between themselves as I intently listened in. Still, no one was aware of my plight, not Dean not Mum, nor anyone else. I just tried to cope with the internal chatter as much as I could... until.

'That'd be 35p please,' said the shopkeeper flatly, as he handed me a copy of the *South London Gazette*.

I could feel the shop keeper eyeballing me as I left the premises and scurried out. When I returned home, I immediately turned to the back pages to view the property section to see what was up, *'For Sale'*. Mum was keeping a check of the neighbouring houses in the event ours was snapped up by some hopeful investor. After checking out the properties on the market, I flicked through to the middle pages of the newspaper.

The headline read: "Nearly ten years on: No closer to fate of poor Missing girl from notorious housing estate."

I saw Lauren's cheeky, smiling, teen-aged face next to an aerial shot photo of our estate, with bold arrows pointing to numerous escape routes where her *'abductor/s' could have made their exit*. At first, I tried not to get lured into reading the story, so I just scanned the columns.

Reading the lies would only upset me like before when the story first broke almost a decade ago. The innuendos and biasedness — namely placing our family in the firing line — was all too much to bear. Yet, I couldn't stop myself: memories of that fateful day began to resurface.

The untimely pursuit of selling our home around the anniversary of Lauren's disappearance most likely had an impact on viewing potential. Hardly anyone showed an interest. With the estate in the headlines again, Lloyd Grossman might want to re-phrase: 'Who'd *want to* live in a house like this?' Even though Mum was bound to catch sight of the reports whirling around in the media, I hid the Gazette under my bed and decided to keep it from her.

A deep sense of emptiness… of loneliness consumed me in the days leading up to the tenth anniversary. Pitiful memories loomed, and my feelings of entrapment were exacerbated. I was desperate to escape the haunting memories that were buried deep within. Year after year more layers of unbridled guilt, hopelessness and tragic fate manifested itself within my psyche. Even though I had tried my damned hardest to display a hard exterior and put on a façade to the world, there's only so long you can keep up the pretence. When pushed so far, rotting walls inevitably start crumbling down.

Dean was due to come around that Wednesday evening, but he called around 9:20 pm to say he had some errands to run for his mum, so "he'd give me a call a bit later." When it had passed midnight, I called Dean's mobile phone numerous times — wanting to hear his voice — wanting him to apologise for his late call. But his phone just rang out. I needed to know he still cared, but his no-shows were becoming a regular occurrence; a pattern all too familiar.

Waiting, hoping, wanting. Longing, waiting, not hearing, hoping, wanting. The times that we *did* speak were brief and the distance between us was clear.

A renewed police investigation into *Missing Lauren* saw tree trunks and lamp posts on the estate and the local surrounding area plastered with her cherubic face. Fresh appeals were made in the local papers for any sightings or new witnesses to come forward. It seemed surreal that the fervour was starting up again. To even think that Lauren *might* or *could physically* come back messed with my mind.

I was finding it increasingly difficult processing the reality of Lauren as a *Missing Person* in the real world, juxtaposition-ed against the *reality* of Lauren's voice firmly in my head — through our conversations — speaking directly to me. The voices at night crescendo-ed.

Chapter 20

Pretty in Pink

'Hi. How can I help?' asked the doctor as a matter of course.

I sat nervously perched on the wooden chair, questioning the real reason I was there.

'Hi. Well, I've been getting really bad cramps in my stomach... around that *time of the month*... I've been taking painkillers to help, but I may need something stronger... It's becoming quite unbearable,' I managed to get out.

'And how long has this been going on?'

'For as long as I... well... since... the last couple of years?' I inflected.

'*Years*?' questioned the doctor.

The doctor hastily scrolled through my medical records on the computer screen, then asked how I was feeling generally. All my responses bounced back somewhat deflated. With a speedy diagnosis, the doctor signed me off with a stronger prescription to help with the pain.

But it came with a warning: Any adverse reactions — *To stop taking the medication immediately and to urgently seek medical advice*. I thanked the doctor and closed the door gently behind me.

Nevertheless, it had appeared that my trip to the doctors created more anxieties than hopeful resolutions. Although the pain and inner turmoil felt intolerable, I was frightened of what was to come. A reliance on pills to make me feel normal again. Whatever *normal* was. Once I'd started, there'd be no coming back.

I stuffed the white box *full of false hope* into the back of my dressing-table drawer, telling myself that I was stronger than that. Telling myself that I could handle the pain inflicted on me without synthetic intervention.

But the following days became increasingly harder. Everywhere I turned people were having conversations about me. Locals on buses sizing me up and down, conspiratorially whispering on street corners as I passed by. No place to free feel or safe. In the days leading up to Laura's anniversary, her face was splashed everywhere in the local vicinity — a reminder that her absence was ever-present — disabling me with overwhelming guilt.

It was Friday evening in Central London. Draped in dark colours, I found myself stood at the bar of 'The Eye'. Dean had finally made contact and although I was eager to get back to where we were, I was still struggling internally. It was the first time Dean and I had been out together since my birthday weekend. But a change from my home environment was welcomed, so I agreed to 'our date'. I tried to remain upbeat. Before we delved into conversation, a voice from behind called out:

'Hey Soph! Oh, my word, I haven't seen you in donkeys! What have you been up to?'

Charlie wore a little red dress which accentuated her slimline waist, with a halter-neck emphasising her bronzed chest. She squeezed me ever so tightly and seemed overly-excited to see me.

'Hi Charlie. Good to see you. I was thinking about you the other day,' I pretended, trying to make conversation. At this point Dean wasn't in sight — he got lost in the crowd and must have slipped off to the toilets.

'You still with Dean?' Charlie asked.

'Yeah, we're still together. He took me away for my birthday weekend a couple of weeks ago. It was really lovely,' I said, trying to clamber onto something positive.

'Really? Ah, that's nice, that's nice,' Charlie repeated. 'Yeah, I was wondering what happened. Whether you were still together?' she continued.

'Yeah, we're good. We're just taking it easy at the moment. What with his work, it can get quite busy.'

'Yeah... yeah,' Charlie repeated. 'So, it was your birthday a couple of weeks ago? Happy belated!'

'Thanks.'

'We'll have to have a catch-up drink to celebrate, Soph!' Charlie offered.

'Yeah!'

'Is Dean here?'

'Yeah... I think he's just gone to the toilets,' I replied, searching the crowd.

'Right, okay. Well, I best get back to my friends. They'll be wondering where I am!'

'Yeah sure. Good seeing you Charlie.'

'Don't forget that drink...! And tell Dean I said, 'hello',' Charlie said as she went.

She slinked off into the crowd. I searched again to see where Dean was. A few minutes later, Dean made his way towards me from another direction. I could tell Charlie was still sweet on him. I flashbacked to that time in the car when Dean and I first met: Dean handing me his business card, then Charlie bombarding me with questions about him, feeling sore about his pursuit of *me* and *not her*.

'You just missed Charlie,' I said.

'Really? When's the last time you saw her?'

'Ages go... She seemed good...'

'*Good*,' said Dean.

There was a pause, and an awkwardness followed.

'You look lovely tonight,' Dean flattered.

'Thanks,' I smiled, taking a sip of my drink.

The change of environment was welcomed and helped if only temporarily to lift the dampening mood that had overshadowed me the past few weeks. My thoughts lingered on Charlie. I thought about trying to search the bar before we left, but decided I'd call her in the next few days instead.

About an hour after our stint at, 'The Eye', Dean and I decided to catch a late-night flick at a cinema in Leicester

Square. Clasping onto our popcorn and soft drinks, we mounted the stairs of the darkened room, ushered to our seats by the friendly cinema attendant. There weren't many cinema-goers in the auditorium, and with an absence of people, we occupied two seats on our row.

As the film rolled on, my eyes became heavier and heavier. Dean would place his hand on mine to try and waken me, but I'd only drift off again after a few seconds. A voice woke me from my slumber.

'Soph... Soph, wake up.'

Dean looked at me and shook his head laughing to himself. I noticed someone had joined our row and sat two seats away to my right. As the final credits started rolling, the person commented on the film:

'I didn't think it would end that way, did you?'

Not wanting to blank them, I proceeded to make small talk.

'No. Well I fell asleep through most of it!' I shamefully admitted, before looking to Dean to share the joke with. Dean stared blankly at me, acknowledging I was still in a sleepy haze.

'I wasn't talking about the film!' continued the stranger.

But when I turned back, the seat was no longer occupied. In a panic, I rotated backwards, then all around, then scanned the row in front. My heart started to palpitate; my chest started to constrict. I clasped the soft drink from its holder and knocked back the last bits of juice to try to relieve the tightness developing in my throat. But the physical aches were mounting.

The lights in the auditorium went up. Dean stood up, ready to leave and I moved quickly from my seat clinging onto him, nervously looking towards the unoccupied seat as I went.

'You okay, Soph? Take your time, you're still sleepy!' Dean joked.

'Please, let's just go,' I anguished.

I studied the roads home, trying to focus on something else to distract my attention away from the wave of negative emotions consuming me. Passing billboard advertisements with signs and slogans informed: *"It's YOU!"* and *"...join our club."* The chatter was constant and relentless.

Dean drove at an accelerated speed, and I pleaded for him to slow down. As much as I tried to hide it, I couldn't conceal my panicked state.

'You wouldn't want to harm me, would you?' I asked.

'Why would you say that, Soph?'

My knuckles clenched tightly onto the sides of the passenger seat. I focused out the window — trying to control my breathing — staring into the night…

…I dashed to the bathroom and purged to rid myself of the sufferable feeling inside. Dean knocked on the locked bathroom door several times, but I didn't let him in — told him it was safer to be alone. I willed the episode to be over, for the voices to quieten down.

I don't remember much after that.

As I opened my eyes Dean was sat upright by my side. The morning light shone through my bedroom window. Dean passed me a glass of water and rubbed my back, studying me with concern.

Standing in my night-dress, my hand reached the side of the bathroom door to steady myself. I felt the rough edges of the wooden frame with my fingers where the bathroom lock had been broken off. I stepped inside, and with the door closed behind me, I collapsed to the floor in a pitiful heap.

After Dean left, I searched for the white box that was hidden at the back of my dressing-table drawer. My hand trembling as I stood there, contemplating. I pierced the silver foil with my nail and quickly popped the pretty pink pill into my mouth, washing it down with the remnants of warm water. At last, I had succumbed.

It was two weeks later. Rehearsals at the dance studio in Kennington had finally started for the event in the city. The rehearsal period seemed a lengthy stint given that the performance would only be for *One Night Only*. Still, I wasn't complaining — three weeks wages and a one-off performance fee weren't to be scoffed at. The production team and cast were friendly enough and I seemed to get on with most people. Things were feeling better, and the dance routines also helped to exhaust me physically and quieten down the chatter.

Plus, of course the pills were kicking in, giving me some relief from my ills.

One evening after rehearsals, I decided to surprise Dean at work; I booked a table at a nearby Chinese restaurant in the city. All arrangements had been made and I had managed to seek clarification from Dean that he would be finishing at 6 p.m. that Thursday evening. After rehearsals, I showered and changed into my evening wear, excited about my unexpected visit and the night to follow. Fellow dance colleagues complimented me on my appearance and wished me a fantastic night out. I boldly navigated my way to surprise Dean, taking the underground to his Managing Consultancy office in Holborn.

Tottering in my heels and over-coat, I walked out of Holborn station and followed the map towards Dean's workplace. A young woman's voice answered the intercom buzzer as I stood on the concrete steps to the offices:

'Hello there, can I take a name please?'

'Hi, it's Sophia Healey. I'm here to see Dean Sutton? Well… it's a surprise,' I jested.

'Dean Sutton?'

'Yes. I'm his girlfriend. He doesn't know I'm coming,' I chuckled, '…I'm surprising him. Could you let him know I'm here, please?'

Even though I felt a bit foolish trying to explain myself, I hoped the receptionist would appreciate my sweet gesture.

'Right... erm... right. Do you want to come in?'

'Thanks,' I replied as I pushed the door open, excited at the thought of seeing Dean's unexpectant face. As I made my way up to the front desk, the young woman looked me at me, perplexed.

'I'm sorry... what's your name again?'

'Sophia Healey,' I repeated.

'I'm sorry Ms Healey, but Dean left our firm about six months ago.'

'Oh... no... Perhaps he's working from home, he has been doing more business from home lately. He probably just didn't tell me he wasn't coming in today!' I jested.

'No. I'm afraid Dean Sutton was *let go*. He hasn't worked here for some time.'

My face reddened. I didn't know how to respond to the *sorry-to-give-you-the-bad-news* receptionist. I pathetically said, *'thanks for letting me know'*, and walked back out of the building as fast as I could, still trying to digest the information.

I dialled Dean's number immediately, but it just rang out, and spent most of the evening trying to call him, until his phone didn't even ring, but went straight to voicemail. I tried to think of all the possibilities for Dean's behaviour, his avoidance, absenteeism and untruths about work.

It was the next day of rehearsals.

'So, go on then, how did he react? Give me all the goss!' shrieked Kay, one of the dancers in eager anticipation as we did our morning workout.

I felt like I was submerged deep under water, scrambling hard to reach the water's surface for breath. I couldn't bear the shame, so I fabricated the whole evening as best as I could, not wanting to reveal the pathetic reality, ending with:

'So… it was great thanks. He was really surprised!'

The end of the day couldn't have come soon enough, and I was glad rehearsals were over for the week.

When I returned home, Mum asked about Dean, but I managed to cover up his misgivings. I couldn't bring myself to tell her about what had happened the night before, and that nowadays I couldn't even get in touch with him half the time. Also, I didn't mention anything about the pills from the doctor — Mum would only worry.

Finally, it was the evening of the event performance in Central London. The clients were full of praise for our night full of entertainment. The theme was *Music throughout the Decades* (50s to the 90s), with my favourite being the 70s with our afro wigs, psychedelic tops and bell-bottom trousers and platform shoes to complete the look! We managed to take some items of costume home, 'courtesy of Wardrobe' for keepsakes.

Dani suggested we go out for a drink in town and persuaded us to wear our newly acquired items of clothing for the night out! We re-touched our make-up and Dani helped to accentuate my eyes with heavier eyeliner and sculptured eyebrows. I completed the look by wearing my red-flamed afro wig. Not one to draw attention to myself, but I let caution to the wind and stepped out into London's nightlife with the throw-back clan in my psychedelic 70s ensemble!

It was now 10:45 p.m. on Friday evening. In jubilant mood, the six of us sang songs from the show as we traipsed the busy streets of Covent Garden — with *Rock Around the Clock, Baby Love and Dancing Queen* as firm favourites – searching for a place to hang out for the night. We scoffed down some fast-food along the way and remembered funny incidents that happened during the show: like when Paul did a double pirouette and his trousers split on-stage, and when Zoe's stick-on hair bun flew off her head during her pas-de-deux, landing on a guest's plate of fois gras, rye bread and fruit!

After swanning 'in and out' of a few places, we stumbled across my usual haunt.

'How about we go in here?' one of the girls suggested.

'The Eye' was busy and buzzing. We queued up outside, and the doorman let us in after a few guests left the premises. At least our eye-catching outfits brought a smile to the doorman's default dead-pan face.

'I love this track,' screamed Dani as Mary J Blige's *All Night Long* blared out from the speakers.

Dani and some of the other dancers formed a circle on the dancefloor showing off their best moves — whooped on by the crowd. Ceri and I decided to rest our legs and perched ourselves on a two-seater sofa near the back of the venue for a chill out.

'So, what's next for you, Soph? You got anything lined up?'

'Nothing yet. I'm still waiting to hear about a job in the West End, but they're still auditioning people for the show apparently,' I resigned.

'Oh, right. Well fingers crossed. You know what they're like, they'll probably tell you, you got the job on a Friday, and they'll see you at rehearsals on the Monday!'

'And you?' I asked back.

'I start a rehearsal block for a film at Pinewood on Monday. Really looking forward to it!'

'Wow, that sounds great.'

'Yeah, thanks. We've got a Hollywood A-lister as the lead, but it's all a bit hush hush at the moment,' she confided.

'Well, you'll have to tell me all about it when the news breaks!' I said, sharing her excitement.

Ceri wrote her number on a scrap piece of paper, and I stuffed it into the back of my bell-bottomed trouser pocket. We continued to *talk shop*, and I was comforted by the ease at which we chatted. The RnB music continued to blare out all around us.

From our position tucked away in a seated area at the back of the venue, you could see people milling by the bar, whilst others were getting down on the dance floor. From behind Ceri's purple afro, I could see the profile of a familiar face in the distance.

'Oh, I've just spotted a friend of mine.'

'Go and say hello then. Or tell them to come over for a drink!' Ceri suggested.

'Actually, do you know what, I'm gonna join the others for a dance before my legs seize up! I'll see you in a minute.'

No sooner had Ceri sprung out of her seat, I adjusted my red afro wig and moved through the crowd towards the bar.

'Hey Charlie!'

Charlie turned around to see me standing there in all my 1970s glory.

'Hey, Soph. I didn't know you were coming tonight!' she startled.

'We had a performance in town — some corporate event in a hotel on Park Lane. It was Dani's idea about wearing our costumes!'

'I was wondering where the guys with the outfits came from!' she said looking nerved by my presence. 'How long have you been here?' asked Charlie, frantically searching the crowd.

Facing the bar with my back to the dance floor, a voice reached over my flaming red afro to Charlie.

'Hey Lottie, have you seen those guys in the retro gear!'

Before she could answer, Charlie's face turned as red as my hair piece, as the outreached hand caressed her naked bronzed arm. I could feel my heart pulsating in my mouth — blood racing through my veins, as a blazing triangle formed.

'Dean. You're here?' I confirmed.

The onset of an internal war rampaged within me, yet at first I spoke calmly. Dean gingerly withdrew his betraying hand from Charlie's arm. He barely looked me in the eye and squirmed like a blabbering fool.

'Sophia. Um, I tried to call you earlier,' he lied unconvincingly.

'Right. And so, because you couldn't get through, you happened to end up here with Charlie?' I asked directly.

'Soph, we need to talk,' a feeble voice got in.

'I'm talking to Dean,' I curtly injected.

'*We* need to talk, Soph,' Dean proposed.

'Oh, so you want to talk now? Well, go on then. Let's talk then Dean! Explain everything to me please,' I insisted. 'Explain your disappearing act and not returning my calls for days on end, not caring about how I might be feeling. Oh yes and explain why you told me you had some fancy job in town, only they got rid of you six months ago! Did you know about that... *Lottie?*' Charlie stood frozen, not daring to answer. 'Yes, and please explain how you ended up here with Charlie — *my* 'friend'. Unless I'm stupid, clearly there's something going on. I guess you didn't bank on me coming here tonight. Thought I'd be stuck at home pining for you,' I raged in tears.

'Okay, okay, Soph, just keep your voice down.'

'*Keep my voice down.* You couldn't be man enough to tell me what was going on. Tell me the truth about what was going on?'

I turned to a quivering Charlie.

'And you. You call yourself a friend. You always liked Dean from the start and couldn't bear the fact that he chose *me* over *you*. You just had to get your own back. So much for the belated birthday drink!'

Just as I was about to lose even more control, Ceri, in her purple afro wig which was now riding half-way back on her head, came striding over, then bridged a wall between us. Surrounding party-goers gave us adequate room in anticipation of mis-placed arms and fists battering the air.

The more Dean stood there as cool as ice the more I wanted to batter him with more than salacious words. Ceri pulled me back as I fought to continue the embarrassing melodrama that was unfolding. Our party of friends watched on in their psychedelic gear as Dean was politely encouraged to *take it outside the premises* by the doorman, followed by Charlie shamefully running out after him.

Black eyeliner was now smudged half-way down my face, and without a care, I whipped my wig off, leaving my head underneath with its stocking top exposed.

'Show's over everyone!' Ceri shouted as she created a trail through the crowd, ushering me towards the little girl's room away from everyone's glare. As we approached the toilets I heard as a bemused Ceri confirm, 'So *that's* Dean.'

Chapter 21

On a 136...

The phone rang incessantly. It had been over a month since I called time on our relationship, but Dean persistently tried every which way to make amends: voice messages, letter-writing, turning up unannounced at the doorstep, flower, chocolates... A betrayal is enough. But with a friend, that's unsalvageable.

A car would hum outside most evenings — but this time it was Dean waiting... hoping... wanting... my every move being watched over, tracked... monitored. History on repeat.

Voices that visited me nightly grew more malevolent, figures from the past swirled in head and poisoned my being... Rasped voices telling me *it'd soon be over*, and *I'd soon be put out of my misery*, continuously rang in my head. Faint echoes of Lauren's voice rang out in the distance trying hard to defeat the undefeated.

The air around me was stifling. My heart began racing as fast as the thoughts running savagely through my mind. One thought overlapping the other — voices interrupting — begging, demanding, dominance. A case of *he who shouts the loudest* always won — in my head. And *my* voice, *my* side, the 'good' side was always defeated. I squeezed my veins in an attempt to get the poison out of my veins, out of my blood...

...Two burly men stood in the doorway waving this pink form in front of me... Mum stood there sobbing uncontrollably.

It was shortly after the anniversary of Lauren's disappearance... I was diagnosed before I was even... before they even put an instrument to my chest... *Psychosis*... they said I had it without even examining me.

On the ward I felt like an inmate... like I was *Inside for a crime I did not commit*.

Chapter 22

Present Day, Hop Farm — Lister Ward

Mum came as often as she could. Devon was flying high still playing semi-pro football up North. He was busy training and locked into forging a new life away from all the drama.

Perhaps the reality of his little sister's demise was too hard to bear. I looked forward to his letters, but I couldn't bring myself to write back. The only time I did write back to was to tell him not to come to the hospital... I was too ashamed to admit where I was — where I had ended up.

But... a precious young life vanished before our eyes. It was my idea to invite Lauren round to the estate. *They said she didn't belong there. It was not a place for someone like her... that's why she was taken away and put in harm's way. And this was my payback.*

I started to believe the voices, and I believe that's when it all began...

...All sorts of people are in here. You name it... we're talking lawyers, doctors from the top right down to the to the basics are here. Half of them in here don't even think that they're ill — that they are not meant to be here in the first place. And half of them don't like the way that they got put in here either.

One day rolls into the next and there is nothing to occupy my mind except my own thoughts — the ones I am desperate to get away from!

But the doses... the doses help to keep the voices at bay... Yes, when the stringent, white-water swirls through my veins I slowly feel the ease... the wind down... the chastened relaxation of thought. Negative thoughts dissipate — the quietened morbid thoughts can no longer infiltrate my weary, tired mind.

'Good morning, Sophia...' greets the nurse.

She places my pills on the side counter and sits there waiting for me to wash the meds down before seeing to another patient...

...I look across at Ruby on the psych ward opposite me. She is always fixated on a spot on the wall. Nothing distracts her from the banal attraction. No one interrupts her *gaze* except when the staff come around with lunch or the nurses come by with routine medication, breezing in and out, loitering by our bedsides for a *monitored* chat. I, on the other hand am always on the look-out, my head turning from side to side not missing a trick or turn, catching everyone's conversations, everyone's body-language, exhaustively noticing, reading and analysing every little detail in absolutely *everything* and *everyone*.

I count the colours of the flowers of those patient's fortunate enough to have 'life' by their bedsides — a gift for better health and speedy recovery from a well-wisher. But flowers soon wither away. Not the best present for the concept of longevity, for the preservation of life.

The gift of flowers decay along with our decaying minds... I choose another coloured flower and count all of those until I count all the different coloured flowers I can see on the ward.

Sometimes I log the colour of the flowers with the highest number and compare it with the lowest and find the difference. Mentally counting the figures in my head and doing the sums.

Sometimes I write them down and keep a tally. And won't be rested until I get my sums right.

Sounds exhausting right? You can imagine how I feel when a nurse comes by and plucks out the withered flowers — meaning I'd have to start all over again. Which is the most popular coloured flower now? Sound crazy? That's how it is... that's how I am. But who's to determine *who's crazy?* The people in power with the clipboards and pens — the dominant ones... the most vocal voices that's who!

Each day I pray for a sign. And I hope one day, when the time is right my mind will be free... to just be... again.

Chapter 23

Old beginnings

It had been over month since I had lived within the white walls of Hop Farm. After one of Mum's visits the nurse spoke to me about a possible day release — a chance to attend a dance lesson once a week. After my weekly visits at the local dance studio, I always returned to the unit on time and the hospital staff trusted that I was on the road to some semblance of recovery. I hoped that I would be trusted to get back to the outside world again — to live my life as fully as possible.

An excitement like no other surged through me. Just being in the dance space, listening to the music, contorting my body in every which way — expressing my creative-self cured more than any pretty pink pill or white liquid ever could.

I sat on the floor limbering up before the dance instructor gave her usual greeting. I always thought it ironic that she'd always ask if we had any injuries — I could tell her a few!

One Tuesday afternoon when we had finished dance class, I picked up my belongings and made towards the exit. A line of women was waiting outside ready to attend the next class.

'Hold on, is that yo, Soph?' a cockney twanged voice rang out.

I turned my head to see a mouth hanging open and staring at me in disbelief.

'Oh my gosh, Car… Car-melle,' I gasped back, with images of us together as children floating through my mind.

She hugged me as tight as she could, burying her afro head into my neck. I hadn't felt a hug like that in a long time and tried hard to keep my composure.

We chatted briefly before she went into class and said we'd see each other again next week and exchange numbers. Although I was thrilled to see Carmelle, I wondered how I was going to get past giving her my phone number.

The weeks continued, and weekly I made excuses about my phone not working etcetera. There was only so long I could keep up the feeble pretence.

One day after dance class, when Carmelle and I spoke, she proposed that we should meet and go out for a coffee. I agreed to go the following week, but from Carmelle's pushed out bottom lip, I knew she didn't believe me!

Nevertheless, feeling on a high from dance class, I hurriedly made my way back to the unit at Hop Farm after dance class. Back on the ward, I lay there thinking about the world outside again. When would I finally be released, live my life again and start afresh?

Sitting on the bed, one of the nurses called out: 'Sophia, we have a visitor come to see you.'
The top of an afro peeked round the door on the ward; I buried my face into my hands and wept. Whether it was out of shame or sheer relief or both I wasn't entirely sure. Carmelle put her arms around me once more and just held me — she didn't have to say a word.

The nurses let Carmelle stay beyond visiting hours and we talked practically the whole night non-stop. For that I would always be grateful not only to the staff but to Carmelle. I told her everything and she told me about being bullied by the South London gyals and that she never wanted to lose our friendship…

Chapter 24

Dying memories

Sophia sits by the window over-looking the children playing in the garden below. A bubble passes by the window and lingers for a while as Sophia admires the colours of the wobbly liquid ball. Then, it disappears from view.

"Soon I'll be a stranger in a strange new place, searching for an old familiar face..."

The music of *Anatevka* soars out of Sophia's old cassette recorder and echoes around the room. Sophia walks to the dressing table and ritualistically lights the candle.

"I belong here..."

She searches the top of her wardrobe and pulls down her old school boater, then picks up the lit candle and walks towards the open sashed window. Reaching forwards — the candle in her right hand and her school boater in the other — a montage of childhood memories flash in quick succession before Sophia's eyes. The engulfing flame grows as Sophia watches the boater burn...

"What do we leave...? Nothing much..."

'...Memories so dear, must die...

Lauren... you were my everything...'

0345 017 9747